Take Me Please, Cowboy

Take Me Please, Cowboy

Cowboy

An 85th Copper Mountain Rodeo Romance

Jane Porter

TULE
PUBLISHING

Dedication

For Megan Crane and CJ Carmichael
thanks for starting this adventure with me 10 years ago!
For Sinclair Jayne
who was quick to jump on the ride and make it better
and my amazing readers
you inspire me every day!

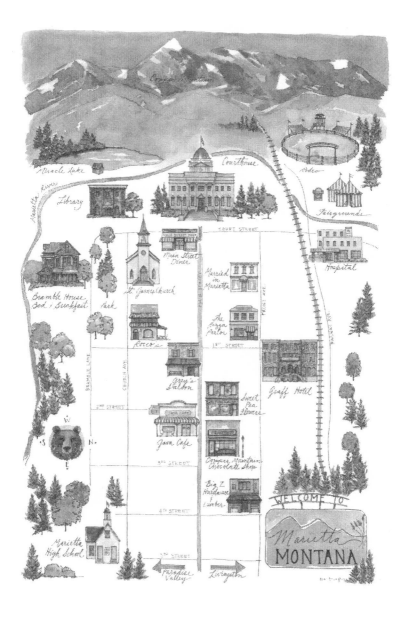

Chapter One

RYE CALHOUN'S 1986 Chevy Silverado overheated four miles east of Bozeman as the sun began to set. It wasn't the first time the blue and white truck overheated, and it wouldn't be the last. But he was so close to Marietta's rodeo and fairgrounds he could taste it. After nine hours behind the wheel, he just wanted to be there. Parked. Settled.

He hadn't slept last night, too worried about his younger brother Jasper's latest respiratory infection. Nineteen-year-old Jasper had been born with cerebral palsy and had struggles, but even with the disease, his infectious smile and endless optimism buoyed the family, lifting them during the darkest times.

Last night had been dark, too. Jasper couldn't breathe. His vest wasn't helping. His supplemental oxygen failed to make a difference. Even their mom, normally calm and together, panicked. There was no ambulance to call. No one to step in. So, Rye, once again, stepped in. Crouching in front of his brother's wheelchair, he gently clasped Jasper's face, telling Jasper to focus on him, and to breathe with him. Rye held his brother's gaze. *Slow breath in. One, two, three. Exhale, one, two, three. Breathe in, one, two, three, four. Exhale slowly, one, two, three, four.*

They faced each other, breathing together. It might have been just a minute or two, but it felt like hours. *Breathe with me. One, two, three.*

Rye ignored the drama behind him. He blocked out his father's voice and his mother's anguish and focused on the only thing that mattered in that moment. Jasper.

Rye didn't know how long it took before Jasper was breathing, his lips no longer blue. The oxygen kicked in, and Jasper gave Rye a small nod of his head.

Then, and only then, did Rye acknowledge his fear. He'd been afraid. They needed to live closer to a hospital. They needed better care for Jasper. Rye had had it with Eureka, a town on the border of Montana and Canada. It wasn't the right place for any of them, especially not his younger brother, but Dad had been born and raised in Eureka and was loath to leave his hometown and his company.

Yet Dad didn't pay the bills anymore. Rye did, and one of these days he and his dad would have to have a serious talk about the future, and Jasper, and his beautiful sisters, twenty-two-year-old Hannah and twenty-year-old Josie, because they had dreams, too. They were smart girls, strong girls, and they never asked anything for themselves, but they should.

Rye had come to realize their dad wouldn't encourage the girls to pursue their passion, which was why Rye had to. Life had to be more than just survival. Because just surviving wasn't enough.

Off on the side of the road, Rye lifted the hood of his Chevy. Steam hissed and water bubbled up from beneath the cap on the radiator. It'd be at least twenty minutes before the engine cooled enough to allow him to continue on. Rye should have replaced the radiator last year, but didn't, not wanting to spend the money, not when it was needed elsewhere.

Pushing back the brim of his cowboy hat, he walked back to the trailer and checked on his horses. Lately, he'd only been traveling with Nickel but one of the barrel racers on the circuit, who'd be competing this weekend in Marietta, had expressed interest in buying five-year-old Topaz, and while Rye was loath to sell a horse he'd hand raised and trained, selling Topaz would help pay Jenna's tuition for nursing school.

NICKLE BOBBED HIS head, acknowledging Rye while Topaz stomped a hoof. Topaz, always impatient and intense, wanted to be free, wanted to run. While Topaz had fire, Nickle was his steady, reliable companion, ideal for roping events.

Rye patted both geldings, giving Topaz one extra because soon he would be gone, before walking back to the front of his truck. Although the steam was slowly evaporating everything still felt dangerously hot.

He felt dangerously hot. Juggling a four-day work week with weekends on the rodeo circuit had worn him down. He didn't hate roofing—it was his dad's company after all—but he didn't enjoy it, and it wasn't what he wanted for himself. Being a rodeo cowboy wasn't his future, either. It was hard on the body and hard on the family. But at least being on the road gave him a chance to escape Eureka for a few days and make some extra money, income needed. But it was hard to be away from everyone when Jasper struggled with and suffered infection after infection.

Rye pulled out his phone, checked messages. Zero. No missed calls, either. That was a good sign. But it didn't ease the hollow ache inside of him. When busy, he was able to ignore the emptiness, pretend it didn't exist. He'd come to tell himself that the emptiness—part resignation, part dread—wasn't real, but rather fatigue, and it would pass. When he became more successful. When he made more money. Always this need for money. He'd been responsible for his family for over a decade, but it hadn't always been so desperate. When his father worked, before his accident, everything had been easier, financially, emotionally. There had never been a lot of money but there had been enough. They had gotten by and even had a few luxuries. Dinners out. A new van that could accommodate Jasper's wheelchair. His sisters had taken dance classes, and Josie had taken some voice lessons, and while there were no trips to Disneyworld, they would drive up to his grandparents' farm in Alberta every summer and they'd all enjoyed that.

But once Dad was hurt, the trips stopped, the lessons stopped, the custom van was traded in for an older model that Rye adapted himself for Jasper.

A truck pulled up behind Rye's on the side of the road. Rye straightened and looked toward the black truck, one of those classic all-purpose work trucks that were neither new nor old, but practical. A man was behind the wheel and a young blonde woman sat beside him. Rye couldn't help giving the woman a second look. In the setting sun, she appeared gilded, her long gold hair an ethereal halo, her slender frame illuminated.

The man climbed out of the black truck, tall and lean with dark blond hair. He headed toward Rye. "Need help?" he asked, glancing at the propped hood.

Rye swallowed his embarrassment. He hated needing help and did his best to never ask for it. "Overheated but should be okay soon."

"So, it's not the first time," the stranger said sympathetically.

"Unfortunately, not."

"Jackson Flint," the other said, extending his hand.

"Rye Calhoun," Rye answered, shaking Jackson's hand.

From Jackson's size and grip, Rye suspected he used to play football. "I've put off getting a new radiator long enough. Clearly, it's time I replaced it."

"Where are you heading?"

"Marietta."

"For the Copper Mountain Rodeo?"

Rye nodded. "You know it."

"I live there. The rodeo's celebrating a big anniversary. Eighty-fifth, I think."

"With some nice prize money, too." Rye looked back at his engine. "Can you recommend a good garage in town? Just in case."

Jackson hesitated. "The Calhouns have a garage. Right at the edge of downtown. Tell them I sent you."

"I will." Interesting that the garage owners had the same surname as he did. It wasn't often Rye ran into any Calhouns. He shifted the bar holding the hood up and then slammed the hood closed. "Thanks for stopping."

"Want me to wait and make sure your truck starts?"

"No, but thanks. You have your girl waiting." It was all Rye could do not to look at the blonde in the truck. "Don't want to keep you."

"Once you're settled in town, come by FlintWorks for a beer. It's on me."

"The brewery at the old depot?"

"That's it." Jackson gave a brief nod and returned to his truck.

Rye watched him walk away before glancing at the girl in the passenger seat. She was looking back at him, a long, assessing look that made him hot and his body harden.

Even though she was someone else's, he still wanted her.

So odd, since he couldn't remember the last time he desired anyone or anything.

He deliberately turned away and climbed into his truck cab, and once Jackson's black truck passed him, merging onto the highway, Rye started his own truck and followed, careful to keep to the speed limit to prevent his truck from overheating.

ANSLEY CAMPBELL HELD her long blonde hair in one hand as Jackson passed the blue and white truck and silver horse trailer, the rugged cowboy in the driver's seat.

The sun's long slanting rays had been like a spotlight shining on Jackson and the cowboy with the broken-down truck. The cowboy had looked at her more than once. Normally, she wasn't interested in being checked out, but the cowboy didn't seem like the flirty type. If anything, he looked alone, tough, and a little weary, but that was also probably her imagination. He was probably just ticked off he was having car problems. No one liked being on the side of the road on what had been one of the hottest days of the month, especially when pulling a horse trailer.

"He's okay?" she asked Jackson, as Jackson picked up speed, traffic moving fast, everyone wanting to get some-where.

"He says he is." Jackson glanced up into the rearview

mirror as if checking for the blue and white truck. "Luckily, Marietta isn't far."

"He's going to Marietta?" she said, before putting two and two together. "He's going for the rodeo?"

Jackson nodded. He looked at her, amused. "Want an introduction?"

"*No*. I'm not interested in dating. Anyone."

He laughed softly. "Simmer down. Everyone knows you're devoted to your uncle and your art."

"I am serious about my art." *And my independence*, she silently added.

She'd only recently come to Montana from Texas, happy to escape her big family of overbearing men. The last thing she wanted was to tangle with another. It was good to be on her own … or almost on her own as she was living with her uncle, taking care of him, but Uncle Clyde was easy compared to her five brothers. "I do appreciate you driving me to Bozeman. I don't know how I would have got that canvas to the Sterbas' law office otherwise. It's one of the biggest pieces I've ever done."

"It was beautiful, and I still think you should have charged a lot more."

"I'll be able to charge more as I get my name out. This sale was just really good for my ego. My first commercial sale."

"In that case, I'm happy if you're happy."

"I'm really happy." She smiled, more than happy.

Finally, she had time to focus on her art. Finally, there was traction in her career. If she kept working hard, she'd have her own gallery in the next year or two. Marietta would be the perfect place for an art gallery. There was money in Marietta, wealthy ranchers, tourists, as well as all the affluency from the East and West Coasts who came to Montana for their own piece of land with a mountain view.

Jackson signaled, taking the exit to Marietta and Paradise Valley. He'd picked her up from the ranch this afternoon as Uncle Clyde didn't want her driving his truck and the painting didn't fit in her small car.

"How is your uncle?" Jackson asked. "Still challenging?"

"I was warned he'd be difficult." Ansley tried not to think about the dustup with her uncle this morning when she asked—begged—to borrow his SUV.

He wouldn't even consider it and she lost her temper, upset that she'd lose her sale. Marching to the barn loft, she suddenly thought of Jackson, fellow Texan, and all-around good and gorgeous. He'd offered to help her should she ever be in a bind and today was most definitely a bind.

Jackson's brow creased. "Did no one else from your family want to come out and help? Why you?"

She shrugged. "They all had careers."

"And your family didn't think you did?"

Ansley swallowed a sigh. "They think it's a hobby. Something I dabble at, something I'll stop as soon as I grow up."

"Maybe I should commission something for the brewery."

Ansley grinned. "Maybe you should. What would you like?"

"Surprise me."

"How big should it be?"

"That's your call. You're the artist."

"You're serious?"

He nodded. "It's FlintWorks's tenth anniversary this year. Why not celebrate with some art?"

She couldn't stop smiling. It was easy to brush off the challenges of living with Uncle Clyde while sitting next to Jackson. Jackson exuded confidence—just like her brothers—but unlike her brothers, he'd been a big source of support as she tried to adapt to Marietta. Jackson had also been raised in Texas's Hill Country, but he had a *real* job, managing the family's popular brewery FlintWorks while she pursued a path of her own, a path not respected by her family of overachievers.

Fifteen minutes later, Ansley pointed out the gravel road outside Pray, the road would take them up to Cold Canyon Ranch. The sun had set, and twilight engulfed the mountains, turning the landscape lavender and gray.

As they approached the ranch entrance, Ansley felt the whisper of loneliness that came from still being an outsider in a small town. Maybe if she lived in town, she'd feel more comfortable, but Cold Canyon Ranch was exactly what it sounded like—a ranch high in the mountains, in the shadow of Emigrant Peak, where the sun rose late and disappeared early. The wind blew through the canyon almost constantly, shaping and stunting the few trees. If the ranch was cold during the summer, she couldn't even imagine how frigid it would be in the winter.

Hopefully, she wouldn't still be here at Uncle Clyde's come winter, but she didn't know who would live with him if she left. She didn't want to return to her family's place outside Last Stand, Texas, but living in the middle of nowhere long term wasn't going to be good for her mental health—or creativity. She missed her friends, and she missed her family, her mom in particular. But at least she was being productive here on the ranch. One of the first things she did in early June was set up a studio for herself in the barn loft. Uncle Clyde couldn't use the space anymore and he gave it to her with his blessing. She loved having her own place, a place no one went but her. Ansley had never had her own dedicated space to draw and paint, confined to either her childhood bedroom, or sharing her mother's sewing room. But now she had a huge loft with wonderful light, and she could paint to her heart's content—or whenever Uncle Clyde didn't need her.

Jackson pulled up in front of the single-story farmhouse, a 1920s white house with a big, covered porch and the tall windows of the period. The house looked dark, which made her anxious. Hopefully her uncle was fine. She was later than she intended but she'd make a quick dinner for them, pasta probably, and with any luck, he'd disappear into the TV room until bed.

"Thank you again," she said to Jackson, climbing out of the truck. "You saved me. I'm so grateful."

"My pleasure. It gave me a chance to catch up with my friends over at Montana Ale Works."

She closed the door, lifted her hand in a final wave, and watched as he continued around the circular driveway, headlights cutting through the darkness.

Letting herself into the farmhouse, Ansley found her uncle was waiting for her, not in front of the TV, but at the vintage square oak kitchen table with its twisted legs. Two straight-back ladder chairs flanked the table and Uncle Clyde was in one. He'd made a point of telling her when she first arrived that there had never been four chairs, only two, because there had been no need for more. It had always been Uncle Clyde and his wife, and as they'd never had children they didn't entertain, either.

"You're late," her uncle said brusquely as she entered the kitchen. "Wasn't sure if you were even coming back."

Ansley held her breath. Her uncle was in one of his moods and she didn't have the energy to argue with him. "You knew I was taking one of my big canvases to a law office in Bozeman. I told you it would take several hours."

"You didn't tell me it would mean I'd miss dinner."

"You haven't missed dinner. I just haven't made it yet. Give me a half hour—"

"You know I like to eat by six."

"Then you should've made yourself something. You're not helpless. Before I came you made yourself dinner all the time."

He glared at her. "I knew this was a bad idea having you come here. I knew—"

"It's not a bad idea as long as we both agree to get along. You're the one in a bad mood. I came home happy—"

"As well as late."

She shook her head. "Stop being such a grouch and let me make dinner and everything will be fine." Her voice was sharper than she intended, but she was tired of taking whatever her uncle dished out.

She'd never even met him until she arrived Memorial Day weekend, late May. It had been an interesting summer living here, and there were times her uncle was good company—well that was going too far. He was satisfactory company—but there were other times, like tonight, when she didn't know why she was even here.

It wasn't as if she was being paid to be his live-in companion. She was here as a favor to her parents, not that her dad would ever ask her to stay with his brother on the family ranch, but her mother had taken pity on Clyde and had also seen it as an opportunity for Ansley to get out and spread her wings a bit. So, here she was, trying to keep an eye on her uncle as his health had begun to fail and no one knew what would happen to him—or the Campbells' Cold Canyon Ranch—which had been in the family since the 1930s.

At the sink, Ansley washed her hands before drying. "I was thinking of just making some chicken and pasta. Would you like chicken Alfredo? Lemon chicken? What sounds best?"

"Whatever is the fastest. I'm hungry."

"They're both quick. We'll be eating in thirty minutes."

"I don't know if I can wait."

"Then how about a yogurt to tide you over?"

His lips pursed. "I just want dinner."

He reminded her of a small petulant child, and her lips twitched picturing him in a high chair, waving his fists, having a tantrum. "I know. The message has come through loud and clear. Since Alfredo is your favorite, I will do that. But are you sure you wouldn't like a snack to hold you?"

"You're being patronizing."

"And you, Uncle Clyde, are being a little demanding," she retorted, "but I'm going to put it down to low blood sugar or high blood pressure as I know you wouldn't normally be so difficult." Then she gave him her sweetest smile. "I'm going to quickly change, and I'll be right down, and dinner will be ready before you know it."

Then as Ansley headed out of the kitchen, she shouted back to him, "And my trip to Bozeman went really well, thank you for asking. I stayed to see them hang the painting on their conference room wall. It was pretty awesome."

FORTY MINUTES LATER, they were at the table finishing dinner when her uncle cleared his throat. "Did you take any pictures?" he asked, voice gruff.

Ansley blinked, confused. "Of?"

"Of them hanging your painting in the office."

She slowly smiled. "I did. Would you like to see?"

He nodded, and she went to get her phone from where it was charging on the hall table. Returning to the kitchen, Ansley pulled her chair closer to his. "I took a half dozen, haven't even looked at them yet, but this is Jackson Flint carrying the painting into the law office. Jackson is huge and that gives you an idea of just how big the painting was."

"I don't know him," Clyde said.

"He's been in Marietta four years now, maybe a little longer. He manages FlintWorks, the brewery his older brothers founded in Marietta's train depot."

"I knew the name sounded familiar."

She flicked through a couple photos of the building maintenance moving furniture to clear space for the painting and then hanging it. "Here it is up," she said, handing her phone back to him. "It really fills up the wall."

Clyde studied the photo. "The Bridger Mountains. The west face."

She nodded. "Mr. Sterba was raised at the foot of the mountains. He said it's his favorite view."

Her uncle was still examining the photo. "You did a good job. Must have taken you some time."

"Weeks, but I enjoyed it. We don't have mountains like this in Texas."

"You don't have any mountains in Texas."

"We do have the Hill Country," she said, turning off her phone.

"Huh. Those are barely hills."

She smiled because he was right. Compared to the Rocky Mountains, Texas was pretty much a flat state.

"I see now why you needed my truck. I'm sorry I reacted so badly."

"It's okay."

"I should have asked more questions."

"It's behind us."

Uncle Clyde's gaze searched hers. "Are you sure?"

She nodded.

"So, how did you sell this landscape?" Clyde asked. "How did Sterba see it? Do you have a website?"

"I have a landing page, and my Ansley Art Instagram account. I use both to direct all traffic to my Etsy store. That's where a lot of people find me."

"Etsy?"

"It's an online store for artisans. They get a lot of traffic and I've been able to sell smaller things through them. But Mr. Sterba's wife saw my work at the farmer's market in Marietta. I've had a little booth a couple of times and have sold things through that, mostly to tourists wanting a souvenir, but it's made me money."

"I always wondered what you were doing out in the barn."

Ansley laughed. "You knew I was painting."

"Yeah, but I didn't know you were good."

"That's nice of you to say so." She rose and began gathering their dishes. "Do you want any dessert tonight?"

"Do we have any of your brownies left?"

"We do."

"I'd like one of those if you don't mind." He pushed up, moving slowly. "Can I help with dishes?"

"No, I've got this. Go relax."

But when she carried a dessert plate in to the TV room later, she discovered her uncle slumped in his leather recliner, the television on mute.

"What's wrong?" she asked, swiftly moving to his side.

"Just light-headed."

Ansley set the dessert plate on his side table and carefully touched his forehead. He wasn't hot or cold. He didn't feel clammy. But he did look pale. "Any other symptoms?"

"No. I'm just dizzy. I was dizzy earlier—"

"You didn't tell me."

"I said I was hungry."

She sat down on the edge of the couch. "Do you want to go to the doctor?"

"No."

"Do you think this is related to your heart issues?"

"No."

She frowned, uncertain. "How do you know?"

"Because it passes."

"How long has it been happening?"

"For the last six months or so. But it's fine. I'm fine. I think I'll just go to bed. I'll feel better in the morning."

She glanced at the dessert plate on the end table. "No dessert?"

"Maybe put it in the freezer and I'll have it tomorrow."

He was struggling to rise, and she hovered, wanting to assist but not sure how.

On his feet, he sighed and shook his head. "If you don't see me tomorrow morning, I might have gone to meet my maker."

"Uncle Clyde, don't say that."

"Just a joke."

"It's not funny. I'm worried about you."

"Everything's fine. You deal with the brownie, and I'll deal with myself."

But in bed that evening, Ansley couldn't sleep, her thoughts returning to her uncle.

What if he really wasn't well and needed medical care? What if he needed help now? She didn't want to lie in bed, updating her Instagram account if he needed her.

Troubled, she slipped from bed, tiptoed down the hall, and quietly opened his door. His room was dark. She heard snoring. He was asleep. He was okay. Feeling encouraged, Ansley returned to her room and wondered again what her uncle's future was, as well as the future of Cold Canyon Ranch, which had been in the Campbell family for almost a hundred years.

The Campbells were a Montana family, and always had been since emigrating from Scotland at the turn of the century. Her dad, Callen Campbell, was the first Campbell to leave Montana, turning his back on the family property, but that was because of a deep rift between him and his brother. They hadn't always been antagonistic. Growing up, her dad and uncle Clyde had apparently been close. They were also competitive like most brothers, with Clyde a little more competitive. But even then, no one expected him to swoop in and steal his brother's girlfriend when Callen joined the army.

Her dad refused to forgive Clyde even after he'd met Ansley's mom and had fallen in love. They'd been happy together—obviously with six kids, five boys and one daughter over a fifteen-year period—and were still happily married. But Callen wouldn't forgive his brother and Clyde made no attempt to repair their relationship, either, not even when widowed. There was no fixing the past, and no hope for the future, which also put the future of the Campbells' ranch in jeopardy.

Callen still owned half the ranch. Their dad had left the property to both his sons, but Callen did nothing to help it, and he never took the income from it, leaving it all in the Campbell trust.

It was Callen's wife, Andi, who felt sorry for Clyde. Andi was the one who sent Clyde a Christmas card every year, and a card for Clyde's birthday. When Clyde's neighbor, rancher Melvin Wyatt reached out to the Texas Campbells, it was Andi who answered the phone. Melvin was calling to let them know that Clyde was not well, and the Cold Canyon Ranch was falling into disrepair. Melvin said he and his boys were patching fences and checking in regularly on Clyde, but he needed help, someone who could be there daily, as his dementia was worsening.

It had been a shock to Ansley's dad that his younger brother had vascular dementia. The last time Callen had seen Clyde they were both in their mid-twenties. Now they were men in their late sixties. Callen didn't feel like sixty. He didn't feel fifty. He was still fit and strong and riding every day. He worked his ranch every day. Discovering that his brother wasn't healthy shook him. He and Andi made a trip to Montana and spent a weekend at the farmhouse. Clyde was better by the time they left, less confused, more lucid, but he was easily agitated and would get frustrated by change.

Back in Texas, Callen gathered his family and said that this next year was critical. They needed to help Clyde, and they needed to figure out what to do with the ranch. Andi suggested Clyde move in with them, but Callen wasn't going to go that far. It was one thing to be concerned about his brother's welfare, and another to have him under his own roof.

There was much discussion amongst the boys, Ansley's brothers, about the Montana property. How many acres? How many cattle could it support? Were any crops being grown? Could it provide a living? Despite the intense conversation nobody was ready to move to Paradise Valley, not when everyone had work, and relationships in Texas.

But then Ansley surprised them all by raising her hand. "I'll go," she said. "At least for the summer. We can decide what happens after that later."

Summer had come and gone, and no one mentioned relieving Ansley. Her parents hadn't returned for another visit. It was as if Clyde and Cold Canyon Ranch were no longer an issue. No one needed to get involved. Ansley had the situation well in hand.

Ansley turned over in bed, squishing her down pillow beneath her cheek. Oh, if only they knew.

Chapter Two

THE POUNDING PENETRATED his sleep, interrupting his dream. Pounding close by.

Rye opened his eyes, looked around, remembered where he was. His trailer. Marietta fairgrounds. The pounding was coming from his trailer door.

He glanced at his phone as he swung his legs out of the narrow bed. Six fifteen.

Rye grabbed a T-shirt, tugging it over his head, then adjusting the waistband on his sweatpants before opening the door.

A bloody young cowboy stood outside in the dirt, swaying on his feet. "I think I need stitches," he said, slurring the words a little, but the slur didn't hide his Southern drawl.

"What happened, JB?" Rye asked, stepping out to get a better look at the youngster who was a great kid when sober but a hothead when liquored up.

"Had some words with a knucklehead." JB squinted through the blood. "I was winning until he hit me with a bottle. Cut me pretty good."

"Let me get my boots and keys. I'll be quick." Rye was quick, too, back outside in less than a minute. He walked JB to the passenger side of his truck and opened the door for him. "Where did you get hit? There's so much blood I can't tell."

JB settled in the seat. "Can't say exactly. It all hurts."

Rye closed the door and went around to the driver's side. Once behind the wheel, he started the engine and pulled away from his trailer. "What about your eyes?"

JB tipped his head back. "They were brown last time I checked." He managed a smile. "You flirting with me, cowboy?"

Rye wished he could smile, but this wasn't the first time he'd dragged JB's sorry self to the hospital. "You've got to stop drinking, JB. You're going to tangle with the wrong dude one day—"

"He started the fight, Calhoun. I didn't want to fight."

Rye said nothing. Most of the other cowboys now kept their distance from JB, not wanting to be drawn into the Mississippi kid's drama, but JB was just nineteen, his brother Jasper's age, and Rye couldn't help being concerned. And exasperated.

Marietta's hospital wasn't far from the fairgrounds, and Rye drove up to the emergency room's entrance and parked in front of the sliding glass doors. "I'm going to wait in my truck," he told JB. "I'll drive you back when you're done."

JB hesitated. "You don't want to come in?"

Rye had spent far too much time in hospitals, far too much time in ER. He'd do it for family, but JB could handle this on his own. "You'll be fine. You know the drill. Go check in and they'll do the rest."

JB staggered out of the truck and slammed the door behind him. Rye watched him disappear through the sliding glass doors and approach reception. Smothering a yawn, Rye did a circle, looking for an open parking spot. Most of them were assigned to doctors but there were some visitor spaces and he took one of the open ones, backing into the spot so he could keep an eye out for JB, although Rye didn't expect to see him for a good hour or two.

Parked, engine off, Rye leaned his seat back and closed his eyes, thinking another hour of sleep would be appreciated.

He was dozing when his phone rang and with a start he opened his eyes, grabbed the phone, checking the number. His mom. Rye's stomach fell. She normally didn't call him when he was on the road.

He answered immediately. "Everybody doing okay, Mom?"

"Yes, sweetheart. We're doing just fine."

"How about Jasper?"

"He's better. I promise." She hesitated. "Did I wake you up? Am I calling too early?"

"I've been up for a while," he said, returning his seat to an upright position. "What's on your mind?"

"It's nothing really. I suppose it could wait. But I thought, if it's not too much trouble..." Her voice faded.

She didn't finish the sentence.

"Spit it out. No need to be embarrassed."

"I've overdrawn the checking account. I thought I had enough in savings to cover, but I don't. Is there any way you could transfer some money into my account? I'll reimburse you back next payday."

"Of course," he said, knowing he'd never accept her money, and she knew it, too, although they never discussed it. "How much do you need?"

"Two thousand. That way I have enough for all the utilities—you know I've been running the air conditioner a lot more for Jasper—"

"You don't need to explain."

"But I do. And then there are the credit card payments. I don't want to be late again."

"I'll transfer money now, as soon as we hang up."

"Thank you, sweetheart."

"No problem, Mom."

They hung up, and Rye immediately went to his bank app, tapped transfers, and moved money from his account to his mom's. While there, he checked his sisters' accounts. They both had a couple hundred, which wasn't a lot, but they were frugal and had part-time jobs to help pay for gas and books at the college.

He closed out of the bank app and closed his eyes, but sleep evaded him this time.

All he could see was his family home in Eureka, and the

wraparound porch with the ramp for Jasper's wheelchair. For a time after his dad's injury, his dad was in a chair, too, but thankfully, he'd recovered enough not to need it anymore. But his dad was still incapacitated, forever unable to work. There had been disability checks in the beginning but after a few years those stopped. His mom worked as much as she could considering his father and brother were dependent on her.

So, Rye worked, and worked hard.

He didn't mind working, either. He was one of those that liked being busy, needed a purpose, but the fact that the family couldn't survive without him, and that every check he earned, whether from roofing or competing, was required for his family's survival created a pressure of its own. He didn't resent his family or the pressure, but that didn't mean he didn't feel it. Thank goodness he had big shoulders, a thick skin, and a high tolerance for pain. It allowed him to keep going when others might have quit. There was no quitting for him, though. He loved his family. He was glad he could help. But it did mean his options were limited.

He wouldn't ever move away from them. He couldn't.

He wouldn't take work that didn't pay the bills.

He was always aware he couldn't afford to get injured, not seriously, as his family would suffer the consequences. And so, when he entered his rodeo events, he always told his mom he'd entered the safe events. But there was big money in bull riding, and every now and then, he'd slip an additional event onto his schedule, thinking an extra hundred or two would go a long way toward groceries, or an extra physical therapy for his brother. The physical therapy sessions weren't covered by insurance anymore. Very little was covered by insurance.

Rye had begun opening the bills before his mom could and handling the insurance as well. Far better he shield her from the negativity. She didn't need it. It would wear her down and then she'd struggle emotionally, and he wouldn't allow that.

He glanced at his watch. Almost eight thirty. He'd need to feed his horses soon and get them some exercise. He needed exercise. The rodeo itself didn't begin until tomorrow, which gave him time to get his head together. He knew what was important. He knew to stay focused. Which was why he'd become a loner on the circuit. He didn't drink or date. He didn't go dancing. He couldn't afford to go out to eat with the others. Being social wasn't as important as taking care of his family, and until his family no longer needed him so desperately, friends could wait. Women could wait. His dreams could wait. There would be time for all of that one day. Someday. God willing.

An ambulance arrived, siren off but lights flashing. A few minutes later, a second ambulance pulled in. Rye's gaze narrowed as hospital staff streamed out to meet the EMTs, assisting the patients as EMTs rolled the gurneys into the hospital through an entrance reserved just for them.

There was a lot of staff moving, and a rather dazed-looking woman climbing out of the ambulance, shouldering her purse, trailing after a gurney.

HE'D JUST CLIMBED out of his truck to stretch his legs when he spotted a young woman in a baseball cap trying to push a wheelchair. The man was big and slumped to one side. She was struggling to keep the chair rolling. She seemed to be hitting every crack in the asphalt, catching the wheelchair's front casters and bringing it to a jerky stop.

Rye shouldn't get involved. He didn't need to get involved, but it was hard to ignore someone struggling when Rye had so much experience with wheelchairs. The least he could do was get the old man into ER safely.

Crossing the parking lot, he approached the pair. "Can I help?"

The young woman looked up at him from beneath the brim of her cap, and he felt a jolt of recognition. Her blue eyes widened at the same time. She recognized him, too. It was the beautiful, sun-kissed blonde from Jackson Flint's truck. A beautiful sun-kissed blonde that was also probably Jackson Flint's girlfriend. "You're Jackson's girl," he said.

"No, just a friend of Jackson's." She took a frustrated breath. "I don't know what I'm doing wrong. I keep getting stuck."

"You're doing fine, it's the parking lot that's the problem, not you. Let me." He grasped the handles on the back of the chair, tipped the chair backwards slightly, freeing the small front casters. It didn't take him long to get the wheelchair onto a smoother surface and as he pushed the chair towards the emergency room entrance, the young woman walked quickly next to him.

"Almost there, Uncle Clyde," she said, patting the old man's shoulder. "Hang in there."

The old man's eyes were closed, his features creased with pain.

The woman looked up at Rye, alarmed.

Rye just focused on getting the wheelchair past the two ambulances parked beneath the hospital portico, and then up the small ramp to ER. "I'll follow you," he said as the glass doors opened.

She nodded and headed to the reception and spoke to the nurse at the desk. Rye glanced down at the older man in the wheelchair. The old man looked pale, and his eyes were still closed.

The young woman turned and gestured for Rye to push the wheelchair forward. He did. She leaned down to speak to her uncle. "I need your wallet. Did we bring it?"

"Pocket," the old man gritted. "Back on the right." He tried to lean forward, and Rye quickly retrieved it, handing the wallet over.

The beautiful blonde flashed him a grateful look and returned her attention to registering her uncle. Once that was done, another nurse came over and took the old man's vitals and asked the young woman questions. She didn't seem to know the answers to most and then an orderly claimed the old man, and wheeled him away, taking him to an examination room.

His niece rose to go, but her uncle grunted something about privacy and for her to stay, and then the wheelchair and patient were gone.

For a moment, there was just silence and then the beautiful girl looked at him, and had tears in her eyes. "I was so scared," she whispered. "The whole drive I just kept praying. I didn't know what was happening and wasn't sure he'd make it."

"You couldn't call an ambulance?"

"We live thirty miles away, up in the mountains. I couldn't wait for an ambulance to come." She struggled to smile, wiping moisture away from beneath her eyes. "Besides, it looks like they're all here anyway."

"You did good," Rye said. "And your uncle will get great care here. Marietta Medical is a great hospital, but I'm sure you already know that."

"I didn't know that. I'm still relatively new here, arrived late May."

"From where?"

"Texas. My family lives in a small town called Last Stand in the Hill Country."

"I've been there."

"You have?"

He nodded. "Right next to Fredericksburg, yes?"

"Yes." She smiled at him, some of the tension leaving her face. "I'm Ansley Campbell," she said, extending her hand.

He was happy to take it. Her hand was soft, smooth, her skin cool. "Rye Calhoun."

"I've never met a Rye before," she said, taking her hand back, slipping it into a pocket of her jeans.

"You're my first Ansley."

Her smile widened. "So, what brings you to Marietta Medical?" Her gaze skimmed over him, as if looking for blood or an injury.

"I brought a friend. He's back there somewhere getting stitches. I'm just waiting for him."

"I didn't think the rodeo had even started yet."

"It hasn't."

"What happened?"

There was something about her voice that made Rye's chest tighten, making him feel. She didn't exactly have an accent, but he wasn't surprised she was Texan. Her voice was warm, a little husky, a little breathless, and it made him feel a little warm. A little restless. "JB has a mean horse," Rye said, not wanting her to know that JB had been fighting. It didn't seem suitable for her ears somehow.

Ansley's eyes widened. "His horse kicked him?"

"I told you he was mean."

She looked at him, her dark blue gaze searching his. "Are you being serious? Because I'm not sure I believe you."

Rye sighed. "Okay, JB was in a fight. I brought him to get stitches."

She pushed up the brim of her cap. "Why didn't you just say that?"

"I was trying to protect you."

Ansley laughed. "I have five brothers, including one that's a fighter pilot. You don't have to protect me. I've heard it all and seen it all at this point."

Rye heard her, but looking into her face with those exquisite cheekbones, full lips, and perfect chin, he didn't think she knew as much as she thought she did. It wasn't a criticism, either. She struck him as sheltered, innocent, and he wasn't going to be the one that broke her trust.

Before he could speak, the swinging door opened and JB emerged, face clean, dark stitches running through one eyebrow and then down his cheek, his skin mottled with emerging bruises. He also looked as if he'd sobered as his eyes locked with Rye's, his expression chagrined as he crossed the waiting area.

"Thanks for waiting, Calhoun," JB said gruffly, folding his discharge papers and shoving them into his denim pocket.

"No problem," Rye answered.

JB looked at Ansley, appreciation in his eyes. Rye wasn't about to introduce him. "Let's get you back to your trailer," he said, clapping JB on the back.

He got JB moving toward the door and then Rye turned to look back at Ansley, who was still standing there in her baseball cap, pink T-shirt, snug jeans, and white sneakers. She looked like a college cheerleader. Fresh, pretty, young. So fresh and pretty it was hard to walk away from her.

He felt another twinge, the pinch in his chest catching him by surprise. What was she doing to him? "Want coffee?" he asked.

She nodded.

The tightness in his chest made it hard to think. "How do you like it?"

"Milk and sugar."

"I'll be back."

Her eyes locked with his. She seemed to be trying to make a decision, curiosity and wariness warring in her eyes. Curiosity won because her lips curved, and she nodded again. "I'll be here."

WHILE WAITING FOR an update from the medical staff, Ansley paced outside talking to her mom on the phone, updating her on everything that had happened. Her mom was calm as always and reassured Ansley she'd done everything right, and there was no reason to beat herself up. She asked Ansley to let her know when there was news and then they said goodbye and hung up.

Ansley forced herself to stop pacing and sit down inside and try not to replay the morning's events over and over in her head but being woken by her uncle's shout, and then running to discover him on the floor had shaken her to the core. It had been hard getting him to her car, and hard to focus on driving when he'd groaned off and on for thirty minutes. Then, reaching the hospital, there had been no-where near the entrance to park what with the ambulances and commotion, so she fetched a hospital wheelchair but just getting her uncle into it made him hiss with pain. He'd broken something, she was sure of that. But just what he'd broken she didn't know.

The sliding glass doors to ER's patient entrance opened and Rye walked in, tall, lean, handsome. Focused. He also had two large paper cups of coffee with the Java Café logo. Her heart thumped with gratitude, glad to see him, and not just for the coffee. She welcomed the company, needing the distraction. It was hard not knowing what was happening in the exam room. It was hard not feeling responsible. Uncle Clyde's bathroom had grab bars at the toilet and bathtub from when Aunt Sandy had cancer. But her uncle fell before he even reached the bathroom. She wasn't sure how to help him or protect him. Maybe a walker would help, something to lean on when he left the bed.

"Any news?" Rye asked, handing her a cup.

She shook her head. "Nothing."

"By the way, it's not a drip coffee. The girl at Java Café insisted I try the vanilla caramel latte, saying it was a special drink in celebration of the eighty-fifth Copper Mountain Rodeo. I didn't know how to disappoint her."

"Is that what you have, too?"

He looked shamefaced. "No. I have a black coffee. I'm not much for sweet things in the morning."

"Whereas I love everything sweet—pancakes, waffles, French toast, cinnamon rolls. The more sugar the better."

"Then you might like the Copper Mountain Rodeo latte."

"I just might." She took a sip. The latte was strong, creamy and sweet, and exactly what she needed after the rough morning. "It's good. Really good. Thank you."

"You're welcome." He gestured to the bench outside. "Want to sit there? It's nice out. The air is fresh."

"Good idea."

Outside as they sat down, Rye extended his legs, boots crossed at the ankle, cowboy hat shielding his eyes. He hadn't been wearing a hat earlier. For that matter, he hadn't been wearing the blue plaid western shirt, either.

"How did you have time to change?" she asked.

"I'm fast."

"Is that a good thing or a bad thing for a cowboy?"

"Fast reflexes are good. Fast rides, not so good."

She didn't want to stare but it was hard not to keep looking his way. He was tan, fit, muscles tightening in his forearm as he drank his coffee. "I appreciate you bringing me coffee when I'm sure you have more important things to do," she said, suddenly feeling shy.

"I don't, not yet. Later, I'll head to the arena, do a little riding and roping to get a feel for the stadium, but today is essentially a rest day."

"Do you compete in a lot of rodeos?"

"Almost every weekend."

"It's what you do full-time?" She persisted, curious about him, more curious than she'd been about anyone in a long time. There was something mysterious about him, something that made her want to ask questions and discover who he was, and what secrets he kept.

"MONDAY THROUGH THURSDAY I'm a roofer. Thursday afternoon I'm on the road heading to my next rodeo."

She hid her surprise, thinking it sounded awful, as well as exhausting. "When do you rest?"

"Usually at night, when I'm in bed."

Ansley grinned, amused. "Where is home?"

"Eureka." His mouth quirked, correctly reading her blank expression. "It's a small town on the border of Montana and Canada."

"But it's in Montana?"

"It is." He stretched an arm along the back of the bench.

"What about you? What do you do?"

"I'm staying with my uncle on his ranch in Paradise Valley. He's a widower and doesn't have any kids. I'm supposed to be taking care of him but as you can see, I'm not doing a very good job of that."

"What happened?"

"He was dizzy last night when he went to bed, but he assured me he'd be fine in the morning. Yet, when he got up this morning to use the restroom, he fell." Ansley felt another stab of guilt and remorse. "I really hope he didn't break anything. I could barely get him to the car he was in so much pain."

"You can't blame yourself. These things happen as we age."

"Then I don't want to age! I don't ever want to be dependent on others."

Rye gave her a look that was impossible to decipher. "There are worse things."

His voice was deep, rather flinty, and she sensed she'd touched a nerve. For a moment she didn't know what to say, but then Rye filled in the silence. "Brothers, sisters?" he asked.

"Five older brothers. I'm the youngest."

"Six of you," he said.

"Yep."

"And five big brothers? Wow."

"It was a lot," she agreed. "Most of them are gone now,

but when they come home, they still act like they're in charge."

"Ranchers or farmers?"

"Two of them are. The other three do different things. But they're all very alpha, and I pity their wives."

"They're married then?"

"No. Well, one was but he's on his own now." She was ready to take the focus off her family. Her brothers had always stolen the limelight, including her parents' attention. They were smart and successful, and considered really good-looking, which didn't help their egos. "What about you— any brothers or sisters?"

"There are four of us. I'm the oldest, then two sisters, and my brother Jasper is the youngest."

"Do you get along with everyone?"

"We're pretty close," he admitted.

She envied him for being close with his siblings. Maybe if she'd had a sister, or a brother who'd wanted to play with a sister, she wouldn't have been so lonely.

The sliding glass doors opened, and Ansley quickly stood but it wasn't anyone for her and she slowly sat back down, trying not to be anxious. Uncle Clyde was with doctors and nurses, and they'd help him, far better than she could. But he hadn't had breakfast yet, and he liked to eat early every day.

She glanced at Rye and made a face. "Sorry. I know I'm not very good company right now."

"You're great. Don't apologize."

"I don't have a lot of experience with hospitals. This is my first visit to an ER. Now, my mom was always driving one of my brothers for stiches and concussions, broken collarbones, broken leg, broken fingers."

"You never broke anything?"

"No. I was the proverbial good girl. Quiet and boring."

Rye smiled, a deep dimple forming in his cheek. "I can't imagine you quiet or boring."

Ansley was fascinated by the dimple, fascinated by the flash of even white teeth, fascinated by his strong tan throat and the hint of an equally tan chest visible above his open button. She wished he'd left a few more pearl buttons open. She imagined he had a rather spectacular chest to match his wide shoulders.

"I think you'll relax better with me gone," he said, standing. "But I'm going to give you my number so you can call me when your uncle is discharged. I'll help you transfer him into the car, and be happy to follow you home to help get him in the house."

"You don't need to do that," she said, rising.

He shrugged. "If I can make things easier for you—or anyone—then I should."

A lump filled her throat, and she looked up into his eyes, the brown irises flecked with gold. "I've never met anyone like you before."

"I'm sure you have."

"No," she said, shaking her head. "Most people don't go out of their way to help others."

"But wouldn't the world be a better place if they did?" His lips twisted in a vaguely self-mocking smile. "Let's make a deal. If you want a hand, call me. I'm not far, just over at the fairgrounds, and don't if I'm being presumptuous. The last thing I want to do is make you uncomfortable."

"You don't, and I'm terrible at asking for help, but in this case, it might be nice to have a hand getting my uncle settled."

"I hate asking for help, too. I've always figured it was because I'm the oldest."

"And I always figured it was because I'm the youngest and sick and tired of being bossed around." Ansley shyly handed him her phone. "Do you mind putting it in my contacts? That way I won't lose it."

She watched as he added his name and cell number to her contacts before tapping done and returning the phone to her. "I really do appreciate the kindness," she said, a catch in her voice.

He looked at her for a long moment, searching her eyes and then he nodded. "Happy to help. Let me know when your uncle is ready to leave. I'll be here in five."

She nodded and walked as he turned away and walked to his blue and white truck. Her brother Colm had one very similar, except his was a rusty orange and white. Cowboys and their old work trucks. She didn't know if they drove them because they were cheap, practical, or they knew they looked sexy in them.

Maybe not all cowboys looked sexy in their beat-up truck, but Rye Calhoun did.

Rye Calhoun was something else.

Chapter Three

T HEY WERE GOING to keep her uncle for the next few days. He had broken his wrist from falling on his left side, but there were other concerns, more urgent concerns, like Uncle Clyde's blood pressure and worrying results from the MRI indicating that her uncle probably had had a stroke, and apparently it wasn't the first. Dr. Gallagher promised to phone Ansley as soon as he had something concrete to share.

Ansley exited the hospital slightly dazed. Her uncle was in good hands, but she was surprised. It hadn't crossed her mind they would want to admit him, and now that they had, she wasn't sure what to do next.

There was nothing forcing her back to the ranch, not immediately. No animals to feed, no uncle to keep company, nothing specific she needed to do. For the first time since arriving in Marietta, she had twenty-four hours to herself. It was a heady thought, and her work ethic told her she ought to return to the barn loft at Cold Canyon Ranch and get painting, while another part of her rebelled against the ranch's isolation.

Ansley thought about calling Rye and letting him know but held back, fearing he'd think she was trying to orches-

trate a date—and she didn't want a date. She was drawn to
Rye, and the physical attraction was pretty electric, but she
still wasn't ready to get romantic with anyone. Relationships
were hard work and breakups brutal. Better to avoid entanglements until she was more settled and financially
independent.

Heading to her car, Ansley thought about her options
and the reluctance to return to the ranch spoke volumes.

Thinking of living on Cold Canyon Ranch long term
with an irritable uncle worried Ansley and so she did her best
not to think past Thanksgiving when she'd hoped to go
home for the holiday and find out what her family intended
to do about her uncle and the ranch.

It wasn't that Uncle Clyde was a bad person. He didn't
lose his temper with her too often, but he wasn't a cheerful
person, and it was far easier for him to complain than look
on the bright side. Ansley needed the bright side. She needed
sun and warmth and smiles. She'd never tell her family how
hard the transition had been, moving in with Uncle Clyde. If
it wasn't for her art, she didn't think she'd still be here now,
three months on.

So no, she wouldn't go back to the ranch yet. It felt too
good to be off the property. She rarely had time to just be in
town and explore, and with the rodeo taking place this
weekend, there was so much to do and see. She drove toward
Main Street and snagged the first parking spot she could find
as Main Street had already been blocked off for the barbecue

and street dance.

Marietta had never looked better. Hanging flower baskets overflowing with zinnias, begonias, and petunias adorned each of the old-fashioned looking light fixtures. Flags were flying, and patriotic red, blue, and white bunting decorated many of the storefronts. Despite the barricaded Main Street, town buzzed with visitors and locals. She stopped in front of the pharmacy to read the poster in the window. The family style barbecue was from five to seven here on Main Street. Afterward, there would be a live country band—actually two country bands—and dancing. It sounded fun, almost like the Fourth of July in Last Stand. People, music, laughter ... everything she'd missed since coming to Montana.

Ansley sighed, rather frustrated and torn.

What she really wanted to do was see Rye, and yet she wasn't going to chase him, especially as she wasn't looking for anything. But he'd been good company this morning, and he'd felt like a friend, someone she could trust, someone she could talk to. He'd lifted her spirits earlier, and even though going to the hospital had been stressful, talking to Rye had been ... fun. Was it bad to want a little more fun?

Taking a deep breath, she opened her phone and texted him. *This is Ansley*, she typed. *It looks like they're checking my uncle into the hospital for the next few days. Thank you so much for all your help this morning. I really appreciated it. Good luck tomorrow. Don't break anything!!*

She reread what she wrote and then deleted the last line

about breaking something. That wasn't necessary.

She hesitated, thinking the text wasn't what she wanted to say. She wanted to see if he'd meet her for dinner tonight on Main Street. She loved barbecue. She thought it would be fun to listen to the bands with him. She'd been raised on country music, and an outdoor concert when weather was this nice was pretty much her favorite kind of evening. But suggesting they meet was forward, and she didn't want him to think she was looking for something, much less intimacy. She hadn't been with anyone since Clark and couldn't imagine getting close to anyone for a long time.

Blinking back the sting of tears, she pressed send before she could reconsider the text. He'd asked her to let him know the outcome and now she had. The ball was in his court.

Ansley's stomach growled. She was hungry. Maybe she could get an early lunch before heading back to the ranch. She was trying to decide where to go when a deep male voice spoke her name.

Ansley turned around and Rye was right there walking towards her.

"How's your uncle?" he asked, his Stetson shielding his eyes as he closed the distance between them.

She felt a flutter of excitement. He was still wearing the blue plaid western shirt and Wranglers, but he'd added a big silver belt buckle and dress boots and, freshly shaven, he was so good-looking it made her breathless. "They're admitting him. There's evidence he might have had a stroke, as well as some concern about his blood pressure. The doctors want to run more tests." She flushed, heat rising into her cheeks. "I actually just sent you a text letting you know."

"I left my phone in the truck while I was doing the signing at the meet and greet."

"Meet and greet?"

"The Mercantile is one of this year's rodeo sponsors so a bunch of us have meet and greets. I just finished my shift. Always happy to support the local businesses, but I'm also relieved to have the appearance over."

"Why? I bet kids love meeting you." And women, she silently added, thinking he had to have a lot of fans.

Rye had striking features, but he exuded strength and a masculinity she suspected women had a hard time resisting. She was having a hard time resisting his pull.

"There are bigger names here than me. I always feel like an imposter."

"But you win, don't you?"

"Sometimes." His firm mouth compressed. "More than sometimes, but I rarely go to Vegas anymore for the National Finals Rodeo."

"When was the last time?"

"Three years ago, maybe?"

"That's not that long ago."

His shoulders shifted and he changed subjects. "So, what are your plans now that your uncle isn't coming home today?"

Ansley tried to ignore the flutter of butterflies in her middle and the frisson of excitement racing through her. He wasn't asking her out. He was simply asking her plans.

"I don't know yet." She nodded at the poster in the Bingley's pharmacy window. "I was thinking of maybe coming back later, checking out the bands. I like country music."

"I do, too. What about barbecue? Like that?"

Her pulse thudded, awareness and desire, which was so baffling because she'd only just met him and yet in some ways she felt like he'd known him forever. "I'm Texan. Of course, I like barbecue. Brisket, ribs, chicken—what's not to love?"

"I was thinking the very same thing," he agreed, an appreciative gleam in his eye.

Warmth rushed through her, coiling in her belly, making her tingle. "Now as far as I'm aware, Montana does not have a significant barbecue culture."

"No, but that doesn't mean we can't enjoy great ribs."

"You're a rib man, then?"

"I'm a if-it's-really-good-I-want-it man." He smiled, his faint but very sexy smile that revealed his dimple. "We could meet for dinner tonight, if you feel like company."

She would definitely like company, *his* company. Rye made her feel eager and hopeful. He also made her feel safe, not something she consciously thought about, but he was just solid and real. She'd never related to the phrase salt of the earth before, a phrase her mom used often when Ansley was growing up, but it fit Rye. He was good and honest ... salt of the earth. He didn't strike her as one of those men who would overstep boundaries, or force attention on a woman. There were a lot of men who did, and it was one thing to head out for an evening in Last Stand, where everyone knew she was Callen Campbell's daughter, which meant, if you messed with her, you'd have to deal with her dad and five angry brothers. But here, no one knew her. In fact, few people seemed to even know her uncle. She wondered why. Had he and her late aunt not made themselves part of the community?

"I'd love some company," she said. "If you're free."

"I'm free." He glanced at the poster in the window. "Looks like dinner is from five to seven. What if we meet at the diner at six? Would that work for you?"

"Sounds great."

The afternoon passed slowly for Ansley. Once back on the ranch, she made herself a sandwich, then cleaned the house, changed the sheets on her uncle's bed, added a vase of white roses from the garden to his bedside table, before taking a glass of iced tea to the loft. She had plenty of time to get some work done. But sitting in front of her easel, she didn't feel inspired.

After an hour fussing at her easel, she gave up, returned to the house for a long soak in the tub, and then switching to the shower feature to wash her hair.

Tonight wasn't a date. This wasn't a romantic thing, and there was no pressure. They were just meeting up, two people in a new place killing some time.

There was no need to be nervous, she reminded herself, blow-drying her hair and then touching up some of the natural waves with her hair iron.

It was important she go in with zero expectations than be hurt, or disappointed.

Or hurting or disappointing Rye, because honestly, that was sometimes worse. Being the bad guy. Being labeled selfish. Self-centered. Insensitive.

Ansley wasn't looking for a relationship. Nor was she interested in hooking up with a stranger. She didn't do hookups, and when she dated, things tended to get serious quickly. Her last serious relationship was very serious. Clark had wanted to get married, but even after two years together she didn't feel ready. He waited one more year, asked her again, and when she still said no, he ended things. Angrily. Brutally. It had been a messy and painful end to three years together, and as much as she hated disappointing Clark, she just couldn't commit to marriage. Not even to an engagement.

Perhaps one day she'd marry, but she wasn't ready anytime soon. She thought of her mom's life, the six kids, the endless dishes and loads of laundry, the hours in the kitchen, the hours driving carpool, never mind all those parent-teacher meetings and the overseeing homework, the focus on grades. The Campbells were good students, too. It wasn't like Callen and Andi had raised a bunch of troublemakers, but with five sons, the Campbell boys sometimes got into it. They were smart and ambitious, but they weren't perfect. So no, Ansley wasn't rushing toward marriage or children.

She was finally out on her own, away from her family, which loomed large in Last Stand. As the youngest, they'd loomed large over her.

Growing up, she'd been shy, and her dad had always said she was sweet, but beneath the shy sweet exterior, she'd been a fiery little girl who was fed up with her bossy brothers, perplexed by her cheerful but overworked mother, and a little intimidated by her tough dad who loved and disciplined in equal measure.

Montana provided a new start. Montana meant she could find herself, figure out her own path, pursue her own interests and dreams, whatever they might be. Even if they weren't fiscally intelligent.

Her dad had always harped on making good financial decisions, and yes, being wise with one's money was important, but not to the exclusion of all else. Life was more than paying bills. Life was filled with beauty and art, and she loved her art. Painting gave her tremendous satisfaction. Creating made her feel complete, like the person she was always meant to be, and if she only made a little money off of it, fine. If she was able to keep a roof over her head, why not do what she wanted to do?

Ansley finished dressing, tucking her sleeveless red blouse into the waistband of her jeans. She added a number of necklaces, layering them to fill the deep *V* of the blouse's neckline before pulling her hair back into a long ponytail. No, she'd leave it down tonight, the long, feathered layers her ode to the seventies. Ansley loved the seventies and early eighties—the music, the fashion, the sense of possibility. From everything her mom had told her, it was such a different era than today. She wished she'd grown up then, before there was social media and technology that blared bad news all the time.

She sat down on the edge of her bed, put on socks and then her boots. She wasn't trying to pretend bad things didn't happen, but sometimes it was hard to find the good things in America with all the negativity, and yet she knew there were good people, and great things being done. But the good news didn't get the attention of the bad news, and there were times Ansley felt overwhelmed by the problems of the world, problems she didn't know how to fix. Which was yet another reason she'd come to live with Uncle Clyde for a while.

She wanted to focus on what she could do—which was create beauty. And maybe art wasn't as important as other things, but art and beauty could make others feel good. Beauty could inspire, and her art could maybe make people happy. It was a way she could give back to the world. It was a way she felt useful and productive. Her dad didn't get it. Her brothers didn't get it. She wasn't sure her mother understood, but it was enough that she knew what Ansley wanted to do. Ansley had too much she wanted to accomplish to spend time defending her choices to her family. Better to move here and just get busy, doing what she wanted to do, being who she wanted to be.

Ansley grabbed a jean jacket from her closet, turned out her bedroom light and scooped up her small leather backpack. After locking the house, she got into her car and began the half-hour drive to Marietta. It used to take her even longer, but she'd become more comfortable with the narrow winding road that took one down the mountain. At least on the highway it was easy driving, the highway in excellent condition. Highway 89 was a major route for those going to Yellowstone, which she hoped to see one day soon.

Ansley was on the outskirts of Marietta when he called her. "You're going to have to park off Main Street a few blocks," he said. "It's pretty busy down here."

"I'm not far away, so I'll start looking for parking once I'm in town."

"Take your time, I'm not going anywhere."

Rye's words wrapped around her insides, warming her. "See you soon."

Hanging up, she focused on navigating the neighborhood east of Marietta's historic district. Her uncle had told her there had been a lot of development in the past ten years with new neighborhoods created northwest of town, with new housing developments, schools, banks, and shopping centers. But Marietta had done a good job retaining its historical character with its red brick buildings and turn-of-the-century Western façades.

Marietta reminded her of small towns you'd see in rural Texas, and she liked that. She liked the charm, and the history of turn-of-the-century America. Someday, she wanted to paint the courthouse, and majestic Copper Mountain properly. She'd sketched the mountain peak a couple of times but didn't feel as if she'd done it justice yet. She was still new to mountain landscapes, which was why selling the Bridger Mountain piece had meant so much to her. She might not be rich and famous, but she loved her art, and was getting better every day.

Ansley found a parking spot three blocks over, near the corner of Second and Bramble. It was a small spot, but she had a small car and even though she wasn't the best parallel parker in the world, she got the job done.

Shouldering her small leather backpack, she walked quickly down Second to Main Street, coming out very close to the diner. Despite all the cowboy hats dotting the crowd, she spotted Rye Calhoun almost right away. He wasn't necessarily taller than everyone else, he wasn't necessarily bigger, but he radiated strength even as he stood still, thumbs hooked over his leather belt. He commanded attention. He commanded *her* attention. Her insides did that flutter again, a whisper of adrenaline that made her heart pound.

The attraction baffled her. Why him? Why now?

She didn't know the answers, only that she was compelled to be with him, and eager to see him smile at her, the smile that made her feel ... special.

RYE WATCHED HER walk toward him through the crowd filling Main Street. The sun poured down on her, a spotlight that haloed her, making her long hair even more golden, kissing her lovely face, and bare shoulders, a gilding that made her shimmer and shine. She was beautiful, remarkable. He had beautiful sisters, sisters he cherished, but Ansley ... she took his breath away. The sun adored her, too, seeking her out above all others.

He didn't quite know how to internalize his response to her. She elicited such a strong reaction that it bewildered him. She was too golden, too lovely, too untouchable.

She wasn't for him. He didn't deserve a Texas homecoming queen. There was no room in his life for such radiance. His world was full of hard things and tough choices. He should want to keep her from that, shielding her from his reality. And yet, here she was, smiling at him, her dark blue eyes full of light as well.

"Hello," he said, stepping forward, to greet her.

She was still smiling up at him, and as she lifted her face, he kissed her cheek, the brim of his hat brushing her forehead. Without even thinking he took her hand, her fingers slipping between his as if it was the most natural thing in the world.

Rye glanced down at their hands and then out to the crowd, chest tight, filled with bittersweet sensation. "You look lovely," he said gruffly, his voice deepening further.

She gave his hand a light squeeze. "Thank you. You look quite handsome."

He didn't know what he was feeling, only that he was feeling, and they were strange emotions, big and fragile at the same time, reminiscent of the boy he was once with a million hopes and dreams. "I hope you're hungry, because I am."

She nodded. "Very. I've only had a sandwich today wanting to be sure I had a big appetite for tonight."

He grinned, delighted by her confession. She wasn't just gorgeous, she was smart, sweet, and strong. Ansley had backbone, grit, spirit. He liked her feistiness. He liked her. Rye wasn't easily distracted from his goals or sense of purpose. He normally had tunnel vision—work, work, work. But today had been such a surprise. She'd knocked him off-balance with that smile of hers and the humor in her blue eyes.

He offered to get her coffee so he could spend five more minutes with her.

He'd lingered in town after his meet and greet hoping he'd hear from her.

This—walking with her, holding hands with her—was exactly what he'd wanted. Time, as well as a reprieve from his unrelenting schedule and the unrelenting demands. Perhaps it was corny, but it was a joy to break free and do something different ... unexpected. She was unexpected and having an evening to just relax and get to know Ansley better was a vacation in itself.

But like all vacations, they eventually ended, and one was forced to return to the reality of the ordinary world. He'd return to his reality soon enough. So tonight, he wasn't going to be practical, and he wasn't going to think of Sunday when he drove back to Eureka. That was still two days away. Tonight, he was just going to enjoy Ansley and enjoy this— dinner with a beautiful woman in a small town celebrating a significant anniversary.

He was proud of being from Montana, proud of his heritage as a fourth-generation rancher, although his grandfather's addictive personality had meant that he made bad choices with the ranch in Eureka, forcing his dad to sell off the most profitable land and turning to construction to support his family. They still lived on part of the property, but it would never be what it once was. Rye always vowed that once he had enough money he'd buy a proper ranch, land that would allow them to make a living from it, rather than this piecemeal life of construction and competing.

One day he wouldn't have to compete at all.

One day he wouldn't have to be on the road, away from

everyone he loved.

One day.

"You're a million miles away," Ansley said, reaching across the picnic table to put her hand on his.

He dipped his head. "I am."

"What are you thinking about?"

"Nothing. Everything."

"Come on. You can do better than that."

"Thinking of my family, and the property we have outside Eureka. Thinking that one day I won't be on the circuit anymore competing."

"Why?"

He shrugged. "It's hard on the body, and hard on the family."

"You miss your family when you're gone?"

"I worry about them," he admitted, unwilling to say too much tonight. He really didn't want reality to overshadow the Friday night street party. He turned her hand over, stroked the inside of her wrist with his thumb. "But I'm glad to be here. With you."

Her blue gaze met his. Her cheeks were pink. "You are?"

"I love small towns. I love being here for the eighty-fifth rodeo." He hesitated, his thumb drawing slow circles over her pulse. "I don't know if I told you, but I was here ten years ago, for the seventy-fifth Copper Mountain Rodeo, and it was one of my worst weekends ever."

"You didn't qualify for the Sunday finals?"

"Worse than that. I was thrown off my horse in my very first event, and then stepped on. I ended up in the ER, needing surgery to set my arm." He winced, remembering. "I broke it in three places. It took forever to heal."

She never looked away from his eyes. "Ouch."

Ouch indeed, but now he was here, older, harder, no more stars in his eyes, which made this moment even more special. Beautiful moments were far and few. With any luck, tonight would never end. "But here we are," he said, "and my gut says it's going to be a good weekend."

"I like the way you think," she said, smiling at him.

And he liked the way she was looking at him, as if he were someone wonderful, as if at any moment he'd transform into a superhero. No one ever looked at him like that. He wanted to ask if she could come to the rodeo tomorrow but that would be jumping ahead too quickly. He had to slow down and just enjoy this evening, enjoy her.

"Have you heard from your uncle?" he asked.

She shook her head. "I did call the hospital on my way here, but Uncle Clyde was sleeping. I'm planning on going to see him in the morning. I'm not certain he'll be ready to come home, but I'll at least be able to talk to his doctors face-to-face."

Beautiful, kind, compassionate.

The whole package.

Slow down, Calhoun. Don't get ahead of yourself.

Rather than think about tomorrow, he watched her expressive face and listened to her voice, amazed at how it wrapped around his heart, making him tender. If they were somewhere else, he'd pull her into his arms, but that was dangerous. It was so much better—smarter—to remain here in public where nothing could happen. As it was, these past two hours had done a number on him. He was feeling things, feeling alive, and he'd forgotten what it felt like to feel … open. Human.

Feelings were things that he kept locked up and put away, but somehow, Ansley had a secret key to the lock on his heart. She made everything feel easy. Being with her was effortless. Being with her, he felt younger, stronger, as if he weren't thirty and trapped in a life he hadn't asked for—

No, that wasn't fair. That was harsh. He didn't want to be ugly. This all—these past thirteen years—had been his choice. He'd volunteered to provide. He'd insisted that his sisters go to college, even if part-time. He'd wanted Jasper to have the best care possible. But that didn't make the commitment painless, and it didn't take away the struggle and the quiet whisper of resentment. *What about me? When will it be my turn?*

Inner conflict was the hardest of conflicts because there was no one to blame. There was no fire or storm creating havoc. There was no destructive wind. Not even a slippery roof in his case. There was just him, and his struggle between being strong and giving, and small and bitter.

He refused to be bitter. He was a better man that that.

But still, it had been a while since he felt like a good human being. So much of his energy was spent just keeping all the balls in play that he rarely had time to just be, much less be in the moment, and this night with Ansley was everything a special night could be. So close to perfect that he couldn't slip into analysis. Better to just let it be what it was—a wonderful escape. A respite from his rigid routine. He had to enjoy it, because it wouldn't last. How could it? He'd leave Sunday night and then there would be work on Monday and another rodeo at the end of the week, this time in Oregon. He wasn't complaining. He would be ashamed of himself if he complained as it was a privilege to be able to take care of his family.

And yet, this, tonight was wonderful. He felt younger, happier, and free. As if anything was possible and magic existed in the world.

Impulsively, Rye lifted her hand, pressing a kiss to her knuckles.

"Yes, cowboy?" she said breathlessly.

"Want to dance?"

She nodded and smiled, the smile that made his chest ache, the smile that made him feel like the luckiest man in the world. "I've been dying for you to ask."

"Can't have that." He rose, their hands still locked. He wasn't about to let go of her.

As they threaded their way through the crowd, he spotted Jackson Flint, the guy who'd stopped to help him yesterday when his truck overheated. He was with a beautiful woman and clearly only had eyes for her.

Rye smiled faintly and held Ansley's hand a little tighter. He could tell folks were watching them, and they were probably wondering how a beat-up cowboy like Rye could have snared a gorgeous creature like Ansley. He didn't know, either, but he felt good and proud. It wasn't just because she was beautiful. It was her confidence. She was a straight shooter. No beating around the bush, no silly protests, no games. It felt good not to play games. But honestly, right now none of that mattered. The only thing that mattered was drawing her into his arms, holding her close, his left hand low on her waist, his right hand taking hers. It was one of those western dances where everyone knew the steps. He knew the steps, but the dance wasn't important. She was, and she felt incredible in his arms, her hips against his, her long legs matching his steps.

Neither spoke during that dance, and as the sky grew darker, the night indigo with a swath of stars, Rye drew her even closer until it felt like they were one. One dance turned to two, and still no words. There was no need for conversation. They were in a world of their own, and the world was magical.

And then the music stopped. The band announced they were taking a ten-minute break and the couples on the dance floor began to return to their seats, but Rye and Ansley remained where they were, his arm still around her waist.

"You're a good dancer," she said, tipping her head back to look up at him.

"It's you," he said. "You make it easy."

"With the right person, dancing is easy."

Just like that, his body hardened, the desire hot and intense. He swallowed, battling the need, shocked by the strength of it. He wasn't a kid. He had tremendous control over his body, and yet he felt a craving that went deeper than just the physical. He wanted to know her, he wanted—

He stopped there.

This wasn't going to happen. He was a fool to tease himself, never mind tempt fate.

He should walk her back to their table, but he was loath to break the contact when her long legs fit perfectly against his, between his, her breasts against his chest.

Not even aware he'd made a decision, he dropped his head and his mouth covered hers. He hadn't intended to kiss her, but her lips were so full and pink. They were warm and soft beneath his. It would be so easy to keep kissing her but instead he pulled away and shook his head.

She looked up at him, a question in her eyes.

"I probably should have asked," he said, lifting a hand to lightly stroke her cheek.

Her lips curved, tremulous. "I would have said yes."

"Still, it would have been more respectful if I had."

She leaned closer, her breasts crushed to his chest. "You're very respectful. And I only have one problem with the kiss."

"Oh?"

"It was too brief."

It was the last thing he'd expected, and the corner of his mouth curved. "I'm sorry to disappoint."

"It was a little disappointing." Heat and humor warmed her eyes. "You see, I couldn't tell if you were a good kisser or not." She lifted a brow. "These are important questions. A girl always wonders."

His body tightened, his chest full of a tender pain. He felt desire but also something else, something far more unsettling, something that made him aware that he had to take things slow. He had to be careful with her. He wasn't promising her anything. There was no future. There was just this weekend, and it was lovely being with her, but there was no way he could take her home, and there was no way he was staying here. There would be no long distance of anything, even if she was willing to try. He wouldn't be willing. He'd done that before and it was a disaster. No, love and relationships had to wait. His future would wait. But how did one explain that to someone like Ansley that made him feel like Superman? As if he was a hero and could do anything?

"The kissing will be a problem," he said, his hand low on her back, close to the curve of her butt.

"And why is that?"

"I think once we start kissing properly, it's going to be very hard to stop."

"You are assuming you're a good kisser," she said, mischief and blaze of fire in her stunning blue eyes.

"You want me to say I'm a good kisser." Air bottled in his lungs, his heart thumped slow, heavy, matching the ache in his body.

"No, I don't want you to say it. I want you to prove it. And, not that it matters, but I don't say this to all the boys. I don't go out anymore. I haven't had a date since my boyfriend and I broke up two years ago."

Rye took her hand and led her back to the table where they'd been sitting. Their beer was still there. The dishes had been cleared away.

"Why not?" he asked, sitting on the bench and pulling her down between his legs. He put one hand on her thigh, unwilling to let her go.

"Not interested in anyone. Not interested in getting involved or getting hurt. Not interested in any of it." She turned her head and looked at him over her shoulder, the blue of her eyes darker, deeper. "Love isn't a game. I don't want to be won. And I don't want to capture or conquer anyone."

"You sound like someone burned you good."

"Not at all. I was with my boyfriend for three years. We met each other at UT. We were happy together, it was a good fit, but then he wanted to get married, and I didn't."

"And then what happened?"

"It ended, and it sucked. I'd hurt him and I loved him. He was the last person I'd want to hurt."

"So why not marry him?"

She suppressed a shiver. "I wasn't ready. And to be honest, I wasn't sure he was the one for me, not forever." She shifted away from him, scooting back on the bench, turning her body so she could face him.

They were now both straddling the bench, her knees against his knees, her blue eyes looking into his, trying to read him. "Forever is a long time, and people change. I was changing and he wasn't, and he wanted the Ansley he met in college, but that wasn't who I wanted to be."

"Who did you want to be?"

"Independent Ansley. Self-sufficient Ansley. I wanted choices. I wanted to be in charge of my own destiny, not just someone's pretty little wife."

Her words felt like a punch to his gut, not because they were wrong, but because they resonated so strongly with him. He, too, wanted more choices. He craved freedom, but Rye wasn't in a position to pursue his dreams. He'd shelved them for now, possibly forever.

"Have I shocked you?" she asked trying to read his expression.

He shook his head. "No. I'm impressed. It takes a lot of courage to say I want, and I need, and it takes strength to hold out for the right person who will give you those things."

A HALF HOUR later, Rye walked Ansley to her car. He was holding her hand, but they weren't talking. They hadn't said very much since that conversation about Clark and freedom and not just being someone's wife. Ansley feared the conversation had gotten too honest, too real and had killed some of the evening's magic and mystery.

She shouldn't have mentioned Clark. There was no reason to bring up regrets and mistakes, not when she and Rye were just getting to know each other.

Ansley wished they could go back to the kiss and the sizzling seductive energy that had made her burn, her veins full of heat and need. The kiss had been amazing. He'd lit her up and she was still humming.

At her car, he waited while she unlocked it and opened the driver's side door.

"Thanks for coming tonight," he said. He was standing a good two feet back, thumbs hooked over his leather belt, hat on his head, the brim and the night shielding his features.

She hated for the evening to end this way. She wasn't ready for the weekend to end, either, not when he would still be in Marietta two more days. "I'm sorry if I overshared—"

"You didn't."

He'd answered too quickly, and he seemed even more detached.

"Then what happened? We were having fun ... weren't we?"

"I—" He closed his mouth, jaw hard.

She lifted a brow, prompting, "You?"

"You're incredible."

"And?"

"I don't want to lead you on. You deserve someone who is going to be around for a while, but that's not me. When the rodeo ends, I'm on the road again, and once I'm gone, I'm gone. I won't be coming back."

She wished she could see his face, wished he'd let her in, but that apparently wasn't going to happen. "I'm not looking for a commitment, Rye. I'm twenty-five, and very happy being single. Just because we had fun tonight, doesn't mean I want you to put a ring on my finger, because I don't. I could easily be married now, but it's not what I want. I have plans, and dreams, and they don't include becoming a wife or a mom anytime soon."

He nodded but didn't speak, and Ansley stood in front of her car, arms folded across her chest, struggling with indecision.

"I'd hoped to go watch you tomorrow if I wasn't needed to drive Uncle Clyde home. But if you don't want me in the stands—"

"Don't say it like that. Don't make this about me. I'm trying to protect you."

"Yes, from you." She stepped toward him, closing the distance between them until she could easily reach out and touch his chest. "You must think you're pretty destructive if you have to warn me off like that."

"I don't date. I don't seduce women. I'm not a player, and yet I feel as if I've played you."

"How? By kissing me? Big deal." Her head tipped back to try to see beneath the brim of his hat. "I have five big brothers. I understand guys. I know how you work. Just because we flirted a little bit doesn't mean I'm planning a future for us."

"If I lived here—"

"But you don't," she snapped. "I had fun tonight. I've been pretty lonely since moving from Texas. I've made no friends yet. I rarely leave my uncle's ranch. Don't make me feel bad for enjoying your company. That's not cool, or fair."

He reached for her, pulling her against him, his hand low on her hip, fingers curving around her butt. "I don't want you to feel bad. Not tonight, not tomorrow, not Sunday, not ever."

"Then let me make decisions for myself. Trust that I'm old enough to know what's good for me, and what's not." She was still trying to see his eyes, still trying to figure out who he was and what motivated him. "I mean that nicely, too. You have a lot of pressure riding on those big handsome shoulders. I shouldn't be adding to that pressure. I'm not interested in being a burden—"

"You're not. Not at all. I enjoyed tonight, very much."

"Good." She smiled crookedly. "I should go, though. It's late."

He kissed her forehead. "I don't want to say good night.

Or goodbye."

"Then don't. Just say I'll see you tomorrow." She hesitated. "If you don't mind me going to watch you compete."

"I don't want to disappoint you. Anything could happen in the ring."

"Win or lose, I'll still love being there, your own little fan section."

"My fan section of one."

She laughed and stood up on tiptoe to kiss his mouth, his lips firm, cool, and then he kissed her back, and the sweetness turned to an impossible craving, absolute fire. He wrapped his arms tighter around her, almost lifting her off her feet. His tongue parted her mouth, teasing her tongue, tasting, demanding, and pleasure coursed through her, wave after wave of want, wave after wave of need. No one had ever kissed her like this. No one had ever made her feel so fierce and bright and alive.

She didn't know how long they kissed but she was lost to the world until a car passed behind them and a bunch of teenagers whistled and catcalled.

Rye ended the kiss, and Ansley staggered back, hot and cold, her legs trembling, heart pounding so hard she could only hear the blood rushing in her ears. "I don't know what you do to me," she breathed, "but it's ridiculous." She pushed a heavy wave of hair back from her face. "Insane."

"I'd invite you back to my trailer but it's not very comfortable."

"And we wouldn't sleep, which wouldn't be good for you tomorrow."

"I can handle myself, and we would sleep. I have excellent self-control."

She slowly smiled until she felt as if her chest would split with joy. "You make me laugh."

"I'm actually quite serious."

"I know. But that makes me laugh, too." She moved close and kissed him quickly on the mouth. "Good night, Rye Calhoun. I'm looking forward to seeing you tomorrow."

Chapter Four

I N HIS SMALL trailer at the fairground, Rye turned out his
light and stripped down to his boxers since the night was
hot and there was no fan or air-conditioning in his trailer. In
the dark, he stretched out on his narrow bed, arms folded
behind his head, and looked up at the ceiling, moonlight
spilling through the narrow window, patterning the metal
ceiling.

He tried to relax, but he was amped up, emotions not at
all manageable. Tonight had been a roller coaster, mostly
highs, but he was aware that the highs would lead to lows.
He didn't want the lows. He didn't want to expose Ansley to
lows, either. Perhaps it was old-fashioned but it was his job
to protect those in his life, and now Ansley was one of the
ones he needed to protect.

She didn't understand his world, or how complicated it
was. He didn't want her in his world, didn't want her to be
part of the struggle. Better to keep the walls up than let her
in, because if she got in…

He shook his head, not wanting to continue the train of
thought. He'd not open his family to criticism or ridicule.
And maybe Ansley wouldn't make any of them uncomfortable. Maybe she wouldn't be uncomfortable, either, but he

wasn't taking chances. He loved his family too much to render them vulnerable.

His phone vibrated with a text. Was it Ansley letting him know she was home? He hated how his pulse quickened as he reached for his phone.

It was.

Pleasure filled his chest, a warmth that undermined his discipline and intentions. He didn't often feel warm. Pleasure was as alien as joy. He shouldn't be feeling, but Ansley had cast a spell, his lovely magician, and he found himself wanting to hope.

But hope was a dangerous bedfellow. Hope, so seductive, could also disappear in the morning, never to return.

Glad you're home, he answered. *Sleep well.*

You, too, she replied, adding an emoji of a smiling face with hearts. He wasn't sure what the emoji was supposed to mean, but a smile and a heart was sweet. She was sweet.

And she was trouble.

Rye woke up in an upbeat mood. He stretched, and yawned, surprisingly well rested. It might have taken him a while to fall asleep, but once he did, he slept deeply. This morning, he didn't remember his dreams—he never did—but they must have been good because he felt good.

But checking his phone he saw a text from his sister Josie and his sense of well-being vanished. *Call Mom*, the text read. *She's having a hard morning.*

Gut knotting, he texted his sister first. *What's going on? Jasper?*

No, she answered. *Dad.*

What's Dad doing? Rye asked.

He's in one of his bad moods. It was awful last night. I hate it when he feels sorry for himself.

I'm sorry, Rye responded.

It's not your fault. You're not the one complaining, making everyone miserable.

Thanks for the heads-up. I'll call Mom.

Love you, Rye.

Love you, too, Josie.

Rye boiled some water making a simple pour over coffee. He wasn't about to make a call home without some coffee in him. He drank half a cup quickly, while it was hot before phoning his mom.

He almost didn't think she was going to answer, but finally she picked up. "Hi, honey. Good morning. How are you?"

The words were right, but her tone was off. She sounded flat and down. He hated for her to be down.

"I'm good," he answered. "How are things there?"

She hesitated just a moment. "Fine."

"Hmm. You don't sound very convincing."

"There's nothing you need to worry about. You've got your events today and fingers crossed you'll do well so you can compete again tomorrow."

"Win or lose, I'll be back home tomorrow night."

"Exactly. So focus on what you have to do. We're surviving without you."

Rye carefully thought through his answer. "I want more

for you than that, Mom. You deserve better than that."

She sighed. "It was a hard night, but it's a new day. Everything is better already."

"Dad's sleeping it off?"

"Rye."

"Be honest."

"He's never his best when he drinks, no. But at least he's not angry when he drinks. He doesn't get violent. He's just ... you know, Rye, you know how he gets."

"Pitiful."

She sighed again. "I don't like that word."

"It's true."

"Yes, he can be exhausting, but he isn't your problem. You didn't marry him. He's your dad, not your husband. I love him and I will take care of him—"

"And who takes care of you, Mom?"

"Why you do, Rye." She laughed, the sound full of anguish instead of humor. "You always have."

"That's my job."

"No, sweetheart, it's not your job. It's never been your job. You should be independent. You should be dating and falling in love, starting a family, not worrying about all of us. I hate that you have so little freedom, and even less spare time—"

"What would I do with free time, Mom? Play video games? Shoot pool? I don't think so." He sat up, swung his legs to the floor. "I'm happy with my life. I love you all. I'm not complaining."

"No, you never have, but that doesn't mean it's not stressful. There's a lot of pressure on you, and I can't help wishing you could be like the other cowboys. I wish you could have that freedom. I'd love for you to be carefree, not always calling home, not always rushing home, not always giving up all your money."

"You're my family. You come first. End of story."

She drew a low, unsteady breath. "What would I do without you?" she whispered. "I don't think I would have been able to handle all of this without you."

"That's not true. You're strong, Mom, and you've taught me to be strong. It's all good. Now, don't get all weepy. Dad doesn't like to see you sad. He'll feel guilty and today won't be any better than yesterday."

"You're right." She took a bigger breath, a steadying breath. "You have such a good head on your shoulders, Rye. You make me so proud."

"Thank you, Mom. Now, I'll be home tomorrow. If I'm in the finals, it'll be late. If I'm not, well, you'll see me early afternoon."

"I'd rather you place in the money."

"Me, too, and hopefully with big money."

"Stay safe."

"I try my best."

"Don't need both of my sons in wheelchairs!" she laughed, trying to make it a joke.

"That's not going to happen."

INSTEAD OF GOING to the morning parade in Marietta, Ansley woke early, had coffee, and got to work. It was a gorgeous morning, and although it'd be quite warm later, it was perfect right now. The sky was blue, and a fragrant breeze rustled through the trees, scenting the air moving through the loft.

Montana had its charms. She focused on her canvas with the dark blue Yellowstone River snaking through the valley floor. She'd taken photos of the scene and had those clipped to the side of the easel for reference. But the photos didn't do the stunning landscape justice. It was more powerful on a larger canvas with the mountains looming large, and the river gleaming against a backdrop of golden alfalfa fields.

She took a fine brush to touch up the split-log fence in the distance. She was lucky the Bridger Mountains sold to the Sterbas, because these big canvases were expensive, and they took so much longer than the little ones, but she was falling in love with the bigger pieces. They challenged her and intimidated her, but it was exciting to do something new and hard and when it was finished she felt ... amazing. Invincible. No longer that sweet blonde girl who kept to herself, but Ansley the artist, Ansley the creative.

No one else in her family did what she did. No one else

was particularly creative and her parents used to scratch their heads and say, where did she come from? Where did the passion come from? Ansley would just smile because she didn't care … she didn't think her love of painting had to come from anyone. Why couldn't it just be her thing? Why couldn't she just be herself? An original?

Cleaning her little brush, Ansley caught sight of the time. Almost noon. The rodeo would be starting soon. She had to get going. She didn't want to miss the beginning, not sure when Rye would be competing, but she wanted to be there for everything.

HE'D BEEN IN Marietta ten years ago for the seventy-fifth Copper Mountain Rodeo. He'd ended up in the hospital, wasting money instead of earning money. This time Rye was going to take home some big money, not just because he needed the money, but he needed the satisfaction. He needed the distraction.

The rodeo's opening ceremonies were about to begin, and he joined the other competitors waiting to ride in for the national anthem. Even from behind the gate, he could see Ansley in the stands. She was impossible to miss with that long golden hair. She was beautiful and it blew his mind that she'd even taken a second look at him, never mind kissed him with so much sweetness and desire. He'd forgotten the pleasure of kissing, the pleasure of being close to someone that made him feel.

He liked how she smiled at him even when he said nothing funny. She smiled at him as if he wasn't the hard-ass he was, but a man of wit and warmth, which everyone knew he was not. The fact that she could smile at him when he didn't feel like smiling, made his lips curve ever so slightly, easing the heaviness within him, making room for other emotions, and much-needed light. She was sunshine and warmth, and she had so much it just spilled over onto him, illuminating his world.

At the signal from the rodeo organizers, Rye and the cowboys and cowgirls raced into the arena in a line, showing off the rider and horse's athleticism. Once in the arena, they formed a solid square and hats were removed for the national anthem and prayer. He glanced up into the stands just before they were dismissed, and Ansley's gaze met his. He felt a rush of emotion, need, and possession. There was no denying how much he wanted her. In the ideal world, she would be his. But he didn't live in fairy-tale land. His personal world was far from ideal. He could want her, but he wasn't going to let it go further than that.

The cowboy in front of him left the arena at a gallop, and Rye nudged his horse and they were riding out, too.

Showtime.

ANSLEY ARRIVED AT the fairgrounds in time to catch the very end of the mutton busting, and holding her program close to her chest, she squeezed into the bleacher seat, moving down to an open spot. The sun was high overhead but almost everyone was wearing a cowboy or baseball hat, and the heat wasn't bothering anyone. If anything, the atmosphere in the stadium was like that of a party. She skimmed the program. Rye was competing in four of the seven events today. Bareback, steer wrestling, saddle bronc, and tie-down roping. Bareback would be immediately after the opening ceremonies and those were beginning now with everyone rising as the announcer kicked off the eighty-fifth Copper Mountain Rodeo, and the cowboys and barrel racers came tearing in on their horses.

Ansley spotted Rye toward the back, and her heart thumped extra hard. He was gorgeous, so handsome in his leather chaps with the black leather vest over his fitted light blue shirt. Some of the guys were smiling, but not Rye. His jaw jutted, and his expression was fierce, and she found it seriously appealing. She liked his toughness and his reserve. But even more so, she loved how she could make him smile … and laugh. He needed to laugh more, too.

She knew the moment he spotted her in the stands. He lifted his hat, his gaze locking with hers. How he found her in the crowd was beyond her, but she shivered with pleasure as he acknowledged her. She was glad he knew she was there. Now, fingers crossed, he just did well.

Bareback was the first event, and he'd be seventh. She watched as cowboy after cowboy was thrown, or unceremoniously dumped, until two had decent rides and then it was Rye's turn. She hoped for his sake that he could stick all eight seconds just so he could get some points. She knew he hoped to do better than that. He wasn't here to charm anyone or make friends. He was here to win. She admired that as she'd been raised in an extremely competitive family. If you were going to do something, do it well. Don't just show up. Always strive to be the best. It was a lot of pressure, but it had paid off for her brothers.

Her dad wasn't so sure about her.

She smiled grimly, which made her think of Rye's smile. Rye really didn't smile often, but when she got him to, she went warm on the inside. Even just a small lift of his lips felt like a victory. She wondered what made him happy, this serious cowboy who knew the other competitors, but didn't want to hang out with them, or drink, or party.

Except for one other competitor, it was proving rough going, with cowboy after cowboy bucked off. She prayed Rye would do better than that.

The chute suddenly opened, and Rye and his horse came flying out, the horse leaping, hindlegs kicking, while Rye dug in, boots forward, arm back, determined to stick.

And he did stick.

He made it all eight seconds despite the furious flying horse beneath them, the horse's hooves barely touching the ground between each kick. But Rye had hung in there, doing everything he was supposed to do, and once the buzzer sounded, he untangled his hand, swung his leg over the back of the horse and jumped off, boots clouding the dirt.

She didn't know what the judges would award for points, because at least he'd get points, and hopefully enough points he'd be in the finals tomorrow. Once the score was posted, the crowd erupted. Ninety-two. The second highest score so far.

Rye's hat had come off in his dismount, and as he bent down to pick it up, he glanced her way. She waved, and he was far away so she couldn't be sure, but it looked as if he'd smiled, that small unwilling smile that made her feel good. She hoped he felt good. He'd done very well just now.

The rest of the afternoon flew by. With the Copper Mountain Rodeo events tightly scheduled, there was little downtime, and with Rye competing in three more events, she always had something to look forward to. When he finished at the top of the leader board in steer wrestling, she knew he'd be competing tomorrow. He'd done well in everything but tie down, so she hoped he was pleased with his efforts. Now she just wanted to see him.

She wasn't sure how she'd find him later, but halfway through barrel racing, he appeared in the stands, and folks made room for him to squeeze in next to her.

Ansley slid her hand into his and gave it a squeeze. "You did so good. I was so impressed."

He dropped a swift kiss on her lips. "You were my lucky charm. I don't always do so well."

"Then I'll just have to travel to all your events to make sure you take home money!"

"You'd make all the guys jealous. You're too pretty to be hanging out with beat-up cowboys."

"Fortunately, I'm only interested in one beat-up cowboy, and that's you."

His gaze met hers and held for a long moment. "You know I leave tomorrow."

She held her smile even as her heart plummeted. "Tomorrow's not here. Let's just enjoy today."

"I don't want—"

"I know," Ansley interrupted, squeezing his hand. "You don't want me getting attached. I got it. I understood last night. I know what's happening tomorrow."

He gave her another long look then turned his attention to the barrel racers. Ansley pretended to watch as well, but her heart and thoughts weren't on the rodeo anymore, but the big, rugged cowboy sitting next to her, his denim-clad thigh pressed to hers, his rough calloused hand holding hers. It all felt right. He felt right. But he wasn't going to be keeping her around. He'd made that abundantly clear.

When the rodeo ended, everyone stood and began rushing from the stadium. Rye wasn't in a hurry to be part of the jostling crowd and so he and Ansley hung back and waited for the stands to empty. Tonight was the big party in

Crawford Park and she mentioned it to Rye, not sure if he'd be interested.

"There's a steak dinner tonight here in town," she said. "I could get us tickets if you thought it sounded fun."

He didn't answer right away. "I like steak." His eyes narrowed as he looked toward the exits which were finally clearing out. "Are you up for the crowd?"

"Not necessarily, but if that's how I get to spend time with you, I won't complain."

His lips curved, a smile briefly warming his eyes. "I'd rather just hang out with you. If you don't mind."

"I definitely don't mind."

"You could come to the farmhouse," she said. "I'm not a great cook, but I know how to throw some steaks in a cast-iron skillet."

He nodded. "I like that. Should I follow you? We can stop and pick up steaks on the way."

"I wanted to stop in at the hospital before heading back. What if I meet you in thirty minutes or so at the turnoff for Miracle Lake? You'll head south on Highway 89, and it'll be on your right a few miles out of town."

"Don't rush your visit with your uncle. I'm going to take care of my horses and clean up. What if we meet in an hour? That way there's no stress."

"Perfect."

UNCLE CLYDE WAS napping when Ansley arrived at the hospital. She sat next to his bed for ten minutes, but he never stirred and even when a nurse came in to check his vitals, he didn't wake. Ansley waited another ten minutes and then rose to go, but as she gathered her things a doctor entered the room.

"I heard you were here," he said, extending his hand. "I'm Dr. Maida, one of the cardiologists here at Marietta. I've been hoping to bump into you."

"I kept calling to get updates," she said.

"The messages were passed on, and we've done our best to keep your uncle comfortable." He paused. "Is there anyone else you'd want me to speak with about his condition?"

"His wife passed away a number of years ago. I've moved in to help care for him. He hasn't felt well all summer, but he refused to get a checkup."

"It would have been helpful. Your uncle had a stroke Friday morning. But it wasn't his first. In fact, he's probably been having a series of mini strokes for months."

They'd stepped out of her uncle's room and were standing in the hallway. Ansley exhaled hard. This wasn't what she'd expected.

"I had no idea. He's not the best communicator and when there is a problem, he's stubborn."

"I don't believe he's intentionally deceiving you. The stubbornness can also be a result of his VCI."

"VCI?" she repeated, bewildered.

"Vascular cognitive impairment. In the past, the medical field referred to it as vascular dementia, but I prefer VCI as it better reflects the cognitive changes within the patient, and how side effects can vary from mild to severe, particularly with decision making and communication."

Ansley wasn't even sure what to say, or where to begin and was glad Dr. Maida just continued.

"We can see from the MRI the damage. It's been over time, but the damage is cumulative and permanent."

"Will he recover?"

"His mobility should improve with physical therapy, but there is evidence of clear cognitive decline." The doctor paused. "The dementia will get worse with time, but physical therapy could help him with mobility. Besides communication difficulties, how has his mood been?"

"Not good. He's frustrated most of the time. Extremely short-tempered."

"Depression coexists with vascular cognitive impairment. Treating the depression would definitely help his quality of life. But I think it's important we be frank, and since you appear to be the primary caregiver, you should know that he's not capable of living independently. If you go for errands, you might want to take him, or have someone stay with him."

"How did this happen?"

"He has a history of heart disease. The series of strokes

have compounded the problem."

Ansley shook her head. "Wow. I'm ... shocked."

"High cholesterol, high blood pressure, and diabetes have weakened his heart, creating a perfect storm for heart disease and the resulting strokes."

Ansley's chest felt tight and heavy. Everything the doctor was telling her was scary. Uncle Clyde was going to need real care soon, not just her in and around the house, and decisions on what to do with the ranch would need to happen sooner than later. If Clyde couldn't manage it—which he hadn't been—someone in the family needed to step up, or the ranch needed to be sold or leased. She was willing to help manage her uncle's care, but she drew the line at ranch management. "When ... when can I bring him home?"

"Probably Wednesday. He's hoping to get home sooner, but I'm not sure that's realistic. Before we discharge him, we will want to make sure he has sufficient mobility once he gets home, which means sessions with a physical and occupational therapist to prepare him for returning home."

"Will he need a wheelchair?" she asked, glad she had a few days to get things in order for his return.

"He's been up on his feet. The nurses have made him walk a little, but he needs support, preferably a walker, but that will have to wait until his wrist has healed."

She'd forgotten his wrist. She'd forgotten that initially she'd thought he'd only hurt his arm. Instead, it was so much more serious than that. "Thank you for taking such good care of him."

Dr. Maida smiled. "That's what we're here for. Any questions?" he asked.

"It sounds like he might need a wheelchair, and if not a walker, then a cane."

"Again, it depends on how well he responds to physical therapy. That's going to be important for his recovery."

"I need to do some reading and research. This is all new to me."

"There's plenty online, and it wouldn't hurt to visit the Alzheimer's Association's website—"

"He has Alzheimer's, too?"

"No, but there's a good section on VCI on their site. It would help you prepare for what's to come."

What's to come.

How forbidding that sounded. She stiffened, her heart falling. It was time to get her parents involved. Her dad and uncle did not speak, but this was bigger than their feud, and she needed her mom and dad's involvement.

Leaving the hospital Ansley checked her watch. Forty-five minutes had passed since she entered the hospital and yet it felt like hours. Flattened, she walked to her car and took backroads to the highway, avoiding the traffic downtown.

She reached the turnoff for Miracle Lake before Rye arrived, and instead of phoning her parents in Last Stand, she used her phone to go to the Alzheimer's Association website feeling as if she needed more information before she talked to them. Ansley skimmed different pages, skipping around until she found the section on VCI. Everything listed was what Melvin Wyatt had reported to her parents last April. Changes in thinking and personality, impaired planning and judgment, the declining ability to pay attention, and difficulties functioning socially.

Mr. Wyatt had observed it all and had insisted someone from the family come to Montana, as something had to be done. Her dad, a former military man, was as alpha as they came, and didn't like being told what to do, but he'd grown up with the Wyatts, and had been a friend of his sons, playing ball with them and riding all over the mountain— and so he flew out with Ansley's mom, and they spent a long weekend at the house with Clyde. It was the first time Clyde and Callen Campbell had been in the same room in almost forty years. Ansley didn't know particulars of that weekend, and could only imagine the tension in the farmhouse, but by the time her parents returned to Last Stand, they'd agreed with Melvin Wyatt that Clyde couldn't be left alone, and they'd send one of their family members to stay with Clyde for the summer until more permanent arrangements could be made.

None of her brothers volunteered to go to Montana for the summer, so Ansley agreed to do it. But her parents had never scheduled Clyde for a doctor's appointment, and Ansley hadn't done it, either. She regretted her lack of foresight, because if her uncle had been seen by a medical professional, surely the doctor would have picked up on the symptoms.

Troubled, Ansley closed her phone and got out of the car to go stand in the shade of the big pine trees which smelled like Christmas and the forest, one of her favorite smells. But it was hard to feel good when her insides were heavy with worry. She felt guilty for not taking better care of her uncle, but also angry, because shouldn't her parents have done more? Why would they think she'd know how to handle Clyde's declining cognitive skills best? Families needed to take care of each other, and in this instance, Clyde was her dad's brother. Her dad needed to let go of the hostility and try to have a relationship with his younger brother before it was too late.

The sound of a vehicle pulling off the highway drew Ansley's attention. It was Rye in his blue and white truck. She crossed to the driver's side and leaned into his open window, mindful of the traffic flying past behind her. "Follow me to the exit for Emigrant. We'll get steaks there."

He kissed her. "Great. Now get back in your car where you're safe."

The kiss made her warm, and she felt the rush of heat all the way through her. She couldn't resist reaching out to touch his hard jaw with the bristle of a beard. "You are so handsome."

"You need some glasses."

She laughed. Rye had a way of making her feel good. He just … did it … for her. Back in her car she drove the six miles to Emigrant and then with steaks and potatoes purchased, they were back in their cars heading to the Campbell ranch.

Rye parked next to her car in the gravel driveway. His gaze swept across the barn and outbuildings and then to the old white farmhouse. "This place has been here a long time."

She nodded. "About one hundred years, settled here in the 1930s."

"They don't make farmhouses like this anymore." His eyes narrowed. "You're in desperate need of a new roof, though. If it isn't leaking now, it will soon."

"Haven't been here through a heavy rain, but winter is coming."

"Just have someone come look at it. Better to know the cost ahead of time."

"Will do. Now let me show you where the grill is, and you can start the fire."

While Rye used the charcoal to get the fire going, and then seasoned the steaks, Ansley microwaved the two potatoes for five minutes before wrapping them in foil and adding them to the grill and then made a quick summer salad with tomatoes, cucumbers, and onions.

Once the steaks were on, Ansley and Rye sat on the covered back porch and relaxed, reliving today's events at the rodeo, discussing what Rye expected tomorrow, and then as

Rye rose to flip the steaks, Ansley blurted out what the doctor had told her at the hospital this afternoon.

Even though his back was to her, she could tell Rye was listening, and once the steaks were flipped, he turned to look at her. "That wasn't the news you expected," he said quietly.

She shook her head. "I thought they'd tell me I'd have to cut back on sodium on his food, or something like that. I didn't realize he had dementia, and I didn't realize he'd had a series of strokes. By not getting him treatment, I made everything worse—"

"I don't think you can take the blame. It's bigger than you. You said you hadn't even met him until Memorial Day weekend."

"Yes."

"How did you find out your uncle was doing so poorly then?"

"The Campbell ranch butts up to the Wyatts' property. Melvin Wyatt's sons grew up with my dad and Uncle Clyde, so he'd stop in every week or two to say hello, aware that my uncle was struggling after my aunt passed away. Mr. Wyatt was the one who noticed my uncle's decline. He tracked down my dad and insisted something be done, that it was a family matter, and family needed to step in."

"He was right," Rye said.

"He was. Without a doubt." She chewed on her lip a moment. "Now I have to call my parents and let them know it's worse than they thought. My uncle needs significantly more care, and I'll be honest, I'm not the right person for that. I don't mind cooking and cleaning the house, but I'm not comfortable bathing him, or dressing him, and he's going to need that in the coming year or so. I don't actually know the timeline, but Dr. Maida said my uncle can't be left alone anymore."

Rye checked the potatoes and then moved the steaks from the grill to a plate. "Can your family afford care?"

She nodded. "I don't know Uncle Clyde's financial situation, but my dad has done well. He's also a savvy investor. While he might not want to be here, I can't imagine he'd refuse to pay for help."

"That's good. Not everyone can afford to hire an outsider."

"I know. We're lucky." She rose. "Do you want to eat out here on the porch or in the house?"

"Out here, if you don't mind. I like the view."

She looked past him to the rugged golden hills and the aspen trees just beginning to change colors. "It is beautiful. I thought the Hill Country was pretty, but this ... this always takes my breath away." Her gaze skimmed the fence and the distant windmill before glancing back at Rye. "I'll grab the salad and dishes and will be right back."

They ate sitting on the top step of the porch, their plates balanced on their laps. "This is nice," Ansley said with a contented sigh. "I wish Uncle Clyde wanted to eat outside, but he has a routine, and we don't vary from it."

"I take it you're more of a free spirit."

"I'm okay with structure, but he's pretty inflexible. That's hard. But beneath his gruff exterior, he's a good person, and from everything I've heard, was a good husband to his wife."

"That's important to you?"

She straightened. "Of course! I don't really think it matters how successful someone is, if he or she isn't good to those they say they love."

Rye's brow raised. "You're sounding cynical about love."

"Not about love per se, but about people. It's easy to say you love someone, but the hard part is showing up, behaving in a loving way."

He set his plate on the step next to him. "Do your parents have that kind of marriage?"

Ansley hesitated. "That's a good question. I think they're happy, but it's not the marriage I'd want."

"Why not?"

"It's a little too traditional. I think Mom is content, but I wouldn't be. Dad controls the dynamics a bit too much. He's not unfair, but he's just the alpha, the head of the family, and sometimes it doesn't seem as if there is much room for Mom."

Rye studied her a long moment. "But if she's happy?"

"Exactly. She was raised in a family a lot like ours. Her dad was a military dad and they moved around a lot. Mom has always taken her job as the wife, mother, homemaker seriously, and she's been good at that, and it apparently fulfilled her. I just—" She broke off, and weighed her words. "Want more." Her gaze met Rye's and held. "And why not? None of my brothers would be satisfied staying home, cleaning house, organizing the pantry, canning peaches every summer. Why should I have to be satisfied doing it?"

His gaze was warm, amused. "You don't."

"That's right."

"You can be whoever and whatever you want to be."

"*Exactly.*" She laughed, then smiled at him. "Do you really believe that, or are you just humoring me?"

"I really believe that. And if you met my sisters, you'd know that's how I feel. I want them to pursue their interests and have the financial freedom that would allow them to be independent, not just of our family, but of needing to depend on a man. It's important women have the ability to decide if a relationship isn't right for them, but it's hard to do that if you have no way to support yourself."

Ansley set her plate behind her. "You're a good brother."

"They're good sisters, good people. I want them happy. And I want them to have options, options that you'd only have if you're not broke or in debt."

Her gaze slowly traveled over his face, taking in the strong brow, the straight nose, the high hard cheekbones. He was deeply tan with faint lines at the corners of his eyes. It was clear he spent his days outside. "They must know how you feel."

"Yes, but one of them, Hannah, is seeing someone for the wrong reasons. She knows I don't approve—"

"What does that mean?" Ansley interrupted.

"He's too old for her. He's got some money. He gives her gifts and acts like he's spoiling her, but he's really controlling her, and I don't like him. I don't trust him. And I know she doesn't love him. But I think she's trying to help the family by not needing my financial support, but I'd rather help her with school and her expenses than have Ron pay her bills."

"How do you know Hannah doesn't love Ron?"

"There's no light or excitement in her eyes when she sees him. There's no … joy. If she loved him, wouldn't she light up a little bit? Wouldn't there be some … spark or warmth? She used to practically dance when she entered the room. Even as a teenager she was always twirling and laughing … sparkling. There's no sparkle anymore. I hate it. I hate Ron's effect on her. He's smothered the light in her and I pray that before it's too late she'll realize he's not the one."

Ansley put her hand on Rye's, her fingers sliding between his. His skin was warm, and she felt an immediate connection. It happened every time they touched. "I hope that, too," she said softly. "For both of your sakes."

Rye lifted her hand to his mouth, kissed the back. "Will you show me where you paint? I'd love to see what you're working on."

"Yes."

"Good. I'd love to see your work."

"I've never shown you?"

He grinned. "We only officially met yesterday."

She laughed. "I did see you Thursday."

"From afar."

"It counts," she said.

"I guess it does. I feel like I've known you forever."

Ansley's insides melted, her pulse quickening. "I feel the same way."

Chapter Five

A NSLEY RAN THE dishes into the house and then led Rye to the big, brown barn which Clyde had told her was easily one hundred years old, if not older. It had room at one end for storing hay and alfalfa, and on the other side, room for livestock. Her loft extended over the haybales rather than the livestock, which was good as the smell of manure on a hot day permeated the entire barn.

She turned on the light and climbed the ladder, waiting for Rye to follow. In the loft, Ansley shifted a few of the smaller stacked paintings, laying them flat out so he could see. "This size is really popular on Etsy. I price them so they're affordable and relatively inexpensive to mail.

"They're stretched canvases," she added, as he picked up one, "and a thinner frame. When I first started, I painted on canvas board, but the boards would bend, and the paint would crack. Customers would be disappointed. So, these lightweight canvases are good for smaller projects."

"I imagine the big canvases are expensive?"

"Yes, which is why I'd like to learn how to make them myself, but that's a down-the-road project. Right now, I buy them in Bozeman at an art supply store."

She watched as Rye continued to wander around her loft, examining everything, and spending considerable time looking at the painting on her easel, the one she'd worked on this morning of the Yellowstone River against the Absaroka Mountains.

"I like this," he said, studying the painting closely, and then stepping back. "It's wonderful. You can paint."

Ansley blushed, touched by the praise. "I'm starting to get the hang of it."

He glanced at her. "How long have you been doing this?"

"I took a couple art classes in high school, and then some at the local college in the evenings, but after a year, I realized school wasn't going to help anymore. I just had to keep painting, and studying different techniques, and so I've kept at it."

"Your parents must be proud."

Ansley didn't know how to answer. There wasn't an easy answer. "Dad's not a fan. Mom wants to be supportive. But they both think this is just a phase."

"Until what?"

"I get married. Have kids."

"Which you don't want to do."

"Not anytime soon, and even if I do marry one day, I'm not going to stop painting. This is who I am and what I love. It's also how I pay my bills."

He seemed surprised. "You can support yourself with

your paintings?"

"I do support myself, and every month I earn a little more." She gave him a challenging look. "How do you think I supported myself? I'm not a trust-fund baby. My parents don't give me money. I am on my parents' health insurance plan, but that's only for one more year. When I turn twenty-six, that's on me."

"And you'll be able to cover it?"

"Yes, and it might not be a lot, but I'm making money, and with me living here, I've been saving most of what I earn. Now when I have my own place, I'll have to pay for rent and utilities, but I can swing it, especially living in Marietta. The cost of living is better here than in Last Stand."

"I wouldn't have thought that."

"Last Stand is in the Texas Hill country, and it's pricey. Lots of the little houses have been fixed up and turned into VRBOs."

"And Paradise Valley is affordable?"

"I'm not looking to buy a ranch. I'd just rent a little house or apartment in town. I've been checking the ads and I'll be able to swing it if I keep working." She hesitated. "I know I've only been here a couple months, but I really like Marietta."

"What makes it special?"

"Besides the fact that I met you here?" she teased, smiling at him. "Well, it's the perfect town, with a historical downtown and beautiful brick buildings and community spaces like the parks and the river walk. And then there are so many trees, I love trees and we don't have anything like this in Texas."

"Sounds like you've fallen under Montana's spell."

"I have, and not just Montana, but Marietta specifically. It has everything I need. Access to an airport, a charming main street, a thriving economy, with a steady influx of money from tourists. I can see myself opening my own gallery here one day."

"Is that your plan?"

"Eventually."

"You might want to get through a winter first. You've only been here during the best months."

"I've heard, but it just makes me more excited to paint the valley during all the seasons. I've never painted snow before, and it's going to be a challenge. The fall colors will be fun, but a frosty Paradise Valley? That's going to be cool."

"You mean cold." He went to her, and pulled her against him, his lips grazing her cheek, the corner of her mouth and then low on her neck. "The snow and wind can be tough but seems like you're up for the challenge."

"I am." She smiled into his eyes, feeling a little dizzy, a little dazed. She loved his arms around her, loved the tingle in her skin, particularly her neck, a tingle that made her shiver against him. "The weather here might be tough, but I'm tougher. Remember, I'm a Texan. We're born strong."

He kissed her then, the most lovely of kisses, so full of tenderness and hunger, heat and pleasure and she just melted into him, arms wrapping around his neck, pressing closer, savoring the hard muscular length of him. He was strong, like she was, and it crossed her mind that she'd been waiting for him her entire life. She'd been waiting for *this*.

In the middle of the scorching kiss, her phone rang, vibrating in the back pocket of her jeans. Rye's hand covered the phone in her back pocket, his fingers warm on her butt. "You've got a call," he said, against her mouth.

She laughed and drew back, but couldn't let go of him completely, not when her head was spinning. "You do that too good."

"As long as you like it."

"Oh, I do." She took another unsteady step back and drew the phone from her pocket. It was her mom. She sighed. "My mom. I'm going to need to call her right back," she said, letting the call go to voice mail.

"I should go anyway. But I've enjoyed myself."

"Me, too." She moved in to press a kiss to his mouth. "Thank you for a wonderful dinner and even better conversation. You're very good company."

"I feel the same about you."

She waited while he climbed down the ladder, and then she glanced around her loft, making sure everything was okay and then followed him down, and turned off the switch at the wall before securing the barn for the night.

Outside, the sky was very dark, a swath of purple black with faraway stars. It looked as magical as she felt. Ansley's throat ached, and she swallowed against the knot of emotion. If only Rye lived closer. She hated to think that tomorrow after the rodeo he'd leave, and she didn't know when she'd see him again. "Thank you for driving here for dinner," she said huskily.

He glanced at her, his gaze skimming her face. "Wouldn't have missed it for the world."

"You say the nicest things."

"You're one of a kind, Ansley Campbell."

She didn't know what to say and wasn't sure she could speak even if she had the words. In just twenty-four hours he'd changed her world. In just twenty-four hours he'd captured her heart, which wasn't a simple thing. She was independent, and ambitious. She had plans and a dream and love weren't part of any of that.

"You know your way back?" she asked.

"I do." He stepped forward and pressed a lingering kiss to her brow. "Good night, babe."

Babe. No one had ever called her that, and she hadn't thought she'd like it. But from him, it sounded perfect. "Good night, Rye. I'll be there cheering you on tomorrow."

She watched as he got into his truck. She waved goodbye as he pulled away, her heart having fallen somewhere between her knees and feet. Once his taillights had vanished, she entered the old farmhouse and slowly locked the front door. Her eyes burned and a whisper of fear pulsed through her veins. Love had been the last thing on her mind and yet suddenly ruggedly handsome Rye Calhoun meant everything.

HE'D MADE A mess of things.

Rye knew it from that smoldering kiss in the barn loft. It was a different kiss than the night before. It was a kiss with emotions, with intentions. It was a kiss that told him things ... like Ansley wanted him. Not just in a physical, gratify-my-craving sort of way, but in the big-picture, real-world way, and it made him feel protective of her. She was so open, so transparent. Her feelings were in her eyes, her face, her voice, her touch.

She liked him, and normally this wouldn't be a problem, because he liked her. But they weren't in the same place, they had different pressures, she only had to worry about herself, while he still had his whole family looking to him to provide for them and make the right decisions for them. Yet his admiration for her only grew. He respected her goals and dreams, respected her determination to be free ... autonomous. He respected her talent, and her drive. She knew what she wanted, she knew what she wanted to be, and she knew where she wanted to live—but that vision left no room for him. Her future in no way resembled his.

He'd never live in Marietta. He could never afford to own something as extravagant as an art gallery. He'd never have the freedom to take the same risks.

He was happy that she could choose her life and path. He was proud of her for working so hard to achieve her dreams. But he didn't have options. He lacked freedom. Their two worlds were as different as could be, and while he supported her dreams, he felt a pang that he'd never been able to dream. And the last thing he'd ever do was tie an independent, successful woman to him. If together, Ansley's creativity would suffer. Her freedom would disappear. And Rye didn't think he'd ever resent Ansley, but he suspected she'd grow to resent him, and that was the worst outcome. It was every bit as bad as Hannah chaining herself to Ron for the rest of her life.

IN THE HOUSE, Ansley locked the front door, and called her mom back, filling her in on everything Dr. Maida had said that afternoon. "It looks like Mr. Wyatt was right. Uncle Clyde wasn't just lonely. He is having cognitive issues, and it's only going to get worse," she concluded. "Mom, we're going to need a plan for Uncle Clyde's care and the ranch. If no one in our family wants this place, maybe it's time to sell it."

"Your uncle owns half. Your dad can't sell it without

Clyde agreeing, and I don't think Clyde would agree. That's the only home he's ever known," her mom answered.

"But he can't take care of it. He can't even take care of himself. He's going to need ongoing physical therapy, probably some occupational therapy. I'm happy to help him, but I'm not a nurse. I can make meals and make sure he's safe, but I'm not comfortable bathing him, or helping him with the toilet stuff."

"Your dad and I don't expect that of you, either, Ansley. I'll begin investigating a home health nurse tomorrow. It is Sunday though and I might not make a lot of progress until Monday."

"Which is fine, since Uncle Clyde isn't coming home until Wednesday."

"That's good, that gives us some time."

Ansley walked with her cell phone down the hall and into the living room. "Have any of my brothers expressed any interest in Cold Canyon Ranch?"

"Not exactly."

Ansley stopped in front of the arched bookshelf flanking the fireplace. One of the shelves was full of small gold framed black-and-white photos. "It's hard for anyone to be curious, much less enthusiastic, after Dad's harsh criticism all these years."

"He has such a complicated history with his brother and that ranch."

"I know, but maybe talk to Dad, let him know Uncle

Clyde is not going to be able to make good decisions for the ranch, and perhaps it's time to come up with a plan because once sold, the money could be invested elsewhere."

"Your uncle might live years yet."

"And I hope he does, for both Dad and Uncle Clyde's sake. I don't think it's right for Dad to leave all of this to you and me. Clyde is his brother. This was his home. He should be here problem solving with us."

Her mom said nothing, but Ansley could feel the emotion on the line, and all the things that no one would say, about two brothers who couldn't forgive, and those around them who couldn't forget. "I don't want to put you in the middle, Mom," Ansley added quietly, "but I've been put in the middle and I'm happy to help—for now."

"I'll call you Monday after I've spoken to a nursing agency. We want someone there by Wednesday?"

"Yes." Ansley hesitated. "Thanks, Mom. I appreciate you."

Her mom's low laugh warmed Ansley. "And I appreciate you. I'm proud of you, you do know that?"

"I do."

Hanging up, Ansley slowly slid the phone back into her pocket, her gaze falling onto the framed photos again. One photo in particular caught her attention. Was that her dad?

She lifted the picture, and yes, it was her dad, but it was also her uncle, the picture taken when they were just boys. There was another photo with their mom, Ansley's grandmother, a grandmother she'd only met once or twice. They were all dressed up, looking as if they were on their way to church, or maybe it was an Easter service since her grandmother was wearing a pretty straw hat.

Ansley had never seen pictures of her dad this young. Back in Last Stand there was a photo of her dad playing football, but he was a teenager in that photo, perhaps in his senior year of high school, but here he was just seven or eight. Her uncle Clyde would've been two years younger. It made her ache on the inside to see them here, smiling, arms wrapped around each other's shoulders. They looked happy, like buddies or best friends. But then, they had been best friends before jealousy and betrayal tore them apart.

Ansley was fairly certain there were more photos somewhere, maybe photo albums in a closet. One of these days she'd have to look for them. Perhaps she'd ask Uncle Clyde, although it might not be something he wanted to discuss.

Troubled, she left the room, switched off the overhead light and, after double-checking the back door was securely locked, went to her room. It wasn't until she'd changed into her pajamas and climbed into bed that she realized she and Rye hadn't made plans to meet tomorrow. But, of course, he had more important things on his mind. Like winning his events at the rodeo.

WEEKS AGO, SOPHIE Wyatt and her sister-in-law the newly-wed, Dr Briar Wyatt, had convinced Ansley that she should volunteer to work the pancake breakfast during the rodeo weekend as she'd meet more people and she'd enjoy the festivities. Ansley hadn't been sure she should work a booth hosted by the Daughters of Montana, as she wasn't from Montana, but as it turned out, this morning she was glad to have something specific to do other than worry about her uncle, and obsess about Rye.

Obviously, Rye had to focus on his upcoming events. It was his job, and it was a dangerous job. He couldn't afford to be careless, and he needed to be focused, but Ansley couldn't help checking her phone every twenty minutes or so to see if she'd missed a call or text.

She hadn't.

Despite Sophie's energy and Briar's quick wit, Ansley didn't enjoy herself as much as she'd hoped. She was doing something useful by volunteering to dish up bacon and sausages to hundreds of people, but her emotions were all over the place. If Rye called, she'd no longer feel blue, but as the morning passed without word from him, she couldn't help feeling down. It worried her that she was falling for Rye this hard. They'd only just met. How could she have such unrealistic expectations?

Ansley felt as if she'd fallen down the rabbit hole. She was getting in too deep, chasing something unlikely, maybe even impossible.

Then, at eleven fifteen her phone finally rang, but it wasn't Rye. It was the hospital calling to say that her uncle was extremely agitated, and he was insisting he be released. The hospital couldn't keep him against his will so could Ansley please come and pick him up? There would be paperwork to do, and discharge instructions as well, but they expected he'd be able to leave by one, possibly two. Which fell right in the middle of today's rodeo finals.

Disappointed, Ansley gave quick hugs to Sophie and Briar before walking to her car, which she'd parked close to St. James. Once at the hospital, she sent Rye a quick text that she wouldn't be able to attend the rodeo today, but she'd be cheering him on from home.

Inside the hospital, she was kept busy signing forms and getting discharge instructions and speaking to her mother who'd talked to a Bozeman based care agency that wanted to know exactly the kind of help Clyde would need, and since Ansley didn't know, she had to request a nurse come and speak to her mom so her mom could get all of her questions answered.

Her uncle had finally resigned himself to the wait, and it was just after two when Ansley was told to bring her car around to the entrance and someone would have her uncle waiting. He'd be in a wheelchair and the attendant would help get her uncle into the car, but then Ansley would need to get him into the house.

Ansley wasn't ready for this. She'd thought she'd have

three days to prepare the house for Clyde's arrival. Instead, he was being returned to her and she didn't have a wheelchair to push him into the house. Apparently, he should be able to walk the few steps into the house with her assistance, but she didn't find the information reassuring. *Should be able to walk* didn't mean he *could walk.*

In the end, after much silent agonizing, they made it back to the ranch, and after lots of slow, teetering steps, into the house, and down the hall to her uncle's bedroom and bathroom. He needed to use the bathroom, and she waited outside the door until he called for her. After he'd washed his hands, she put her arm around his waist and walked him to his bed. He wanted out of his clothes, and she helped him undress to his boxers, and he slowly, painfully climbed into bed.

It was obvious he shouldn't be home yet.

It was obvious he wasn't close to being independent.

But it was also obvious he wanted his own bed in his own home, and she couldn't blame him for that.

RYE SENT ANSLEY a text just before his first event. *Are you here?* he asked.

She didn't answer.

He suspected she hadn't come today, and he was disappointed, but at the same time, pragmatic. She had commitments. He had commitments. Fortunately, he felt good, strong, ready to ride. He was going into today's competition in good shape, with him at the top of the leaderboard in steer wrestling, second in saddle bronc behind Huck, and fourth in bare back. Now he just needed to clinch a couple wins.

Rye adjusted his gloves, resettled his chaps on his hips. He was calm. He knew what he had to do. Briefly his thoughts turned to Ansley before he forced his attention back to the upcoming ride. He had this.

The roar of the crowd and then the immediate collective groan told him the last saddle bronc rider hadn't stuck his ride. It was proving to be a challenging afternoon. Huck Jones had set the bar high yesterday, and had another outstanding ride today, but there was room for Rye to take second. He wanted second—or better.

He climbed up on the chute, waited for the signal and then lowered himself on the bronc. The gate flew open. Rye's vision narrowed and time slowed, allowing him to feel the bronc beneath him, matching every leap and kick, exploiting the bucking of the horse to earn maximum points.

The bell sounded at eight seconds and the stands roared their approval. On the ground, he beat his hat once against his thigh and looked up at the scoreboard. It had been a good ride. He wouldn't call it his best. But would his score be enough for him to take second?

His score flashed. Elation filled him. Yes. It would be

enough. Second place behind Huck Jones was good enough for him. He'd be taking home some seriously good money.

ANSLEY WAS IN the kitchen considering her options for dinner as Uncle Clyde said he wanted real food tonight as he'd barely been able to eat anything in the hospital, but Ansley didn't know what to make him. She wasn't a great cook. She hadn't yet learned how to cook properly yet, and while reheating was in her skill set, making and baking from scratch wasn't.

Ansley closed the refrigerator door and opened the freezer, pulling out a package of ground beef, hoping sloppy Joes or tacos could be considered real food. But as she set the frozen beef on the stove to defrost, she heard a truck approach the house. For a split second she wondered if it was possibly Rye coming to see her, and then she chastised herself, knowing it would be impossible for Rye to be here and at the fairgrounds at the same time.

It turned out to be Melvin Wyatt pulling up in his truck. She liked the Wyatts, and had an extra soft spot for Melvin Wyatt, the family patriarch, a man who'd raised his grandsons when their dad died in an accident that also took Melvin's only other son's life. But you'd never know Melvin had worries or pain. He was always looking out after his neighbors, in particular curmudgeonly Clyde Campbell.

Ansley met Melvin on the front porch. He was carrying a huge soup pot. "Dinner," he said. "Sophie and Summer said they'll also send something over for dinner tomorrow, too."

"That's not necessary," Ansley said, before quickly adding, "but so appreciated. They must have heard I'm not that good in the kitchen."

"Practice makes perfect," Melvin said, as she opened the front door for him. "And in my case, it was a lot of practice." He nodded to the kitchen. "I'll put this on the stove, shall I?"

"Yes, please. Thank you."

In the kitchen, he washed his hands and then faced her. "So, how is our patient?"

"Uncle Clyde seems to be in a lot of pain." Ansley hesitated. "But he's also had all the pain medicine he can take until later. Should I let him have more?"

"I'll sit with him for a bit. If he needs more medicine, I can give it to him."

"Thank you, Mr. Wyatt. I've had a hard time this afternoon." She heard her voice crack and she exhaled hard. "I warn you though, he's in a mood."

Melvin smiled. "But of course he is. Even before the strokes. That's just our Clyde." He patted her on the shoulder. "Since I'm here for the next little bit, put your feet up and relax if you can. I'll let you know when I head out."

But Ansley couldn't put her feet up. She was too wound up to relax, and so she began making lists of all that she needed to do, and things she needed to purchase to make

Clyde's life easier, and hers, too. She'd love a camera system, like a baby monitor, that she could put in his room. They needed more grab bars in her uncle's room, or some kind of frame near his bed to allow him to get up more easily. Would a hospital bed be better? She didn't know.

She was in the laundry room in the back of the house when Rye's voice echoed down the hall. "Ansley? Anyone home?"

Ansley froze, heart thumping. He had come. She'd hoped, how she'd hoped, she'd see him, and then she thought it wouldn't happen, and yet now he was here. She rushed from the laundry room toward the front door where Rye stood on the threshold, late afternoon sunlight streaming behind him. He was holding his hat, wearing a T-shirt and jeans and what looked like comfortable old boots.

He was heading home, and yet he had driven a half an hour out of his way away from his destination to be here. To see her.

"Hey, hi." She reached up and tugged the elastic out of her hair letting the ponytail down. "How did you do?"

"Won in steer wrestling, placed well in two other events."

"Oh, Rye, that's fantastic!"

His smile was bashful. "It feels good to be taking some money home."

"And no broken bones," she said, closing the distance all the way so that she could hook a finger over his leather belt, her thumb sliding across the big silver belt buckle. "That's a win in of itself."

"True. My mom will be relieved."

"You'll have to tell her."

"I will once I'm on the road."

"She worries?"

"About everything, but to be fair, she has a lot on her plate. I don't want to add to her troubles."

"You're not going to get home until it's late," Ansley said, feeling his hard flat abdomen against her knuckles. He was so warm and lean and hard. His body was a thing of wonder. If only he was sticking around another week maybe they would have had a chance to get to know each other better, to grow even closer.

"It will be seven hours if there's no traffic, and I don't expect a lot of traffic. I encountered road work on the way down, that's why it took me forever on Thursday, but not on a Sunday night."

Thursday, was it only Thursday when she first laid eyes on him? Friday when they spoke? Crazy. It seemed like he'd always been in her life, or maybe she'd always wanted him in her life.

Ansley swallowed around the lump in her throat. "Are you hungry? Can I make you anything?"

"Not hungry but I wouldn't say no to something cold to drink."

"I've water and iced tea," she said.

"Iced tea sounds good."

She led the way to the kitchen, not that he needed to be shown how to get there, not after being here last night, but neither of them mentioned last night. Everything seemed so different already.

In the kitchen, Ansley pointed to the big pot on the stove. "If you change your mind about food, I have enough beef burgundy to feed an army. Mr. Wyatt brought it over."

"You mentioned that name last night. Wyatt. Any relation to the professional rodeo cowboy Wyatts? Sam, Billy, and Tommy Wyatt?" Rye asked, leaning against the kitchen counter.

She glanced at him surprised. "Yes. You know them?"

"Have competed with all of them, but Tommy and Billy are in a class of their own right now. They're some of the best ever."

"The Wyatts are our closest neighbors. I haven't met all of them yet, but I do know Joe and Sophie, Briar, who is Tommy's new wife, and Sam and Ivy—"

"I know Ivy quite well. She's an outstanding barrel racer. Her mother was, too."

"Such a small world," Ansley marveled, pouring the tea over ice cubes and presenting him with the glass.

"Especially for those who compete on the rodeo circuit here in Montana."

He was leaning against one of the kitchen counters, looking absolutely gorgeous against the vintage cabinets. Every kitchen needed a handsome cowboy, especially one with soulful dark eyes like Rye Calhoun. "Do you think you'll always compete? It's tough on your body, isn't it?"

His lips quirked. "And I thought I was hiding my limp pretty well."

"Are you in pain?"

"There's always pain, that's just part of the job."

"I'm not sure I like the job then."

He took a long sip of his iced tea. "My goal was to be done at thirty."

Ansley frowned, remembering the stats she'd read in yesterday's program. "I thought you were thirty."

His smile was crooked. "I am. So, hopefully, in the next couple of years I won't need to compete. I'm ready to shift gears but can't afford to leave the circuit yet. But it's the plan."

"And then what? Continue with roofing?"

His smile faded. For a long moment he didn't answer. Rye took another long swallow of the iced tea. "That is the family business."

But there was no joy in his voice, and it struck Ansley that his light had gone. He didn't love roofing. She realized he was doing what needed to be done for his family, and whatever his dreams were, whatever his personal ambition had been, had been sacrificed for the greater good.

It made her heart ache. This beautiful, disciplined hardworking man seemed to put everyone else first.

It made her care for him even more.

"Can I please just make you a sack lunch for the road? I'm pretty good with peanut butter and jelly, and I've got some really good strawberry jam here. Sophie Wyatt makes it for Uncle Clyde every summer."

"You don't need to worry about me."

For some reason that seemed even worse. Not to worry about him? Not care about him? "I'm not worrying, I'm simply providing a PB and J sandwich for you."

"You don't have to fuss over me, babe. I can take care of myself, and I mean that in the nicest sort of way. You've got plenty to do without adding me to your list of concerns."

"What concerns?"

"Um, your uncle?"

"You're not my uncle, and you make me happy. Maybe I'm crazy, but it feels nice to think about someone ... to think about you."

He looked away, jaw working. "I'm used to doing the providing. I'm used to taking care of others. I don't know how to let someone take care of me."

"Not even your mama?"

He looked at her, his gaze slowly moving over her, the top of her head down the length of her body and then back up again. "My mom has been dealt a bad hand in life. It's my mission to make things easier, as much as I can."

"Is that why you live at home?"

"I have my own space on our property. I don't live in the

main house. But before you go thinking I have a cool pad, it's a trailer. It's a pretty rough trailer, but it's mine, and it gives me a little space and helps let me come and go without disturbing the others."

"Who all lives at home?" she asked carefully, feeling as if she was maybe overstepping. He'd been so private, she suspected that his family wasn't something he wanted to discuss.

"Everyone." His lips curved but it was a grim smile, and it didn't reach his eyes. "My parents, John and Jennifer, my two sisters, Hannah and Josie, and my younger brother Jasper." He glanced at his watch and set his iced tea glass down. "Speaking of, I should get on the road."

Ansley nodded and walked Rye outside, to his truck and rig.

For a moment, neither said anything. They just stood next to his Chevy, taking in the twilight. Ansley really didn't want him to go. She couldn't bear to say goodbye. Not yet. Maybe not ever.

She sucked up her courage to ask what had been on her mind almost constantly the past twenty-four hours. "Will you be back this way anytime soon?"

Rye reached out to touch her cheek and then tucked a strand of hair behind her ear. "No. My weekends are all in different directions. Oregon next weekend, Idaho, Washington state, Wyoming, South Dakota."

"That's just the next five weeks. What then? Won't the

season be wrapping up soon?"

"End of October," he agreed. "South Dakota is my last for this year."

"And then?" She'd meant to sound strong, but her voice came out a whisper.

"I'll be working six days a week in construction, getting those roofs on before the snow comes."

"And roofs can't wait." She forced a smile, if only to hold back the sting of tears wanting to fill her eyes.

His head inclined, the briefest nod. "I hate the circumstances—"

"It's okay."

"If things were different—"

"I get it."

He smiled, but he wasn't smiling. He couldn't even look at her, his gaze fixed on a point beyond her shoulder. "It's not because I'm not into you," he said lowly. "Believe me."

And she did.

She couldn't see him lying to her. What would be the point? What would he achieve by deceiving her? He wasn't that kind of man.

Salt of the earth.

The words whispered through her, making her long for a different version of this story, one that ended happily. One where there would be more romance and more slow dancing and more long desperate kisses. That would be a story she'd tell her children and grandchildren. *I met your dad at the*

Marietta rodeo...

Instead, he'd go to Eureka and become the construction worker, putting on work boots and a hardhat.

"Ansley?" His voice had dropped, the huskiness of it stealing her breath.

"Yes?" She blinked hard and smiled because that was what they were doing now. Being mature. Keeping it together. This would not be a dramatic tortured goodbye.

"I'm probably not going to be very good about staying in touch." His brown eyes locked with hers. "It's not personal."

Oh, she wasn't going to keep this up much longer, not with the pain building inside of her, the sadness huge and hot. "I know." She forced a smile. "And I know if we lived in the same place, we wouldn't be having this conversation." She lifted her chin, her smile wider, tears stinging the corners of her eyes. "Now give me a hug and go. You've got a lot of driving to do tonight."

His arms wrapped around her in a tight hug that let her feel the things he wouldn't, couldn't say.

He was so him—so solid and real and good. She understood his strength, understood that he had to be strong for those who needed him. Fortunately, God had made her strong, too. So, she could take care of herself and not be one more anchor on a man. On Rye.

As he held her tight, she squeezed him back. *I love you.* The words were silent but that didn't make them any less real.

She pulled away first, taking a big, and necessary step backward. "Good luck next weekend." She exhaled, still smiling, still fighting the gritty burn in her eyes and throat. "Where in Oregon?"

"Pendleton," he said, drawing out his truck key.

"Good luck. Be safe."

"Always." Then he was climbing into his truck, starting the engine, and driving away.

She waved as he drove and just before he disappeared from view, his window opened and his arm came out, hand high in a final goodbye.

Goodbye.

Ansley crouched down in the driveway, ducked her head, trying to stop the tears but it didn't work. The tears wouldn't stop.

How impossible the last three days had been.

The best weekend of her life had just become one of the worst. And for reasons she didn't understand, she'd never felt even half this pain when she and Clark broke up. And they'd had three years together, not three days.

Chapter Six

T HE NEXT FEW days passed so slowly that Ansley thought she was losing her mind. Since returning home Sunday afternoon, Uncle Clyde had been demanding, irritable, and a bewildering mixture of lucidity and confusion. Although he was supposed to get out of bed and walk every day, getting some exercise, he only left bed to use the bathroom before he'd return to bed. Ansley overheard him talking to someone on the phone that he didn't need help and he wasn't going to be going to any physical therapy appointments.

Uncle Clyde just wanted to be alone, and have his meals served to him in bed. He even resorted to using the bedside urinal, so he didn't have to get up too often. In theory, Ansley didn't mind dumping his urinal and washing it out before returning it to his bedside, but he was supposed to be regaining mobility and independence. He wasn't making the slightest effort to do either.

He asked her to move the TV set into the bedroom, and she agreed, but then worried that if she moved a TV into her uncle's room, he'd have no incentive to become more independent. She tried to call her mom, but she was out, or unavailable, Ansley's call going to voice mail. Ansley knew better than to call her dad. Her dad refused to get involved. She'd always respected her dad so much but his inability to forgive his brother, and his unwillingness to help make decisions for his care and the ranch, deeply disappointed her.

Troubled, Ansley drove to the Wyatts to get advice. Melvin and Summer Wyatt welcomed her warmly, and they sat at the kitchen table having tea and banana bread which Sophie had baked that morning.

"I worry that Uncle Clyde is regressing," Ansley said, feeling guilty for coming to the Wyatts but she didn't know what to do, and the Wyatt family had been neighbors with the Campbells for generations. If anyone outside the family knew how to deal with Clyde Campbell, it would be them. "He's asked me to bring the TV into the bedroom and there's no cable access in the bedroom. I could ask the cable company to come and put in access, but I'm not sure it's the right thing to do. The doctor was adamant that Uncle Clyde has to get out of bed and walk every day. He needs the exercise and stimulation, but he's only getting up to use the bathroom once or twice a day and he won't allow me to schedule the physical therapist. Insurance will cover someone coming here and working with him."

"But he's getting up to use the bathroom?" Summer asked.

Ansley hid her embarrassment. "He'll use it once a day, but the rest of the time he prefers peeing in the plastic urinal the hospital sent home with him. I then empty it for him."

Melvin glanced at Summer who appeared equally concerned. "That's not right. He should be up and moving around, strengthening his legs."

"And working with the physical therapist, doing the exercises," Summer said sternly. "Even I do my exercises."

"I'm glad you've come to us," Melvin said. "You shouldn't have to be dealing with those all on your own. Hopefully your parents will be coming soon. This shouldn't fall on you—"

"Or you," Ansley interrupted carefully. "You have your own family to take care of. I don't want you being burdened. I just hoped you might have some ideas. I've never done any elder care. I never even did much babysitting when I was younger, so this is all new to me."

Summer reached over and placed a light hand on Ansley's. "We have a long relationship with Clyde. His wife Sandy was one of my good friends. We'll start paying Clyde visits. He'll come 'round, you'll see."

Ansley gave Summer's hand a gentle squeeze. "Thank you, but I hope you don't think I'm complaining—"

"No. You're trusting us, which is good," Melvin said. "And I'll be stopping by later today but won't mention that you've been here."

Ansley nodded gratefully. "Thank you, and I should be getting back. It's probably not smart of me to leave him alone."

"You've only been gone twenty minutes or so," Summer

said. "If he's sticking to bed, he should be fine."

But Ansley was already on her feet, reaching for the car keys. "Thank you again—"

"Don't thank us," Melvin said, interrupting her as he, too, got to his feet. "Think of us like family. We've got to stick together and take care of each other. It's the only way to get through life."

Impulsively, Ansley hugged Melvin, and then gave Summer a careful hug, too. "Lucky to have you as neighbors," she said.

"We feel the same way," Melvin said, walking Ansley out to her car.

She opened the driver-side door and hesitated. "If Summer knew Clyde's wife, Sandy, then you must have known my dad and Uncle Clyde as kids."

"I did. My boys grew up with the Campbell boys. They played sports together and competed in amateur rodeo events together, but Sam and JC went pro, and Clyde and Callen had their own careers. Your dad enlisted and he never returned. That was a shame. He was missed."

She looked up at Melvin, curiosity filling her. "You knew why he didn't come back."

"I knew. We all knew."

"Why did he do it?" she asked, thinking of the photo in the Campbell living room of two little boys all dressed up for church.

"You mean, why did Clyde steal Sandy from your dad?"

Melvin sighed. "Why does anyone do anything? Desire, fear, anger, insecurity? But of all those things, I think your uncle truly cared for Sandy. I think he'd always envied Callen's relationship with her—he'd harbored secret feelings for her—and so once your dad was gone, Clyde saw an opportunity and he took it."

"What was Sandy like?"

"Pretty, petite, and very lively. She was raised on a ranch close to the town of Emigrant and she was as social as they came, always organizing picnics and barbecues. In winter, she'd have everyone out at Miracle Lake ice-skating and building a bonfire. She tended to be the life of a party, which I think appealed to Clyde. Clyde was not as outgoing as your dad, and not as confident. Clyde was quiet and shy, and Sandy was the opposite."

"I can't imagine my uncle with someone like that. He seems so ... crochety."

"All I know is that he truly loved Sandy. From the start, he adored her, and after they married, he treated her like a queen. She brought out the best in him, and she was his world, and since they didn't have children, he was hers."

"They didn't want children?"

"Sandy couldn't have them. Summer knows more about this than me, but Sandy was pregnant a half dozen times but none of the babies made it to full term. The losses were devastating. Clyde became even more protective of her."

The miscarriages sounded devastating. Ansley couldn't

imagine going through all that. And how awfully ironic that Sandy would have six miscarriages while her mom and dad have six healthy children. "I wish I'd met her," Ansley said, meaning it. "I'm sorry I never did."

"Not sure if you know, but Sandy and your mom worked for years to create a reconciliation between the Campbell brothers, but your dad wouldn't have it."

"My uncle wanted it, though?"

"From what I understand, yes."

Ansley's heart hurt. "It makes me sad. I don't understand how one can go through life unwilling to forgive."

"Your dad was deeply hurt. He felt betrayed." Melvin hesitated. "Despite the difference in personalities, Clyde and Callen had been close. I'd say they were best friends, which is why your dad felt betrayed."

"But if my dad had married Sandy instead of my mom, I wouldn't be here. None of my brothers would be here." She hesitated. "He probably wouldn't have had a family."

"Exactly. None of you would exist. And it's a wonderful thing you do."

THREE HOURS LATER, Melvin showed up at the Campbell farmhouse, bringing a baked pasta dish for dinner and telling Ansley he intended to spend the afternoon with Clyde so Ansley could run errands or paint, or just take a long nap.

She was free to do whatever she wanted or needed to do.

Grateful, Ansley gave Melvin the biggest hug, thanking him so many times that he patted her on the back. "This is what friends do," he said. "Friends show up."

Friends show up.

The warmth and conviction in his voice made the air catch in her throat and her eyes sting. She'd never needed neighbors before. She'd always had her family, but Melvin was right—people had to be there for each other. People needed community.

Delighted to have a few hours free, Ansley drove to the nearest grocery store, picked up fresh bread, eggs, cheese, and produce, including her favorite, apples. But instead of immediately heading home, she drove one of the old roads that paralleled the Yellowstone River, enjoying the sunlight and shadow dappling the river. Eventually she found a little pullout where she could park and have an apple, and maybe sketch. She always kept a sketch pad and charcoal pencils with her, and leaving her car, found a perfect spot to sit and draw.

It was wonderful to be outside, wonderful to stop thinking, wonderful to just be in the moment. The world fell away. Her worries faded. She spent nearly two hours lost in her work before realizing the time. She quickly packed up and returned to the ranch, finding Melvin and her uncle sitting in the family room together, watching TV.

"I'll see you tomorrow," Melvin said as he left. "I could

tell Clyde enjoyed the company."

The rest of the day passed in a blur of activity, the kind of activity that wasn't memorable but filled the hours, and it wasn't until Ansley was in her room for the night, that she realized she hadn't checked her emails today. At first, there was nothing interesting, just questions and notifications for her account on Etsy, and then a request by someone on eBay asking if she'd consider accepting a lower price for her small Last Stand painting, the one of its historic square, and it had already been very affordably priced. Biting back frustration, she countered the offer and was just about to sign off when she spotted a message she hadn't opened from a Marcia Brixley at The Bozeman Big Sky Gallery.

Ansley read the message, eyes widening as she reached the end. She'd been invited to be part of an upcoming exhibit in one of Bozeman's biggest art galleries.

She sat up and reread the email, trying to process the information and not wanting to miss any of the details. The show would be in just three weeks. One of the original participating artists had a family emergency and was forced to drop out and Marcia, the gallery owner, wanted Ansley to fill the space. She'd heard about Ansley's work through the Sterbas, who were old friends and customers, and was formally inviting Ansley to participate, if Ansley was interested.

If she was interested. Wow.

Wow.

Ansley jumped off her bed, pulse racing, feet dancing. She couldn't believe it. This was huge. *Huge.*

She'd never been part of a show before. She'd never been invited by any gallery to hang any of her work, never mind be a featured artist. She grabbed her iPad and reread the invitation a third time, the pleasure sinking in. There would be an opening night reception with a cocktail party. Ansley was encouraged to invite any of her collectors—this made her laugh. She didn't have any collectors. She'd only recently started a mailing list. But this show could change all that. The email ended with, "I hope to hear from you soon, with an answer either way."

If it wasn't so late at night, she'd call Marcia straight away, and then she wanted to call her mom and tell her, but again it was late. Ansley was so excited, and she wanted to celebrate, but with whom?

Rye came to mind. But then, he was always on her mind, even if she pushed him back, pushing him to the far corners which was where he waited, filling the silence and space, filling her heart with regrets. If he only lived closer. If they'd only had more time. If, if, if…

It was hard to sleep that night.

Ansley tossed and turned, her thoughts filled with the gallery invitation, the pieces she'd display, the significance of the show, of sharing with Rye.

At three o'clock in the morning, she gave up trying to sleep for a while and turned on her iPad to look at her available pieces which she kept track of in an album on her phone.

She'd need a number of significant paintings to show, as well as some works in a different price range. She'd love at least one big statement landscape like the one the Sterba law office hung on their conference room wall, along with several other oversized works. She had a number of smaller ones, but they needed to be framed. She'd have to do a lot of painting in the next few weeks, but she could, especially if she painted late into the night. Three weeks from tomorrow. Perfectly doable if she worked twenty-four hours a day.

Ansley flopped back in bed, feeling the shudder of nerves. *Don't panic. You've got this. This isn't scary, it's exciting.* She had the opportunity to do something she'd always wanted. This was her dream. Nothing would stand in the way of her dream.

Maybe it was good that Rye was gone. She wouldn't want to be at her easel all day and late into the night if he were in town. She'd want to be with him, just hanging out, feeling happy. He made her happy. Or he'd made her happy before he'd ended things.

THURSDAY MORNING RYE entered the family home to grab some milk from the refrigerator since he was out in his trailer. His mom was in the kitchen with her morning cup of tea and her familiar notepad which she used as a weekly shopping list.

"Good morning," she said smiling at him.

"Morning, Mom."

"Looks like you need milk," she said, adding another thing to her grocery list.

"Don't worry about it," he said. "I'm leaving after work tonight. I'll get milk when I get back Sunday."

"You're sure you're ready to compete again?"

"Why wouldn't I be?" he asked, returning the milk and closing the refrigerator door.

"You've been in a bear of a mood. I figured you're hurt and keeping it to yourself."

"I left Marietta in good shape. It felt good to win."

"Then what is it?"

He sipped his coffee and fought for patience. He wasn't in the mood to talk about anything right now. He wanted coffee and some quiet, or at least coffee and conversation that didn't focus on him. "Things are good, Mom."

"Are they?"

"Yes. We've a lot of jobs lined up for the rest of the fall, and we're pushing to get those roofs done before the first snowfall. We're more comfortable financially then we've been in months—"

"Then why have you kept your distance from us?" she interrupted gently, pushing her teacup across the small island's old butcher-block countertop. "You've barely spoken to any of us since you came home Sunday."

"That's not true. I've played a video game with Dad and hung out with Jasper."

"You haven't been home for dinner all week."

"Because I'm working late trying to get the Lewis roof finished before leaving tonight for Pendleton."

She pulled the teacup back. "But when you do come home, you don't eat. I don't think you've touched any of the dinners I left for you in the oven."

"Sometimes I've had a late lunch. Other times, I'm just not hungry."

"Which would be fine if you had weight to lose."

"I ride better when I'm lighter, Mom."

"Perhaps. But you're not sleeping, either. I see your light on in the trailer in the middle of the night."

"What are you doing up in the middle of the night?"

"I guess neither of us can sleep."

Rye sighed and rubbed his brow, pressing hard against the throbbing that wouldn't go away. He couldn't sleep, no. And he had no appetite. He had to hide his phone to keep from calling Ansley. It was killing him not talking to her. It was a fire in his chest, and it burned night and day. He didn't know what was happening. He'd never felt this way. It wasn't a good feeling. He didn't like feeling sick to his stomach. He didn't like feeling he'd failed her. He'd argued against the guilt because she'd been fine when they said goodbye. She'd smiled at him and sent him on his way. He could still see her standing in the middle of Cold Canyon Ranch's driveway waving. Her calm had reassured him. She had her own life, and he had his.

Rye looked at his mom, feeling the weight of her gaze. Her eyes, a lavender blue, were filled with shadows and a sheen of tears. Only Josie had inherited their mother's violet eyes. The rest of them had their dad's brown eyes.

"Mom. Don't." Rye couldn't handle it when she cried. Thankfully she rarely cried. "Things are fine. You're getting yourself worked up over nothing."

"Something did happen. I know it."

He said nothing, determined not to be drawn into this. He had a long day ahead of him and then an even longer drive tonight.

"Did you have a fight with someone in Marietta?" she persisted.

"No. I don't fight, you know that."

"And you're not injured," she said.

"No."

She tipped her head, studied him. "Then it's love."

Rye choked on his mouthful of coffee and nearly spit it out. "No," he said, after struggling to swallow.

"I think you met someone in Marietta."

Rye was not doing this, not today, not any day. "I need to go. I'll be home to hitch my trailer after work, but don't plan on me for dinner."

His mom reached out and caught his sleeve as he passed,

stopping him. "It's okay to have feelings."

He hesitated and then leaned over and kissed the top of her head, her thick dark brown hair beginning to show strands of gray. "I know." Then he was walking out to his truck and a long day on top of the Lewis house, wrapping up the job so he could leave for Oregon. It was a good thing he had a good crew, several of the men having been with Calhoun Roofing since he was a teenager, but everyone always showed up, and the newer guys worked harder, when he was on the job site, too.

But driving to the Calhoun Roofing office, Rye itched to call Ansley. She was constantly on his mind, and he wanted to know how her uncle was doing, but even more importantly, how she was doing. He knew all too well that it wasn't easy becoming a caretaker, and this was new to her. He hoped she was getting support from her family. He hoped the Wyatts were still checking in. It was a lot to ask of a person, but Ansley was strong. She had backbone.

She had more than that.

She had fire and light, warmth and sweetness, courage and a beauty that crawled into his heart and took up space. Considerable space. He was missing her. And thinking of her way too much.

Calling her wouldn't make things easier. Calling her would just make him want to keep calling. He wouldn't detach the way he needed to do, and that was the next step, the most important step. He had to let her go.

It was the best thing for both of them.

But that didn't make it comfortable.

THURSDAY MORNING, AFTER helping her uncle with his morning routine and then arguing with him about trying to come to the kitchen table for breakfast, at least making the effort, Ansley gave in and helped him back to bed. But once he was there, and content with his oatmeal and coffee, Ansley called Marcia at the gallery to discuss the invitation.

The call with Marcia left Ansley even more excited. It was the first time anyone in the art business had treated her as a true artist. A true professional. She hadn't realized how much the inclusion would mean to her, and after discussing the exhibit with Marcia, she agreed she'd want to come see the space—and what section of the gallery would be her space—to make sure she had the right pieces, and enough pieces, to show. But to go to Bozeman, she'd need someone to stay with Uncle Clyde. Ansley resolved to discuss it with Melvin, certain he'd be supportive, and when he arrived that afternoon and she shared the invitation with him, he was so pleased she almost felt as if she was one of his grandkids.

"Do you want to go today?" Melvin asked. "Have you set a time with her?"

"I haven't, but she is working today. But then she's also working tomorrow."

"Do what you want to do. Between Summer and me, we've got you covered."

Ansley called Marcia back, asked if there was a good time to come by the gallery, and Marcia suggested that afternoon if it worked. Ansley said it did and quickly showered and dressed, pulling her long hair into a ponytail to look a bit older, before driving the forty-five minutes it'd take to reach downtown Bozeman.

Marcia was even more lovely in person. She was younger than Ansley expected, early to midforties, with dark hair and light gray eyes, and a crackling energy that made it hard for her to stand still. "This would be your area," Marcia said, walking Ansley across the gallery to a massive wall with a half wall. "I usually encourage the artist to share their vision for displaying their work, but I might have some thoughts."

"Of course. I'm open to anything and everything."

"Good, then I hope you're open to adjusting the pricing for your work. You are seriously undervaluing your landscapes, and I know you do a lot on Etsy and eBay, but consider increasing those prices. Offer Ansley Art merchandise that's affordable, but your originals should be priced accordingly." Marcia hesitated. "Do you have any questions about the commission we take?"

"I'd expect it's the standard fifty percent."

Marcia nodded. "It might seem like a lot, but we're going to market you, introduce you to some of the biggest buyers in Gallatin County, and it's something you'll want to put on your resume. I've worked hard to make this one of the more prestigious galleries in Montana. My sales staff is exceptional and we're in an excellent location."

"I know. And I'm thrilled. I haven't stopped smiling since I got your email."

"We'll want everything to hang a few days before the opening night reception, so have everything to us by the twenty-fifty, maybe?"

"Do you have an ideal number of pieces you'd like me to show?"

"It depends on the size of your canvases, but usually it's anywhere from ten to thirty. I've found that we sell the large 24x36 works well, but you'll want a variety of sizes as everyone has a different preference, budget, and display space."

"Thank you," Ansley said as one of the sales staff flagged Marcia for a call. "And I'll see you soon."

"Can't wait to see what you bring us."

Outside, Ansley sat in her car parked on Bozeman's bustling Main Street, heart thumping, emotion sweeping through her chest. For years, she alone had believed in herself, and for years she had persisted at her craft even when her family suggested over and over that she get serious and buckle down with a real job. Painting was a hobby. She needed a real career. She needed to contribute to society. She had been given a good education and she needed to use it.

The comments and criticisms had hurt, but Ansley knew

who she was, and she knew what she wanted and this show in three weeks was proof that she was on the right track. Her hard work hadn't been in vain. One exhibit wouldn't change the world, but it was a start to making the life she'd always dreamed of, the life where she could be creative and successful.

She'd have to call home and share the news with her parents, but before that, there was someone else she wanted to tell. Ansley pulled out her phone and studied it for a long moment before typing a text to Rye. *I've had some exciting news and had to share. I've been asked to participate in a three-person exhibit at a prominent art gallery in Bozeman. It's my first gallery show. I'm pretty excited. Just thought you'd want to know.* ☺

She waited a minute in case he answered. He didn't.

She kept her phone on her lap while she drove back to Paradise Valley, but he didn't call on the drive, or even while she made dinner, or did the dishes.

Turning out the kitchen light, Ansley told herself it was okay, that he didn't have to call. He knew and that was enough. It had to be enough. Right then her phone rang. And it was Rye.

Blinking back tears, Ansley grabbed a coat from the hooks by the door and stepped outside to the covered porch to talk to him. "Hi," she said, breathless.

"Is this a bad time?"

"No. It's perfect. Just finished dishes."

"How is your uncle?"

"Grouchy but fine."

"Hope he's not taking it out on you," Rye said.

"No, and the Wyatts are being amazing. They're coming every day to sit with him, letting me have some time to myself."

"Good people."

"Yes." She drew a breath. "You saw my message?"

"I did. Congratulations, Ansley. I'm really happy for you."

The warm sincerity in his voice made her exhale with pleasure. "Thank you." She bit her lip, not sure if she wanted to cry or smile. She'd wanted so badly to hear from him and had been so afraid he wasn't going to respond to her text. "How are you?"

"Good. And you?" he replied.

"Better now that you've called." Her voice cracked and she fought to keep all the emotion in.

"I'm sorry to keep you waiting. I was working earlier, and then trying to get on the road for Pendleton."

She knocked away the tears and suppressed a shiver at a chilly gust of wind. "You're driving now?"

"I am. Getting close to Sandpoint, Idaho."

She glanced at her watch. It was almost seven. "How much farther do you have to go?"

"Another four hours or so."

"It's going to be a late night."

"That's alright. I'll sleep in tomorrow. Anyway, tell me

more about your show. When did you find out?"

"Last night." She drew her coat closer. The weather was changing. Fall was coming. The nights were already so much colder. "I wanted to call you right away, but you said no contact."

"You should've called me. This is big."

She paced the porch, glad he couldn't see her or her nervous energy. She didn't want him to know just how much she'd missed him and how afraid she'd been that she'd lost him. "I know I'm supposed to leave you alone."

"Don't put it that way."

"But you'd meant it that way."

"This isn't easy. I'm finding this hard, too."

She leaned against the porch pillar. "Why can't we stay in touch? Even if it's just a little bit? A little bit would be so much easier than nothing."

"Because I want you to meet someone there."

"Well, I don't."

He laughed, half amused, half exasperated. "We can only be friends."

"Then you shouldn't have kissed me like that. You shouldn't have made me feel like this."

"Like what?"

"Like I can do anything. That I can be anyone. You gave me the feeling of possibility and I won't give it up." *I won't give you up*, she added silently, straightening.

"You're the one with magic in you," he said, huskily.

She swallowed. "We need to change the rules. I don't like your rules."

"What rules are those?"

"That we can't see each other and we're not to stay in touch. It's too hard, Rye. Cutting me off, cutting me out, hurts too much."

He didn't immediately speak. She heard him exhale at the other end of the line. "I don't want you to hurt, babe. That's the last thing I want you to do."

"Then don't close the door," she whispered. "Let's leave it cracked open. Let me hope."

Silence stretched again. "Hope is a dangerous thing," he said at length.

"Hope is hope."

"Exactly," he ground out. "We should be responsible."

"How is it irresponsible to care? People need love. People need affection. Even tough guys like you." She'd tried to sound playful, but the words stuck in her throat, the intensity of her feelings making the words come out sharp and raw.

"So, what are we supposed to do?" he asked.

"You said earlier that we're friends. Well, let's be real friends," she said without hesitation. "Let's talk. Communicate. Stay in touch."

"But if we do, we will just get more attached. *I'll* get more attached."

"And you don't want to."

"I don't want to," he agreed.

Her heart fell. She was on such a roller coaster of emotion, so many staggering ups and downs. "Why? How can I be that wrong for you?"

"It's the distance—"

"Distance can be overcome."

"And then it's our backgrounds. We come from different places. You've never said it, but I have a feeling you come from money—"

"You can't hold that against me!"

"I don't, but when I try to picture you in my world, I don't see it working."

Her eyes stung and she took a deep breath, trying to stay focused. "And you can't see yourself in my world?"

"Not the way things are."

She processed this for a bit. "Is there ever a time you could see it working?"

He sighed, sounding terribly exhausted, and more than a little frustrated. "I'd like to say yes, but that would just be leading you on."

Ansley nodded and swallowed, determined to keep calm. Rye would run if she began weeping. "I appreciate your honesty."

"I feel like an ass."

"Don't. Real friends are honest with each other." She paused, gathering herself. "I should go check on Uncle Clyde. Get to Pendleton safely."

"I will. Good night."

"Good night, Rye."

Ansley hung up and dropped her phone into the coat pocket before lifting her face to the moon and the smattering of stars. She didn't want to regret meeting Rye at the hospital during the rodeo weekend, but oh, things would be so much simpler now if she hadn't. She'd be able to focus on her work, and making friends here, and taking care of her uncle. Instead, she was pining for a man who didn't see a future with her, a man who said he cared but wasn't going to let her in.

Oh, Ansley, queen of impossible dreams.

Chapter Seven

ANSLEY PAINTED EVERY free moment, staying up late in the loft on Thursday, but the cold snap made it too cold to paint in the barn. She dragged everything down from the loft and turned an unused bedroom, the one that used to be her aunt Sandy's sewing room, into a studio. The room faced the north and didn't have the good light of the loft, but it was a lot warmer, and her paint dried faster, and she was able to keep a closer eye on her uncle and respond more quickly to his needs.

But as she worked through the weekend, her thoughts frequently, constantly, turned to Rye and the Pendleton Rodeo. How was he doing? Had it been a good Saturday? Would he be competing Sunday?

Saturday night she finally reached out, texting him to ask how he'd done. *Are you competing tomorrow?*

He took just a few minutes to text back. *Yes. It's not my best weekend, but not by worst, either.*

Good, she answered. *I know how you like to cover your gas money.* ☺

You're ruthless, he texted.

No more ruthless than you, she replied.

Touche.

She hearted his message and then chewed her lip, uncertain what to say now. When they were together in person it had felt right. When she'd been with him, she'd felt complete. No one had ever made her feel that way, and she couldn't imagine wanting to be with anyone else now that she'd met Rye. He was by no means perfect. He wasn't the gentlest of men. He wasn't the funniest or the most laid-back, and yet he was right for her ... he just fit. Her and her heart. He was familiar in the best sort of way, as if something deep inside of her recognized him, recognizing who he was and his importance in the world. As well as his importance in her world.

She hesitated then quickly texted, *I miss you.*

He replied, *It will get easier with time. You'll meet someone else.*

Ansley ground her teeth together. *But I don't want to meet someone else. I don't actually want to meet anyone. I didn't want to meet you. I wasn't looking for a boyfriend or relationship but then I did meet you and ... it changed everything.*

He didn't answer.

Ansley held her breath, heart beating unsteadily. *I want to see you.*

He took a long time to text in reply. *We already talked about that.*

Furiously she typed back. *I don't think I really agreed with you. I think you decided that we wouldn't see each other and I just went along with it.*

Every time we see each other it will just make it harder to say goodbye, he texted.

She glared at her phone, answering, *Then we don't have to say goodbye, right? We can just say see you soon or see you later. Why does it have to be so final?*

Ansley. It was just the one word, and it spoke volumes. He was frustrated with her.

Well, fine. She was frustrated with him. *Rye.*

He didn't answer her text. Seconds passed. Seconds turned to minutes. Ansley clutched her phone, wanting him to reply. She wanted to understand this.

And then her phone rang, and it was him. She answered quickly. "Oh, hello, Rye."

She felt his smile over the phone, it was a reluctant smile, but he wasn't angry. "Why are you so stubborn?" he asked.

"Do you want a serious answer, or a smart-ass answer?"

"I'd prefer the serious answer."

"Great. So here it is. You're special, and I'm not going to let you disappear into the universe as if you don't matter."

"We've only just met."

"I can't speak for you, but I know me, and no one has ever turned my world inside out in such a short period of time. I don't fall for guys easily. I'm not a romantic. I don't love love. I love—" She broke off, holding the last word in. But it hung there between them, teasing, tempting, full of aching nuance and meaning. *You.*

"I'll be better about calling," Rye said gruffly.

"That would be nice."

And this time the silence was warm, almost comforting, the silence of understanding and it gave her much needed peace. She loved him. How it had happened, how a weekend could become love, she didn't know but at the same time she didn't question it. "I don't want to keep you up. You've a big day tomorrow. But I'll be cheering you on from afar."

"Thanks, babe."

Babe. He'd said that to her the day he was leaving, and he just said it again, and her heart turned over. She wanted him and wanted to be his.

Hanging up, Ansley leaned against the brass bedframe. She was glad she'd texted, and glad he'd called her. She felt … better. Not necessarily calmer, but better. She was being true to herself and standing for what she could. She'd put herself out there. Only time would tell if he would stay in touch.

RYE RODE BETTER than he expected on Sunday, once again taking first in steer wrestling, second in saddle bronc, and fourth in bareback, which meant he was returning to Eureka with good money. If only he'd enjoyed the weekend more. He hadn't attended any of the social events as he had in Marietta with Ansley. He'd kept to himself except for the cowboy autograph session at the local feed store, and then stayed after for a half an hour visiting with some of the local sponsors. Rye understood the importance of creating good-will on the circuit, and he always made sure to thank the sponsors, because without them there wouldn't be the prize money and he wouldn't have the career. He would have had a good time if Ansley had been there. He would have felt like a million dollars sitting across from her at dinner or walking with her through the fairgrounds. She brought light into his world, light and warmth and a sense of possibility, as if she was like Tinker Bell and could wave a magic wand and cover everything with pixie dust.

His life could use some pixie dust.

He could use Ansley's sunshine and magic.

He talked to her during the drive back to Eureka. They spoke for over an hour and would have kept talking but he'd hit a section of a mountain pass and lost her. He'd warned her that he might lose her, and if that happened, he'd just talk to her tomorrow.

He half hoped she'd try to call him back, but she didn't, and he refrained from calling her because he couldn't appear needy. Needy wasn't a good look and yet she made him feel needs he didn't know how to handle—not just physical needs, but emotional ones.

He did need connection.

He was alone far too much.

He didn't share his worries as he tried to protect others.

Just talking to her made him feel better, closer, even though they hadn't talked about anything particularly deep. It was the kind of call where you talked about nothing and everything, where you talked just to hear the other person's voice, and then wait for the laugh. Ansley had an amazing laugh, too—sexy, warm, generous. Hearing her voice made him ache for her. Her laugh made him crave her mouth and softness.

He wanted to see her. He wanted to taste her and draw her close, wrapping his arms around her delicious, addictive warmth.

Rye reached home just at midnight. After taking care of the horses and unhooking his rig, he showered in his trailer and collapsed into bed. As he closed his eyes, his phone vibrated and he glanced at it. Ansley.

Tell me you're home, she said.

Ansley's text made him smile. *I'm home*, he answered.

Good. I couldn't sleep until I knew you were safe.

You're a hard woman to resist.

The three little dots danced as she typed her response. *I don't know about that. You've done a pretty good job of resisting me so far.*

That's because you've done a good job of wearing my resistance down, he answered quickly.

She sent him a laughing emoji. *Good,* she added. *Life is too short not to enjoy it.* She hesitated and then typed, *I want to see you. I want to meet you somewhere.*

You keep asking for trouble.

I guess you like trouble, she wrote.

For a long moment there was no reply, and then he replied, *I like you.*

ANSLEY HELD HER phone to her chest, holding Rye's words close to her heart.

They had to find a way to make this work, and they would. *Once all my pieces are ready for the exhibit, I'm going to find a way to see you*, she told him.

Ansley held her breath as she waited for his answer, and then it came. *Maybe we can meet in the middle*, he answered.

She smiled. *Perfect.*

The next week passed far more quickly for Ansley now that she and Rye were talking. She felt more optimistic, which lifted her spirits and helped her concentration while painting, allowing her to work longer. Every night she and Rye talked for ten or fifteen minutes before bed, and in the morning, he usually texted her a good morning when he was on his way to work.

He'd be leaving for the rodeo in Idaho Falls after work. It would be another seven-and-a-half-hour drive for him. She knew, because she'd mapped it, and he'd be driving I-15 south, straight through Butte, which was only an hour and thirty-five minutes from Marietta. Two hours from the Campbell ranch. She didn't think it'd be a good idea to try to see him on the way down, but maybe on the return drive Sunday? They could meet for dinner in Butte and he could continue home, and she'd return to Paradise Valley. She hadn't told him her idea yet, but she would when they talked tonight, when he was on the road heading to Idaho.

All day, she felt butterflies, and that electric nervous energy of wanting something so bad she could taste it. She was dying to see Rye. It had been almost two weeks since they'd said goodbye, and on Sunday it would be two weeks exactly. She hoped he'd be receptive to her idea. It didn't even have to be a long dinner. An hour would be perfect. *Please, please let him say yes.*

But that night Rye didn't call her. There was no checking in from the road.

Ansley waited, wanting to give him space, but when she went to bed, she felt puzzled, and hurt. He'd promised to call. Had he broken his phone? Had his truck broken down again? What had happened?

ONE MINUTE, RYE was on the Eureka Fire Department's roof and the next he was flying through the air. Rye only had a split second to react before he slammed to the ground, hurtling himself forward trying to create a ball to protect his back. He hit the ground hard, knocking the air out of him.

Rye never lost consciousness, so he heard the shouts around him. It took a moment to catch his breath, but he knew almost immediately he'd broken something. Or somethings. The pain was severe. It was a similar pain to what he'd felt when he'd broken his shoulder a couple of years ago, only this was hotter, more brutal, and throbbing in more places.

Because he'd been at the fire department, one of the volunteer paramedics raced out to help while another one got the gurney from their ambulance. During the drive to the hospital, Rye created a mental list of things he'd need to do—alert his insurance, let his family know, take a look at his schedule and see what upcoming jobs needed to be shuffled or rescheduled, and then there were three upcoming rodeos he'd have to withdraw from.

And then there was Ansley. He'd have to tell her, he supposed, but didn't want to. She'd worry, and she had enough on her plate.

There was also the lost revenue. The new bills, too, as his insurance wouldn't cover all the hospital costs.

Rye wasn't happy. It was terrible timing with winter coming. The roofing business slowed down considerably during the coldest months. Of course, they tried to work all year long. But there were some weeks where the weather was just too bad and surfaces too icy to get his guys outside, never mind on a steep, slick roof.

Twelve hours later, Rye woke up for a second time. He was still in the hospital, still recovering, the surgery having been lengthy due to bones in his shoulder and arm being fragmented, and fear that the fragments would damage the nerves, ligaments, arteries, and veins in his arm.

In saving his back, he'd done a number on his arm. The

doctor was concerned that Rye would lose some function, but Rye wasn't worried about that. He'd recover. He'd always recover. A broken arm was nothing, even if he'd broken it in three places. He just needed to recover soon so he could get back to work.

Josie and Hannah came to see him together in the morning. Hannah perched on the edge of the chair while Josie sat on the foot of his bed, both sisters watching him with wide solemn eyes.

"Stop with those faces," he said dryly. "The world hasn't ended. It's just a broken arm."

"And shoulder," Josie said.

"It's serious," Hannah answered. "I've been discussing your injury with your nurse. She said you were in surgery for hours."

Rye tried to shrug but it sent pain washing through him. "But I'm here and as you can see, I'm fine."

"Mom is planning on coming later," Josie said.

"Tell her she doesn't need to," he answered.

"You tell her," Hannah said.

He made a face at her. "Find my phone and I will."

Josie sat taller. "What's happened to your phone?"

"I don't know. It was on me when I was on the roof. Don't know where it is now."

"I'll find it," Josie volunteered. "Because you'll want it. They said you're going to be here until at least tomorrow."

Hannah glanced at the whiteboard across from his bed

where his vitals and medicine were written down. "Or longer."

"I'll be home tomorrow," Rye predicted. "You'll see. But I wouldn't mind the phone. I've calls to make."

Josie found his phone, locating it in the bushes at the fire station, and brought Rye's charger from his trailer, handing over both to her brother at the hospital before leaving Rye with a kiss on his cheek so she could make her classes at the community college in Kalispell.

Alone, Rye scrolled through his phone's messages and voice mails. Work calls, a text from one of his cowboy friends, a call from Ansley, and a number of brief texts.

Hey, you okay?
Hope you're alright.
Are you in Idaho?
Rye, are you mad at me?

His chest, with ribs bruised from the fall, hurt as he drew a deep breath. He needed to tell her, but he also needed to tell her the truth.

This wasn't working between them. It wasn't the right thing for him, and it was time he made the break.

Rye didn't blame her, though. He blamed himself. He should have been better about boundaries and sticking with his initial decision.

The whole accident on the roof—that was because he'd become careless. He'd become absent-minded. He'd lost focus and failed to concentrate. Again, Rye couldn't blame Ansley because she didn't know how much of a distraction she was, and she couldn't know that she intruded into his thoughts and life constantly.

He hadn't been thinking about work when he slipped on the roof. He'd been thinking about her. He'd been thinking about how and where they could possibly meet up, wondering if she could break free from the Campbell ranch to meet him somewhere off the I-15. And because he'd been so caught up in the fantasy, he'd failed to take the necessary safety precautions, and then slipped and fell, just as his dad had slipped and fallen.

Thank goodness Rye had rolled, landing on his shoulder and arm rather than his back or his head. But it was the same shoulder he'd injured before and it was as his doctor said, a season-ending break, possibly career ending. Personally, Rye didn't believe that. With new screws and plates, he'd heal and be as good as new, but it would take time and until then he had to stay off ladders and roofs, horses, and bulls. For the next few months, he had to keep his feet on the ground and his head down. Time to be practical.

Which meant, he had to stop the madness. Had to regain control over his heart and head.

He knew his life, knew what he could handle, knew when he was beaten. Ansley was too great of a distraction. She was too beautiful, too appealing, too challenging, too smart, too creative, too fascinating. She was too much of everything, and he found her impossible to resist. He'd loved and hated talking to her this past week. He'd loved and hated hearing her voice and seeing her texts. She made him feel so much. She made him feel so intensely that he lost focus. He lost perspective.

He didn't want to hurt her, and he didn't want her sad. He was doing his best to take care of her but how could he take care of her, when he couldn't even care for himself? He was a mess. A certified, bona fide disaster. He had to cut the communication once and for all.

One day she'd thank him. One day she'd realize he'd saved her from a lifetime of disappointment and sacrifice.

Bracing the phone against the pillow supporting his left arm, Rye carefully typed a text to Ansley.

Sorry to have been out of touch so long. I took a fall at work and needed some surgery. I'm going to be fine but it's ended the rodeo season. I won't be doing any more traveling until spring. I think it's also the right time to step back and make a clean break. You know I'll always be your fan. Take care, Ansley.

He hit send, and after a moment of feeling the most ridiculous lance of pain, not in his shoulder or arm, but in the center of his chest, he blocked her number so the break was complete.

Chapter Eight

IT HAD TAKEN her a full day to realize that Rye had been serious.

He wasn't taking her calls. He wasn't answering her texts. In fact, her calls went straight to his voice mail, and after asking Sophie Wyatt about it, when she stopped by with Summer Friday afternoon, discovered that Rye must have blocked her. *Blocked her.*

At first, she was hurt, really hurt, and then she was angry. Who was he to block her? She'd been a friend. And yes, she had strong feelings for him, but she'd never crossed the line, never behaved inappropriately. Why had he thought it essential to shut her out like that? It was rude, demeaning.

He was rude, demeaning. He'd taken her from such a high to such a painful low. And if this is what he wanted … if this was who he was … she was glad he'd finally shown his true colors, glad he'd cut her loose. Now she could move on. Be free. Meet someone new. Someday.

On Sunday, exactly two weeks after Rye had driven away, the entire Wyatt clan came over to Uncle Clyde's for a Sunday barbecue. They arrived in four trucks, and all spilled out, everyone carrying something. Seeing them gather in the backyard was daunting. There were babies and toddlers, dinner, dessert, and drinks. The men set up folding tables and chairs in the shade while their wives covered them with cheerful yellow tablecloths and adding a vase of daises on each table. The weather had warmed again and one of the younger Wyatts—Billy, maybe?—found an old sprinkler and attached it to a garden hose so the kids could run through it, and they did, shrieking and laughing and getting soaked.

It was colorful and chaotic and just what Ansley needed. Having grown up in a house with a lot of brothers and commotion, it felt good to pretend she belonged, even if she wasn't actually part of the Wyatt family. She'd felt lonely living here, and it had been a struggle making friends, but now she had all of the Wyatts to call friends, and they were friends. They'd been there for her all week and had shared her excitement on getting the invitation to do the gallery show.

But watching the Wyatts, two of them still competing on the PRCA circuit, with Tommy and Billy heading to Las Vegas in December, it was hard not to think of Rye. But she couldn't keep thinking about him, couldn't keep hurting over him. She had to let him go. And yet it was hard to let him go.

How did one let love go?

Sophie had been sitting with Ansley at the end of a table until she saw her kids squabbling and had jumped up to separate them. Ivy, Sam's wife, slid into the seat Sophie had vacated. "Granddad has been filling us in on your gallery exhibit coming up," she said. "That is exciting. Are you ready?"

Ansley shook her head. "No. I need at least three, maybe four, more pieces. I think I can do it, provided I just paint, paint, paint."

"Is the nursing aid providing any respite?" Sophie asked, returning to the table and squeezing in next to Ivy.

"Yes. She's usually here from nine until one, and then your family has been great about stopping by and keeping Clyde company after his afternoon nap so I can get a little more work done. It's been a huge help. I wouldn't have anything ready for the gallery if it weren't for the Wyatts."

Sophie studied Ansley a moment. "So, what's wrong? You seem a little down. Everything okay?"

Ansley shrugged. "It's nothing, at least nothing that important. I'll get over it."

"Feeling homesick?" Ivy guessed.

"No." Ansley flushed, feeling sensitive. "It's a guy thing."

Sophie's eyes widened, understanding dawning. "When you asked me how could you tell if a number was blocked ... is this the same guy?"

Ansley nodded miserably.

"What a jerk," Ivy said. "Who is he?"

Ansley bit her tongue remembering that Rye said he was good friends with Ivy. There was no way she could share any of the details with her, or the Wyatts. As Rye had said, the professional rodeo circuit in Montana was small and close knit. "Just ... someone." She forced a smile. "But don't worry, I'm not letting him distract me. I've got the show coming up and lots to do."

"What do you still need to do?" Sophie asked.

"I'd like at least one more big landscape, and I need to finish two smaller pictures, and then I've got to get them all framed. The big canvases don't have to be framed, but the others do, and framing is time consuming."

"I'm sure one of these guys could build you your frames," Ivy said, nodding toward the four brothers and cousin gathered around the other table. "Most of them can do anything and build anything. Not sure if you know, but Sam has been making furniture this past year. He's become quite the craftsman. He would probably enjoy doing something new."

It was an intriguing idea. "I wonder how much he'd charge," Ansley said.

Ivy shook her head. "I don't think he'd charge you. If you covered the supplies, he would be happy to help."

"Can't do that. I'm not a charity project. You are amazing neighbors and you've done so much, but that would be too much. He should be compensated for his time—"

"You could make a donation to our favorite nonprofit instead," Ivy said. "I'm active in an organization that helps kids with disabilities ride. That way it's a win-win."

Ansley couldn't resist Ivy's confidence or smile. "I'm not

sure it's a win-win for Sam, but getting my pictures framed here, instead of lugging them elsewhere, is a huge timesaver."

"Sam," Ivy called to her husband. "Can you join us? We have something to ask you."

Ansley shook her head at Ivy. "Not now. He's relaxing—"

"He's fine, and this is a good time. He's in between commissions now." Ivy smiled as her handsome husband approached. "He's just finished the most gorgeous dining room table for Bitterroot Designs. There's nothing he can't make." She reached out to clasp Sam's hand when he was at their side. "Ansley needs some custom frames for her paintings, and I thought you might be able to help her." She stood up, vacating her seat for him. "You two talk. Sophie and I are going to serve the dessert."

Ansley watched Ivy and Sophie walk away. They both looked awfully smug. *But I suppose if you had a Wyatt husband you could afford to be a little cocky.* Ansley didn't have that confidence and she apologized to Sam. "Sorry about dragging you into this, Sam," she said as he sat down.

"Tell me what you need."

She quickly explained about her medium and small canvases needed to simply be framed for the exhibit. She pulled out her phone and showed him a few of her finished works. "The frames don't need to be fancy. I can also paint them once they're built."

"Or I can do that if you're running short on time." He paused. "How are you doing on time?"

She hesitated. "Not good. I'm behind."

"When is the show?"

She told him and he gave her a pointed look. "That's less than two weeks away," Sam said.

"I know." Ansley pressed her lips together, feeling anxiety rush through her, but at the same time not wanting to put pressure on Sam. "But I can—"

"No, you can't. I've got it. Don't worry."

"Sam, I—"

"I got this." He raised a hand to fist-bump her. "Don't worry. I won't let you down."

She smiled at him, grateful, reassured, but later that night when in bed she couldn't sleep, thinking of how amazing the Wyatts were, and how lucky she'd been to meet them.

The Wyatts were the kind of neighbor everyone needed. The kind of neighbor that knew when to step up, and when to mind their own business. They'd been stepping up for the past two weeks without making a big deal out of it.

One day, she'd pay them back—somehow. But until then, it was such a comfort to have good people near her. She needed Sophie's smiles and Summer and Melvin's hugs. She needed good people to remind her that she was valuable even as she struggled to heal her banged-up heart. It still stung how Rye had shut her out, but she'd recover. It would just take time.

RYE HAD JUST stepped from the shower when he heard a knock on his door. It was either his sisters or his mom since Jasper and his dad never came out to his trailer. "Hold on," he shouted, grabbing a towel with his right arm, and struggling to wrap it around his hips.

Covered, he went to his door and opened it. His mom stood on the threshold.

"Looks like I caught you at a bad time," she said. "I can come back."

"Everything okay?" he asked.

"Yes. Just wanted to talk to you. It's hard to find time lately for a proper conversation." She gestured to his nearly nude status. "But this is probably not the best time, either."

"I'll dress. Give me a moment." He opened the door wider to let her enter.

A few minutes later, he was back wearing loose sweatpants and a hoodie that he could zip over his shoulder and arm. His mom was sitting on the small couch, hands folded primly in her lap.

"Would you like a drink?" he asked thinking he could use one. He'd only been home from work for a half hour and a beer tasted nice right around now.

"Anything besides beer?" she asked, knowing him too well.

"I can make you a vodka and orange juice."

She considered it then wrinkled her nose. "I'm good. If I have a cocktail, I won't want to make dinner."

"Then don't. Order pizza tonight."

"You have a solution for everything," she said as he disappeared into the tiny kitchen for a beer.

"That's my job," he said, popping off the cap and sitting in the old armchair facing the couch.

He watched as her lavender gaze swept the interior of his home.

"You keep everything nice and tidy." She didn't sound surprised, though. She'd raised him to be organized, to keep things clean, and he, the oldest, had always tried to do what he'd been taught. It was easier that way, less friction between his parents, less drama for the family.

He saw his mother study some of the rodeo ribbons and awards he'd hung on one wall.

"Where are the buckles?" she asked.

"Put away. A little too much bling for such a humble abode."

She smiled. "You remind me so much of my dad. I wish you'd been able to spend more time with him when you were growing up. But considering you didn't see much of each other, it's remarkable how similar you are, and not just in looks. You have the same quiet strength. He was a man of conviction. If he made you a promise, he kept it, always."

It wasn't hard for Rye to read between the lines. His mom had fallen in love with Jonathan Rye Calhoun, imagining he would be her hero, like her adored father. But John was cut from a different cloth, and while he'd once been a hardworking man, setbacks set him back, permanently.

Her smile quavered and, clasping her hands tighter, she added, "Someday you're going to meet the right one, and you're going to want to build a family with her, and what she wants is going to be important, Rye."

Rye lifted a brow but held his tongue.

"Let's be honest if we can. No woman is going to want to live here, in the trailer. And they certainly won't want to move in with your family."

"I would never move my wife into your house, and what's wrong with this place?" he teased her. "It has four walls, a roof, plumbing, even a hot plate in the kitchen—"

"Thank God, I know you're not serious. But, Rye, you have thought about this, haven't you? No young woman is going to want to move here, and I want a daughter-in-law one day, I do, but not if she'd resent us."

"She wouldn't."

"She would if she had no place of her own. I know, because I had to move in with your dad's family here, and it wasn't ideal. Trust me."

Rye had never heard this before and it gave him pause. "You never told me."

"I wasn't going to speak against your grandparents, or your dad. But it was stressful, and it made those early years as a newlywed far harder than they had to be."

Rye held his breath, because what options did he have? None. He'd never abandon his family.

"Have I upset you?" his mother asked, tentatively, voice pitched low.

"No, of course not."

"I want the best for you."

"I understand. Fortunately, I'm not getting married anytime soon so we don't have to cross that bridge yet."

She hesitated. "What about the girl you met in Marietta?"

He frowned. "There was no one—"

"There was."

"In any case, it's over."

Her eyes widened in distress. "Why?"

He couldn't do this. He didn't have the wherewithal to handle questions about Ansley. As it was, he hadn't forgiven himself for abruptly shutting her out. He'd been ruthless, focused on survival, *his* survival, and while survival skills might be useful on a deserted island, or during a zombie apocalypse, it wasn't a quality he admired in himself. He'd put his interests before hers and the regret was enormous.

Instead of answering his mom's question, Rye rose.

His mother reluctantly stood, too. "I was being too nosy, wasn't I?" she said.

He hugged her with his good arm. "You're just being a mom, and you're a wonderful mom."

"Oh, Rye, I totally forgot why I came here tonight!" she

exclaimed, stepping back. "Based on Josie's admittance to the interior design program at Gallatin College, she's been offered a paid internship with a design firm in Bozeman, which would allow her to cover some of her living expenses in Bozeman."

Early in the summer, Josie had been forced to defer her start date at Gallatin due to the financial situation at home. It had been hard for her to wait another year, but the college administration had understood that it was a financial situation and had agreed to let her begin the following fall. "I'm surprised they're offering her a job for next year."

"It's not for next year. The firm would like her to start in January, after the Christmas holidays. The company specializes in universal design and the senior vice president, who is on the board at Gallatin College, was impressed by your sister's ideas and passion for accessibility. He believes she has something to offer now and hates that she's had to put off school based on financial considerations—"

"It's not as if I wanted her to wait another year," Rye growled.

"No, of course not, and Josie understood, but if she's able to cover her cost of living in Bozeman, I think it'd be good for her to move, especially with Hannah now in Missoula."

Not that Ron hadn't done his best to convince Hannah that she didn't need a nursing degree, that Ron would take care of her, but Rye had put his foot down. Hannah needed to finish her education and then she could decide what happened next, but she'd worked too hard getting her associates degree with an eye on transferring to Missoula for her to give up on that goal.

"Won't it be hard for you to lose both your girls at the same time?"

She shook her head. "It's what is supposed to happen. I'd rather them be off pursuing their dreams than doing minimum-wage jobs here."

"I agree."

"So, you'll drive her to Bozeman for the interview? You know she gets nervous over things like this, and I'd feel better if she wasn't making the long drive alone."

"But I thought she already had the job."

"I believe they'd like to offer her the position, but they want to meet with her first."

"I see. When do they want to talk to her?"

"Wednesday. Or is it Thursday? I forget. You'll want to check with your sister."

"I will."

Rye walked her back to the house before stopping by the barn to secure it for the night. As he returned to his trailer, he thought of driving Josie to Bozeman, acutely aware that Bozeman was so close to Ansley.

Ansley. Just thinking of her flooded him with emotion and need.

But Ansley wasn't part of the picture, not anymore, and

he pushed all thoughts of her from his mind. They'd made a clean break of it—he'd made a clean break of it—and that was how it'd stay.

In bed that night, he couldn't get comfortable. His arm throbbed, his shoulder throbbed, and the physical pain could be tolerated as it was nothing new. He'd spent years with aches and pains from his work. What he wasn't used to was the gnawing emptiness in his chest. It was an ache that Advil wouldn't help. It was an ache that exercise didn't alleviate. It was an ache that caught him off guard at all hours of the day, surprising him with the intensity of the loss.

It felt like a death. He, who didn't become attached, had fallen for her. It wasn't an infatuation. It wasn't a crush. It wasn't even lust. It was so much bigger, and deeper, and he was grieving what could have been … should have been.

He missed Ansley's voice. He missed her texts, missed the connection. Missed the warmth and her bright, fierce optimism. It had been a long time since he cared for anybody the way he cared for Ansley. He wasn't even sure he'd ever cared for anyone as much as her. She was just sunshine and hope, and picturing her, he felt some of that sunshine within him. Since he couldn't hold her, he'd have to hold on to that.

Rye finally slept but woke at three, shoulder and arm hurting so much that he forced himself up to get a pain killer. He washed the pills down with a glass of water and watched TV when sleep didn't come. He wasn't really following the program though. Bozeman was so close to Marietta, just thirty minutes' drive. Ansley was just thirty more minutes south of Bozeman on the ranch.

It would be a dangerous, destructive madness to see her.

Seeing her would bring fresh pain, deepen the loss and longing. A sane man wouldn't let that happen, not when he was still missing her so much. Not enough time had passed for him to be indifferent to her. Rye suspected he might never be indifferent to her. But hopefully, with time, the missing and wanting would ease. Hopefully, time would help the memories fade, along with the intensity of his regret.

He closed his eyes, but he saw her.

Ansley.

Rye sat up, moved the pillows behind him, trying to find a more comfortable position, and suddenly he remembered his mom's words about the trailer and how unsuitable it was for his future. Obviously, he knew that moving a wife in here wasn't ideal, but he hadn't expected his mom to have such strong feelings about the arrangement. He supposed he'd never thought of it from an outsider's perspective, and it was strange to think of his mom as an outsider, but once upon a time she had been. She'd been born Jennifer Johnson, raised on a farm close to the town of Sparwood, two and a half hours outside of Calgary. Rye's Johnson grandparents had raised cattle and farmed and been prosperous enough that they could afford to give their children a happy and secure childhood. Jennifer attended college in Calgary and then, after graduating, stayed in the city to work.

It was in Calgary she met John Calhoun who was in town for a construction conference. Apparently, there were immediate sparks and after just a handful of dates, and a half dozen visits to Calgary from Eureka, John proposed. Jennifer accepted. They were married within six months of meeting.

It was not a shotgun marriage. In fact, Rye didn't arrive for eighteen months, and by all account, his parents were delighted by his appearance. He was healthy and happy, and no one imagined that there would be any reason why it would be so difficult for Jennifer to conceive again. They didn't start trying until Rye was two, but it would be years of infertility before Jennifer consulted a doctor, and finally, Hannah was conceived. Josie followed soon after and then Jasper. His mom's pregnancy with Jasper had been normal. There had been no illnesses, or viruses, nothing to make anyone concerned, but when Jasper arrived, something clearly was wrong. There was quiet speculation that Jasper had been injured during the birth, but of course none of the medical team would admit such a thing.

But Jasper turned out to be a joy, doted on by the family, he was endlessly cheerful, impossibly good-natured. Even though his life was filled with scares and complications, he never complained. He seemed to understand better than any of them what a gift life was, and how quickly it could be taken away.

Chapter Nine

JOSIE HAD BEEN incredibly nervous during the drive to Bozeman. They'd left the house at four thirty in the morning on Thursday, getting them to Bozeman by ten thirty, in plenty of time for a quick lunch, a relaxed campus tour, and then her three o'clock interview in downtown Bozeman.

Rye was waiting for his sister at a coffee shop not far from the design firm, and although he'd been keeping an eye out for her, she'd found him before he saw her approach.

"I love them," Josie said, practically dancing around the table. She pulled out a chair and sat down across from him. "They do amazing work. They are leaders in universal design, corporate and residential, and we started talking about how great design should work for everyone, and how accessibility shouldn't have to look institutional."

Rye couldn't remember the last time Josie was so excited. "So, you got the job?"

"It's an internship, and I'll get some college credits—"

"I thought they were paying you?"

"They are, and until school starts, I'll work full-time and then cut back to part-time once classes begin next August."

TAKE ME PLEASE, COWBOY

She paused, drew a breath. "They even know of a place I could rent, it's a little studio here downtown, but walking distance to the office. It's not available until January, but I'd be living in a real city. I'd be part of all this!"

"Too bad we can't see the apartment, make sure the building is safe, and all that."

"We can if we want. Just not today." She gave Rye a hopeful smile. "Why don't we spend the night here, see the apartment in the morning, and then drive home?"

It was on the tip of his tongue to remind her that it would be expensive staying overnight. They'd need two rooms since he wasn't going to share a room with Josie. She was an adult, and he respected her privacy. "It's not a bad idea," he said.

She was immediately on her phone searching for motel rooms. It didn't take her long to find something that could work—a one bedroom suite where she could sleep on the pullout bed and he could have the bedroom.

"I'll take the pullout," he said.

"Not with that arm," she answered. She glanced up at him, still smiling, still so excited. "Should I book it?"

"Yes. Then let whoever needs to know that you'd like to see the apartment in the morning. I won't feel good about you moving here if it's not a good location."

"Rye, you know I can handle myself."

He looked at his beautiful sister, truly stunning with her violet eyes, dark hair, and high cheekbones. His mother must

175

have looked the same as a young woman. "I'd be a terrible brother if I didn't check it out."

"I agree." She sat back and sighed the most contented sigh. "Can you believe this? I was so upset at having to push back school for another year. I think I cried all June, but now I have this opportunity. I can't tell you how lucky I feel."

He was glad. Truly glad. He had been the one to say no, they couldn't afford to send her to college this year. He'd been the ogre who'd pointed out that there wasn't enough for both Hannah and Josie to go away at the same time, and since Hannah was older, she took precedence. He'd felt awful. He'd hated to be the dream crusher but someone had to be practical.

"You've earned this," he said gruffly. "And deserve this. I'm proud of you Jo-Jo."

She grinned. "Thank you. Now let's check into our room and relax a little bit before we get some dinner. What do you say?"

"I say yes."

They left the coffee shop and were walking toward his truck when a poster in a window caught his eye. He stopped and glanced from the poster to the name of the business. The Bozeman Big Sky Gallery. Ansley's show. It was here. The reception was tonight.

"What?" Josie said, stopping next to him.

Numb, Rye nodded at the poster. "I know her."

"What do you mean, you know her?" Josie asked, moving closer to the poster to read it for herself. "Who?"

"Ansley Campbell."

"You do?" His sister glanced at him surprised. "How?"

He wished now he hadn't said anything, but it had been such a shock to walk down the street and see her name. "I met her in Marietta a month ago when I was here for the Copper Mountain Rodeo."

"Really? Then we should come tonight for the artists' reception. I bet she'd love to see you."

Rye made a rough sound, shook his head. "I don't think she'd be that happy to see me."

"Why not? Were you rude to her?"

He growled his frustration. He'd brought his sister to Bozeman, but he wasn't escorting her to a gallery reception. "Not rude, no. But it's not something I want to discuss."

"Why not?"

"Why not what, Josie?"

"Why can't you talk about it?"

"Because it's ... in the past, and once things are in the past, it's better to just let things be."

His sister took a step back, arms folding over her chest. "So, it's like that."

"I have no idea what you're talking about," he snapped.

"You hooked up."

"We didn't *hook up*. She's young, just a couple years older than Hannah. I don't hook up with kids."

Josie couldn't suppress a smile. "You are so worked up. She did a number on you."

"No, she didn't. And Ansley did nothing wrong. She's perfect. She's gorgeous—so beautiful it took my breath away the first time I met her—and she's talented. She's kind and smart and she has backbone. She's ... special."

"So, why wouldn't she be happy to see you? What did you do to make her hate you?"

"I didn't say hate. She just—oh, drop it. I don't want to talk about it."

Josie sighed. "You hurt her."

Rye took an angry step backward. "I didn't hurt her, not like that. After I broke this," he added, nodding at his arm still in the sling. "I realized I couldn't be in two places at once. I couldn't take care of things at home, and make things work with her."

"It's a six-hour drive to Bozeman from Eureka."

"Seven to Marietta."

"Which is nothing for you, so clearly she wasn't perfect, because if she had been, that drive would have been a piece of cake."

"It's a lot more complicated than that, sis."

Josie shrugged. "I just don't believe you, Rye. You would not let a seven-hour drive keep you from the perfect woman. That doesn't make sense because you're the most determined man I know. You never give up. You never quit—"

"This is different. I'm not free to pursue her. I've the

family to take care of." He abruptly stopped talking and turned away, hands on his hips, frustration in the rigid set of his shoulders.

"You let her go because of … *us?*"

The pain and disappointment in his sister's voice wounded him. "Think about it, Jo. Jasper needs better care. He's having issues. I can't help if I'm not in Eureka—"

"But I'm still there. I can help."

"Dating costs money. Gas is expensive. I made you wait a year for college because we didn't have the means to send you, so how do I justify suddenly blowing cash on romance? I couldn't. It didn't make sense. I made the right choice."

"I'm sorry, Rye."

He turned to face her, undone by the sympathy in her voice. She hadn't created any of this and at twenty she shouldn't have to feel any guilt. "I'm good," he said, looking her in the eye. "I am."

"But all you do is work. You should enjoy life a little bit. You should enjoy being single. You're not bad-looking—"

"Thanks."

"And sometimes you have a good personality."

"How you flatter me."

Josie blinked away the sheen of moisture in her eyes. "Let's go to the artist reception tonight."

"No."

"Just for a while."

"*No.*" Rye looked at his sister like she was crazy. Maybe

she was. She was a Calhoun after all. "Didn't you hear anything that I just said?"

"I heard you say Ansley was pretty much perfect, and I have never heard you describe *any* woman as close to perfect. And then you gave me a bunch of lame reasons—well, actually, only two lame reasons, but they're terrible. She doesn't live that far away. It's a drive. Big deal. You drive all the time. And yeah, gas is expensive but so is everything." She looked up at Rye, expression pitying. "Stop being pathetic, Rye. I'm almost embarrassed for you."

He pressed his lips into a hard line, unamused. "Be embarrassed. But there's no way I'm going to invade Ansley's event tonight. This party is a big deal for her. This exhibit is a big deal. She was really excited about it."

"All the more reason for us to go. If the show is so important to her, you must stop by tonight to congratulate her."

"We came to Bozeman for you to do the interview. You've done the interview. In the morning, we head home."

"But since we have no plans for tonight, let's pop in."

Rye was done arguing. He continued walking toward his Silverado which was parked several blocks south of the gallery. From the corner of his eye, he saw Josie take a photo of the event poster in the window, but he said nothing, just wanting the whole subject to drop.

Of everyone in his family, Josie was most stubborn. He'd never met anyone more stubborn. Their mom used to tease her that it was because she was a Taurus, and Rye, who took no stock in horoscopes or astrology, did agree with his mom that Josie could be incredibly bullheaded, but she was also fearless and tireless when it came to achieving her dreams. She wanted to be a designer that helped people, that improved lives. She wanted to make a difference in the world. There was no way he'd stay upset with her, not when Josie had the biggest heart of anyone he knew.

Happily, after a few minutes, Josie seemed willing to let the whole Ansley-art-reception topic go, and they passed a local brewery that specialized in wood-fire pizzas. Josie, who'd been so nervous about her interview with the scholarship committee, hadn't eaten more than a mouthful in days, begged to stop for pizza. They did and had a very nice early dinner of pizza and beer.

By the time they reached their hotel, Rye was ready to call it a night. Josie just laughed at him. "It's not even six thirty," she said.

"Which is why I just want to stretch out, watch the news, maybe a show or two, and then sleep."

Josie shrugged as he closed the door separating the bedroom from the living area. "Suit yourself. Personally, I'm not tired at all."

He should have recognized the challenge, but he didn't. Instead, he assumed she'd pass the evening on her phone, or watching the television in the living room. Instead, when he emerged from the shower twenty minutes later, he saw she'd sent him a text. *I've taken an Uber downtown. Thought I'd see if there was anything interesting happening on Main Street tonight.*

Rye tossed his phone onto his bed and swore under his breath. He knew exactly where his beautiful, lively little sister had gone. He'd like to say he was shocked, but he wasn't. This was exactly the sort of thing Josie did.

He dressed quickly, combed his hair, and drove back downtown. Sure enough, there she was standing in front of the gallery, smiling at him as he approached.

"You took a little longer than I expected," she said, flashing a teasing grin. "But maybe it was a really long shower."

He was not in the mood to do this. "Josie, this isn't cool. I don't appreciate being manipulated. We are most definitely not going in. Let's go."

"You don't have to go inside, but I want to see who Ansley Campbell is. And I'm interested in her art, purely from a design perspective, of course."

"Oh, undoubtedly. Next thing you'll tell me is that you'll be hanging her art in your future clients' homes."

"*If* she's good, yes," Josie sniffed. "But art is a very personal thing. What some might like might not be others' taste at all."

Rye fought to keep his temper reined in. He adored his little sister. He loved that she was warm, and funny, and full of personality. He was glad she hadn't been beaten down by the situation at home, nor was she trying to find someone to rescue her from the situation like Hannah. "What do you want, Josie? Tell me, so we can get this resolved."

"I just want to go in and do a little walk around. We don't have to stay long … ten, fifteen minutes tops?"

He glanced through the window. The turnout was impressive. Lots of people were milling about and while he couldn't see Ansley from here, he was certain it would be different once he entered the gallery. The thing was, he wanted to see Ansley. He very much wanted to see her, but he didn't think it would have a good result. He didn't think he'd leave feeling better about their situation. "Why are you doing this?"

Josie shrugged. "I'm curious. It's obvious you care for her, and if she's the right one? Why let her go?" She gave him an almost pitying look before marching up to the front door and entering the art gallery.

RYE WAS THE last person Ansley expected to see at the gallery's cocktail party.

But even worse was seeing him with a very beautiful woman. For a moment, Ansley couldn't breathe, feeling as if she'd been punched in the gut. Overwhelmed by emotion, she stared fixedly at the wall, as if studying one of the other artists' works, when in reality she was trying to keep it together and slow the dizzying, sickening beat of her heart.

He'd said he was done driving until spring.

He'd said he wasn't seeing anyone.

He'd said he wouldn't, couldn't, get serious with anyone.

And yet here he was on a Thursday night in Bozeman on what looked to be a very cozy date.

Ansley's eyes stung and she swallowed around a stupid lump in her throat, hurt, and betrayed. She'd trusted him. She'd believed him. But apparently everything he'd told her was a lie. She felt like a fool.

She didn't want Rye to see her, and she most definitely didn't want to speak to him. In a panic, she slipped behind a screen that had been put up by the catering company to hide their prep area. She smiled apologetically at one of the catering staff who was behind the screen filling a tray with appetizers.

"I just need a second," Ansley said faintly. "So many people. It's rather overwhelming."

The woman in the starched white jacket and black trousers smiled kindly. "I don't like crowds either, and it's pretty packed in here tonight. Marica has had a great turnout." The caterer looked at Ansley more carefully. "But aren't you one of the artists?"

"Yes, and you're right, it is a great turnout. I just didn't expect so many people."

"Looks like a lot of your pieces have sold. Congratulations."

Ansley forced a smile. "Thank you. It's my first real show."

"And obviously not your last. You should be out there

celebrating, not hiding. Go meet your fans."

There was nothing Ansley could say to that and hanging on to her smile by sheer strength of will, she straightened her shoulders and stepped back into the gallery, only to walk straight into the woman who'd been at Rye's side just a moments ago.

Ansley froze, heartsick. "I'm sorry," she murmured, hating how this beautiful night had turned sour so quickly.

But the gorgeous brunette wasn't going to let Ansley escape. She faced Ansley and smiled. "I'm Josie Calhoun," she said, extending her hand. "Rye's youngest sister. I've heard so much about you."

Ansley's jaw dropped. His *sister*?

Relief swept through her, so intense Ansley felt dizzy. "It's nice to meet you, Josie." Ansley shook Jose's hand. "I have to say I'm shocked to see him here," she said, glancing toward Rye who was making his way toward them. "What brings you to Bozeman?"

"I'm going to be attending Gallatin College next fall, studying interior design, but I've been selected for an internship starting in January. I had an interview this afternoon."

"That's exciting, congratulations."

"Thank you. I'm thrilled. I love design, all areas of design, but as you might expect, I have a soft spot for barrier-free design."

Ansley shook her head, not following. "Why is that?"

185

"Rye didn't tell you about Jasper? Our brother has CP, cerebral palsy, and needs a chair—" She broke off, realizing Ansley still didn't understand. "He was hurt at birth and doesn't walk. He's in a wheelchair but there are a lot of places he can't go because it's not accessible, which is what fueled my interest in universal design."

Ansley glanced at Rye who was about to join them. "I had no idea."

"Rye is pretty private," Josie answered, "and protective. Jasper's had a hard year. We've all been worried—" She broke off as Rye reached their side and gave her brother a dazzling smile. "Rye, look who I found."

Ansley couldn't take her eyes off of him. His chiseled features were every bit as handsome as ever, and yet his expression was shuttered. He didn't look happy, but he also didn't look upset. He just looked like a stranger.

Josie said something about needing to find the ladies' room and slipped away, leaving Rye and Ansley alone. Ansley didn't know where to look. She didn't know what to say. Her heart raced, and she felt a little light-headed. She should have eaten more today. The glass of champagne on an empty stomach probably wasn't the best idea. "Hello," she said huskily.

Rye leaned and dropped a kiss on her cheek. "It's good to see you."

His deep voice was both familiar and bittersweet. It took everything within her to remain unmoved. "This is quite a surprise."

His lips twisted ruefully. "I hadn't planned on coming, but once Josie saw you were part of tonight's exhibit—" He broke off, jaw working. "No, I can't blame this on my sister. I wanted to see you. I wasn't sure it was a good idea, but here we are."

"Why wouldn't it be a good idea?" Ansley asked. "We didn't part as mortal enemies, did we?"

"No, but it wasn't an easy goodbye."

"You blocked my number."

Dark color suffused his cheekbones. "I couldn't leave the door open. I didn't trust myself, not when it came to you."

She searched his eyes trying to see past his polite veneer. Was all the warmth truly gone? Had he managed to smash all feelings?

"Your sister is quite lovely," Ansley said, trying to think of something safe for them to discuss. "In every way."

"Which is another way of saying that she's nothing like me," he said, an eyebrow lifting.

Ansley couldn't repress her smile. "I'm sure you just have different strengths. Yours are just more … manly." She nodded at his arm. "Did that happen in Idaho?"

He shook his head. "Nope. Eureka. Tumbled off the fire station roof."

"Sounds awful."

"Certainly a longer, harder fall than from a horse."

It was hard to keep her emotions in check when she

wanted more, when she longed to feel his lips against her cheek, to smell the clean spice of his aftershave. He was here, so close, but also too far away. "But you're okay," she said.

"I'm going to be fine."

It struck her that maybe they were talking about two different things. Her eyes burned and she looked away. Josie was standing in front of one of Ansley's big canvases studying it intently, and Ansley felt another awful pang, wondering how these two worlds had suddenly collided. This wasn't what she wanted, and it certainly wasn't what she needed. Josie being here was fine, but Rye? She looked up into his face, her gaze meeting his and holding. No, Rye shouldn't have come.

But as their gazes locked, the connection was still there, just as intense and potent as it always had been. A traitorous fire flared within her, the heat making her tremble. She didn't want to feel anything for him, and yet Rye still undid her, every bit as real and potent as the last time she saw him.

But then, nothing had really changed between them. He was who he was, and she responded to him as she always did. He was still tall and tough, hard and handsome, and intoxicatingly male.

She still wanted him, still wanted his mouth and touch, his arms, strength, and warmth. Even after his cold, callous treatment, she still cared.

How stupid, how unfair. There was no justice in the world, was there?

SOMEHOW JOSIE WORKED her magic, inviting Ansley to join them for an after-cocktail-party bite and drinks to celebrate Ansley's first show.

Ansley had tried to get out of it, but Josie was terribly persuasive, and incredibly sweet and wore down Ansley's defenses, just as she did with everyone.

After the gallery party ended, they walked to a restaurant one block over and were able to secure a table. From the moment they left the gallery, Josie and Ansley were deep in conversation, laughing and talking, frequently interrupting the other, which just made them laugh more and talk faster.

He'd never seen Josie out with others, and it pleased him that Josie and Ansley had hit it off so quickly. By the time food arrived, they seemed like old friends, while Rye felt like the stranger. It wasn't a conversation he could contribute to, as they were discussing life and art, and how beauty was essential, and art had the ability to heal hearts and minds.

Ansley was beautiful as always, but it was Josie that moved him. She was so animated, so sure of herself, so passionate about her beliefs. He felt guilty all over again that he'd been the one to insist she wait one more year to move away. He'd been the one to crush her in June. She'd never blamed him, but she could have. For years now, he was the hard one, the practical one. Rye couldn't afford to wear rose-colored glasses and talk about how transformative art was.

He also wouldn't because he didn't believe it.

What changed lives was money. Money created opportunities. Money opened doors. Money meant one had the ability to see the best doctors, get the best care. The lack of money meant one was always dependent on lists and referrals, and then waiting for answers, and waiting for treatment and Jasper didn't have time to wait. He was getting weaker. His body was under attack. There were newer treatments and better doctors, if only they could get him in to see those doctors.

But Jasper wasn't here. Josie was, and Ansley was, and Rye was, too. And even though he was overwhelmed by guilt, it was also wonderful to see Josie in her element, to realize she was finally getting her moment. He was proud of her. He was proud of Ansley. He was glad they were both working to fulfill their dreams.

"So, when do you move here permanently?" Ansley asked as the waiter cleared her wineglass, and the other little plates.

"Probably the first week of January," Josie answered. "They want me to start working by the seventh."

"So, just after the new year."

Josie nodded. "I wish it was sooner, but this will give me time to save up a little more money and figure out what to take."

Ansley smiled at her. "You know I'm not far away, so if you need anything, call me."

Josie nodded again. "I will."

"And once you're settled, if you have time, it'd be fun to get together," Ansley added.

"I'd love that," Josie said warmly. "You'd be my first friend."

Rye tried to ignore the tightness in his chest. He was jealous. Jealous that they could be friends and he wouldn't be part of the future. He stepped away to quietly pay the bill only to discover she'd already paid. How had she already paid? He didn't see her slip anyone her credit card.

Outside on the street he thanked Ansley, before adding, "We were taking you out to celebrate. Dinner tonight was supposed to be our treat."

"You two barely ate anything, and I wanted to treat. If Josie hadn't insisted you come tonight, I wouldn't be celebrating with anyone."

He glanced away, embarrassed, exposed. She was right. This was all Josie's doing. She'd forced him to the gallery, and then suggested dinner, smoothing the awkwardness with her quick smile and sense of fun. And yet, he'd wanted to be here. He'd wanted to see Ansley. He'd wanted—

He couldn't let himself go there. "Josie has ideas of her own," he said flatly, "but tonight she made the right call. I did want to be there. I loved seeing how your hard work is paying off. It's remarkable."

"Glad your sister dragged you here."

He let the jab slide. "I still owe you a celebratory dinner, and it will be on me. I insist."

Ansley's blue eyes met his and held, a challenging light in them. "So not necessary, Rye."

"Maybe not, but I'd like to have dinner with you."

She didn't blink or break eye contact. "Perhaps in January, when you move Josie into her apartment, we can put something together."

How indifferent she sounded. But what did he expect? He'd been ruthless in his rejection. She shouldn't trust him. He didn't trust himself, not when she was so close, and he still wanted her so much. "Sounds good."

Ansley never lost her smile as she turned to Josie. "I'm going to give you my number and please do call when you're back in the area. I want to see you and we will plan something fun."

"I'd like that," Josie said, pulling out her phone, and exchanging numbers with Ansley.

They walked Ansley to her car before heading the opposite direction to Rye's truck. For a long moment neither Josie nor Rye spoke, but Rye could tell his sister was dying to say something.

Once in the truck he looked at his sister. "What? Say it."

His sister's shoulders lifted and fell. "You know what I'm going to say."

"That she's too good for me?"

Josie shook her head. "No. She's perfect for you, perfect in every way. But I think you're scared."

He scowled. "I'm not scared."

"I think you are afraid she'll break your heart. But, Rye, she's not the one breaking your heart. You're doing that all by yourself."

"That's ridiculous," he said, starting the ignition.

"It was obvious she cares for you, and what's ridiculous is that you decided it won't work without actually trying."

He shifted into drive and pulled away from the curb with Josie's words tumbling around his head, knotting his gut. He didn't agree with his sister. She wasn't right.

"You ride broncs for a living, Rye. And when money is extra tight, you ride bulls, even though you promised Mom you wouldn't, and you do it because you're tough. You're fearless on the circuit. You want the challenge, and you believe in your skill. It's what's made you successful. So why don't you believe in yourself now?"

He had no proper answer, at least none that she—or he—would accept.

Chapter Ten

A NSLEY DIDN'T ARRIVE back at her uncle's ranch until eleven thirty. It had been an incredibly long day, after a very grueling couple of weeks, and yet she was so keyed up she didn't think she'd be able to sleep, not right away.

What a strange crazy unexpected night it had been.

She'd hoped for a decent turnout at the gallery. She'd hoped some of her paintings would sell. Reality had exceeded her hopes, and she'd been blown away by the reception. The gallery was packed and except for two of her nineteen works, everything had sold by the end of the party.

She hadn't thought even half would sell, especially marked at the prices Marcia had set, but her most expensive works sold first. Clearly, Ansley wasn't the best one to judge her work or price it, and then before she left to have dinner with Rye and Josie, Marcia mentioned that she'd love to feature Ansley in another show, perhaps in January or February, if Ansley had new work by then.

Ansley would have new work. She'd make sure of that, especially now that she knew there was a market for what she did, and a waiting list for her new pieces.

Ansley put the kettle on the stove, boiling water to make

a cup of Sleepytime tea. She needed it tonight as she didn't feel sleepy, or calm, and the lack of calm was due to Rye.

He wasn't supposed to be there tonight and seeing him had knocked her off-balance. She'd pretended to be fine, but on the inside, she was far from fine. She still felt so much when near him. It confused her that she still cared so much. Worse, she knew he cared. It was clear he cared. So why had he put them both through all the pain and drama?

As if thinking about him could conjure him, her phone rang, and she knew it was him. Taking her phone from her purse, she was right. His name flashed. He'd unblocked her. She was tempted to ignore his call. She should ignore his call. She shouldn't give him an inch. But when it came to Rye, Ansley was weak. She answered the call, picturing Josie, remembering what Josie said about their brother Jasper. Apparently Ansley still didn't know the real Rye.

"Hi," she said, shifting the kettle off the hot burner before it could begin to whistle in earnest.

"Just want to make sure you got home safely."

"I'm home. Safely."

He hesitated. "I'm truly proud of you, Ansley, and I'm glad I got to see you in your element. It was impressive. You're going to be incredibly successful."

"Is that a bad thing?" she asked, leaning against the counter.

"No. Why would you say that?"

"Because it's not a competition between us. We're both

successful, just in different areas."

"I don't feel competitive with you."

"Then why did you push me away after you broke your arm? Why did you choose then to block me?"

He didn't have an answer, not at first. "It wasn't about you, it was about me, and the fear that I was losing focus and failing to take care of my responsibilities."

"Meaning, your family."

"Yes."

"You support everyone."

"For now, yes. Someday, my sisters will be independent and then it will just be my parents and brother."

"Jasper will always live at home."

"Yes."

"Why didn't you ever tell me this?" She wasn't angry with him, but rather, it would have helped to know his world, to understand his commitments. But she couldn't know him if he didn't let her in, and he'd never been willing to do that.

"I don't discuss my family with others, and it has become a habit to protect them. But I wish I'd talked to you, or tried to explain what was happening. Instead, I cut you off thinking it was the best thing for both of us."

She pushed away from the counter and poured hot water over the tea bag in her cup. "You shouldn't think for me. I have my own brain and it's a good one."

"I didn't think of it that way. I believed I was tackling

the problem head-on, making the necessary decisions—"

"You do realize that's rather condescending."

"My dad was injured when I was seventeen. I became the breadwinner in my family then. I had to figure out how to make things work for my family, which wasn't easy when we were deeply in debt. I didn't know how to make money, not as a high school senior, but I learned, and I figured out what I needed to do, and I still tend to make decisions first and then deal with the consequences later."

She sighed and wrapped her hands around the hot mug. "As long as it works for you."

"It doesn't. I think you know that."

Silence stretched, filled with unspoken meaning.

"I'm okay," Ansley said after another long minute. "You don't need to worry about me. You have a lot of people to take care of, and a lot of pressure on you. I don't want to add to that. I refuse to be a burden—"

"You've never been a burden. You were the opposite. You were like sunlight and oxygen." He stopped talking, exhaled. "Next thing I'll be saying is that art is transformative. I'm sorry—"

"Don't be. I'm glad we're talking. We should never have stopped talking. Communication is everything."

Rye coughed, clearing his throat. "So, are you seeing anyone else?"

"Seriously?" She laughed incredulously. "Not really into dating anyone right now. The last guy banged up my heart a bit. I figured I'd avoid entanglements until I'm ready for fresh rejection."

"I never stopped caring for you. My feelings for you have never changed."

"Don't say that. You're making it worse. The fact that you could cut me out while having *feeling*s blows my mind."

"Why?" Rye asked, voice low.

"Because if you could do it once, you could do it again, and that's a risk I couldn't take."

"Fair enough."

"So that's that. We say goodbye—"

"No." He softened his tone. "I don't want to do that, not tonight, not ever again. I can't, not when I care this much for you."

"How much?" she demanded.

"I want you to come to Eureka and meet my family. I've never introduced anyone to them, but I want you to see where I live, and what I do, and meet my parents, and Jasper."

"What about your other sister?"

"Hannah is going to school in Missoula, but I'll ask her to come home. I want you to meet everyone."

"Why now?"

"Because I have to stop protecting you by making decisions for you. In my mind Eureka was not good enough for you. My situation at home didn't seem good enough, either."

"How can you say that about your own family?"

He seemed to struggle with his words. "It's better for me to just invite you to come see us, and let you meet everyone, and decide how you feel, because Eureka is my home. I can't move everyone, and the only way you and I could work, would be if you thought you could be happy in Eureka with me ... and us."

"No pressure," she said, trying to make a joke of it.

"I'll be honest, Ansley, it's scary inviting you up. But there's no other way to know if you could be happy in my world without letting you in."

FOR THE NEXT month, they texted and talked daily. Rye drove down to see here in Marietta, staying for a night at the Bramble House on Bramble Avenue. Ansley couldn't leave her uncle alone all night, so she returned home even though she wanted to stay with Rye.

Things were good between them again. Things were better than they'd ever been. The sparks and chemistry were still there, but they'd also begun to talk, really talk, and sharing their feelings created more trust and a deeper bond.

"It's my turn to come see you next," Ansley said on Sunday when Rye prepared to head back up to Eureka. "Tell me when it would be good for you, and I'll come up. It's only fair."

"How would you leave your uncle for a weekend?" he asked, keeping her securely in his arms.

"My mom arrives this week. She's going to stay until Thanksgiving."

"That's good. But you don't want to leave your mom, not after she's only just arrived."

Ansley pressed a kiss to his neck, breathing in the scent of skin and man and a teasing hint of his aftershave. "One of the reasons she's coming is so I can come see you and meet your family."

"Oh." Rye drew back to meet her gaze. "Well, in that case, just let me know when you're on the road. I'll be there, waiting for you."

WITH HER MOTHER settled in the Campbell farmhouse, and comfortable with Uncle Clyde's routine, Ansley was free to head to Eureka.

She didn't pack a lot as she was only staying for a couple days. She did include her paints, charcoals, and a number of canvases in case there was time or inspiration to work. She set off at dawn and made good time, which added to her nervousness. Ansley hadn't told him yet she was coming, thinking it'd be fun to surprise him. But what if it wasn't a good surprise? What if his brother wasn't well? Or if Rye had changed his mind about her coming?

But this was exactly why she had to go north. She had to see Rye in his hometown. She had to see him in his environment and, hopefully, seeing him in his world would answer the nagging question—could she be happy there? Because that was what it would come down to. She'd have to move to live with him. With them.

Would his family like her?

Would she be welcomed into the family?

Would she be comfortable with them?

When Ansley had met Rye, she hadn't been looking for forever. She wasn't in a hurry to marry and settle down, but Rye had changed all that. It wasn't that he'd changed her, but he'd made her feel stronger, happier, even more creative, and those were all good things.

Could they make it work? That was the big question, and it was what compelled her to Eureka today.

Ansley had never thought of herself as a risk-taker. At home in Last Stand, she'd been quiet, always trying to fly under the radar. But there were things worth fighting for, and Rye Calhoun was one of those things.

She didn't know where he lived in Eureka, but she'd found an address for Calhoun Roofing online. From what she could tell, Calhoun Roofing wasn't the biggest roofing company, but they'd been around since the early nineteen eighties and had solid reviews. Of course, there was always a review or two by a disgruntled customer, but the company had responded and apologized and said they wanted to make things right and would be in touch.

Ansley half smiled, thinking that sounded like something Rye would say. Or maybe it was just how the Calhouns were—straight up good people.

She tried to imagine Rye's reaction when she showed up on the office doorstep. He'd be shocked, but then pleased. She knew he'd be pleased. She shivered in anticipation. Just three more hours and she'd be there.

RYE COULDN'T BELIEVE his eyes.

Ansley was here, in Eureka, in the tiny construction office on Dewey Street. His dad had opened the office in the early 1980s and when things had gotten tight, had sold off the biggest chunk of space to a window company, built a wall to divide the two businesses, and turned the small section into a very small office, usually manned by Carol, but with Rye hurt and unable to climb onto roofs, he'd sent Carol off on a much-needed vacation and he'd taken over playing office manager.

He was in the middle of doing office manager things like taking calls and placing orders for materials when Ansley walked in, and because he was being given the runaround by a supplier when the door opened, he didn't immediately look up, but when he finally did, sunshine flooded the doorway, haloing beautiful golden Ansley. He hung up on the supplier and crossed to the door.

"What are you doing here?" he asked, taking her in his good arm, the other still was in a sling.

She smiled shyly. "Came to see you. Did I come at a bad time?"

"No. A great time. I was about to cuss someone out. You saved me from losing my temper."

"Then I'm glad I arrived in the nick of time."

"Me, too." He kissed her, and then again. "Let's get out of here and get some lunch. That is, if you're hungry."

"I haven't eaten yet."

"Good. I haven't, either."

THEY ATE BURGERS at the little burger joint in downtown Eureka and shared an order of fries. Rye wanted to know how long she'd be able to stay and asked her if there was anything in particular she wanted to do or see.

"Just you," she answered, stopping herself from reaching for another fry. "And obviously your family. But if there's a scenic drive we could do, or something pretty to see, I did bring my paints. Just in case."

"I'll have to think about that," he answered.

"Are you working tomorrow?"

"No. Not now that you're here."

"Don't close the office because of me."

"It's slow right now. I'm not missing anything, and I would miss you if I went to work and left you alone."

"Well, I wouldn't be alone. I'd have your family for company. I can't wait to see Josie again."

"Actually, she's not here right now. She's visiting Hannah in Missoula."

"That will be fun for her."

"From what I understand, Hannah's boyfriend is planning on proposing soon. I'm hoping that's not this weekend."

"You don't like her boyfriend?"

Rye slowly shook his head, expression grim. "No. And it disgusts me even calling him a boyfriend. He's twice as old as she is. He's not attractive. He's not fun or interesting. He's not good enough for her. He'll never be good enough."

Ansley's brows rose. She'd never heard Rye speak of anyone like this. "So, why does she love him?"

"I don't think she does. I think she's confused." Rye's jaw worked, the muscle near his ear tightening. "He has some money. He's showered her with gifts, with all the things she's never had, and it's turned her head."

Ansley reached across the table to take Rye's hand. "But if she's happy?"

"Then I'd be happy, but I don't think she's happy. I think she's being a sacrificial lamb." Rye pulled his hand away. "She'll marry Ron because he can pay for things, and that would ultimately make things easier on me."

Ansley was glad when lunch was over and Rye suggested heading over to the house to show her around and introduce her to Jasper and his parents. Rye's negativity toward Ron had been a shock, but as the big brother, he was of course protective and invested in Hannah's future. She could only imagine how her brothers would react if she brought home a man twenty years her senior, a man who was spoiling her with gifts. They'd be uncomfortable, too, and her dad would have plenty to say as well. She almost asked Rye how their dad felt about Ron, but he got a call, and he took it, saying he'd be back in the office on Monday, and by the time he hung up, she forgot about her question.

Ansley drove behind Rye's truck, following him to his house. He gestured for her to park off to the side, while he parked next to her.

Her heart sank a little as she took in the house. She hadn't expected anything fancy, but it was a very dark brown block, two stories high with a sharply pitched roof and plain square windows. If the house was painted a lighter color, and there were shutters and perhaps some landscaping, it would have more curb appeal, but as it was it just looked utilitarian, as did the flat overgrown yard.

A wide ramp led to the front door, the brown stain quite scuffed on the bottom third. She wondered if the marks were from Jasper's wheelchair. Of course, she wouldn't ask, but anxiety bubbled up, anxiety that this was Rye's home, and she might possibly be living here with him one day. He opened the front door and stepped back so she could enter. The house was dark, the blinds on the windows were drawn. It was all Ansley could do to stand there when she already felt like she was suffocating.

"Dad likes to keep the curtains drawn," Rye said, closing the door behind them. "But when Josie's here, she's opening up everything. But with her in Missoula, he's got it all buttoned down."

A female voice sounded from the back of the house. "Is that you, Rye? You're home early."

"I know. I've brought someone to meet you."

"Let me just comb my hair and put on some lipstick," his mother answered.

"Take your time," he called back, before turning to Ansley. "She's going to be really happy to meet you. I've told her about you, and Josie is convinced you two are going to be best friends."

Ansley smiled, trying to hide the tenderness inside of her. She felt unsettled, almost bruised.

"I hope she'll like me," Ansley said.

"Of course she will. How could she not?"

BUT IT WASN'T Mr. and Mrs. Calhoun who were the problem. It wasn't Jasper, either, as he was absolutely lovely.

The problem was Ansley. All afternoon, and then all

through dinner—they were having a bucket of KFC and mashed potatoes and gravy in honor of her being there—she struggled. She wasn't comfortable.

Worse, she finally understood what Rye had been talking about all this time, and why he had pushed her away, trying to make decisions for her—and them. He wasn't ashamed of his family, but he understood the realities, and it was clear he understood that it wouldn't be easy for someone to assimilate into this world, not the way it was. His dad wasn't just disabled from his job injury, but he was also struggling with depression.

Ansley couldn't imagine a dad just abdicating all responsibility for one's family, leaving the job to his son. But Rye, wonderful, courageous, selfless Rye had stepped up to fill his father's shoes and be the person they needed him to be. He'd done this since he was just a teenager, which made her admire Rye even more.

But it was hard to see how little he had for himself. How little he had financially, how little freedom and space, never mind emotional space.

She couldn't imagine her brothers having to contend with the world Rye inhabited. She couldn't imagine any of them willingly sacrificing their own futures for their family, and maybe she was wrong, maybe if confronted by a tragedy, each of her brothers would step up and make hard choices. But they hadn't needed to do such a thing and the Calhoun family benefited daily from Rye's effort. They all benefited from his work and his income and Rye had been doing this, paying for everything, for years.

And he, himself, had nothing to show for it.

He lived in a dreadful little trailer. His parents had the main house, but it was incredibly rundown. Yes, the interior was clean but there were no special touches, nothing to make it homey, or personal.

Ansley, the artist, Ansley the woman who craved beauty didn't think she'd survive in this place, and she'd made a terrible mistake coming to Eureka. After dinner was over, she retreated to Rye's trailer, overwhelmed by Rye's family's struggles.

Perhaps if Josie was here, Ansley could talk to her, and ask questions. Like why didn't Rye's father do anything to help the family? She'd watched him that afternoon sitting in front of the TV, and then watched him again at dinner, and he was helpless, practically as dependent on the others as Jasper.

Ansley didn't know enough of the situation, and so she couldn't judge. She shouldn't judge. But she found herself questioning why Mr. Calhoun didn't still try to manage his roofing company. Maybe his back had been hurt, but couldn't he do the books, or handle sales calls, or order materials? Couldn't he go into the office part-time and represent Calhoun Roofing? Why just abandon it completely, leaving it all to Rye?

Further, why didn't Mr. Calhoun work on increasing his

mobility? Perhaps if the family purchased a newer car, one with a ramp to the driver's seat, perhaps living more independently would help him with his self-esteem. Obviously, she didn't know the full extent of his disability but from what she'd seen, Mr. Calhoun needed help standing, and he needed help moving around the house, and instead of a cane or walker he leaned on his wife or one of his children. Or resorted to a wheelchair. But if he was going to be in a wheelchair, he should push himself. He shouldn't insist his family push him about. He shouldn't force everyone to wait on him. Couldn't he see the damage he was doing to his family? To his wife? To Rye? Was there a medical reason he couldn't walk, or would physical therapy allow him to get back on his feet?

Ansley covered her face, dismayed by the intense emotion flooding her. She was too upset, too invested. If she already felt this critical and frustrated now, how would she feel in six months? Six years?

"It's awful," she said to her mother, having called her mom while Rye was still out. "I shouldn't have come. I don't belong here."

"I don't understand," her mother answered. "Isn't Rye there?"

"Yes, he is, and he's exactly as he's always been—a hardworking man who doesn't complain—but Mom, his home, his life, it's nothing like I imagined. I know it makes me sound incredibly privileged, but I'm really uncomfortable here. There are so many problems, and it all falls on Rye. But how is he supposed to take care of them all, and have a life? He's not ever going to be free of his responsibilities to them. They will always come first."

"You preferred the version of the story where there was just the two of you," her mom said.

Ansley's eyes burned and she rubbed at her temple, trying to ease the tension. "Yes." She felt heartsick, physically ill. "I pictured something totally different, but I was wrong. There is no room for me."

"Has he said this to you?"

"He doesn't have to. He's thirty years old and he still lives at home. Yes, he's in his own little trailer, but it's not far from the house. Until recently, both of the sisters have lived at home, and that was to save money so they could go to school, but Rye pays for virtually everything. He supports his mom and dad. He takes care of his younger brother Jasper. He helps cover his sisters' expenses when they need it."

"Rye sounds like a very strong man."

"He is. He's amazing. But Mom … I couldn't do what he does, and I couldn't be happy here. I don't want to live here, not like this. I don't know how he does it."

"I think you're getting ahead of yourself, honey, because he hasn't asked you to do it."

"But that's why I came. He invited me up to meet them and see his world. He wanted me to know more about him and his life, and I thought it would be fine. I thought Eureka wouldn't be as cute as Marietta, but I'll have Rye, and we'll make it work. I was wrong, though. This isn't the life I want. I don't want to live under someone else's roof, I don't want to love someone and not have time alone with him. I don't want to be second fiddle, and in this case, I'd be third or fourth fiddle."

"Then it's a good thing you went up there and understood his commitments. Far better to make a break now, than later."

The idea of saying goodbye to Rye killed her. They'd been through so much and when it was just the two of them, it worked. They'd always worked. It was the rest of the stuff, the outside world and his mountain of obligations that kept them apart. "I love him. I do. But is love enough to make this work? I'm no longer sure."

"You're twenty-five. You're only just exploring the world on your own terms. I don't blame you for being overwhelmed by his situation at home. It's a lot. And it would be a lot to take on, should you two decide to move forward together."

"He would never forgive me if I reject his family."

"Ansley, you're not rejecting his family. You are being honest about the complexities in his world, and how you would fit in, as well as where you'd fit in."

"Why do I feel like such a mean person?"

"There's a difference between being mean and being realistic. You've taken off the rose-colored glasses, and you're looking at the situation from a long-term perspective. You've always said someday you want a family, and now you've discovered Rye already has a family he's quite involved in, a family he financially and emotionally supports. In the back of your mind, you have to be asking how does he support them and the family you would create? How does he have time for your children and all of his other responsibilities? How does he have time for everything?" Her mother paused. "And if you're not thinking that, you should. Because as people age, they have more health issues. If his dad is unable to function without help now, he's just going to be more dependent later. The younger sisters heading to college probably won't ever move home, but Jasper won't ever be independent."

"Jasper's situation I understand. That's not an issue for me."

"So, what troubles you most? Dad? Or the economic situation?"

"Both. The Calhouns' life is hard. Financially, they're strapped. I didn't realize until I came here, just how much I had, and how much financial stability we had compared to others."

"You've lived in a bubble. Your dad worked hard, and he's been lucky. He went to college in Bozeman, then served in the military, leaving with excellent benefits. He's had his health, and he's competitive, always pushing himself to do more, and that's a trait that comes from within. Not everyone has it, and not everyone needs to be ambitious."

"I agree with you, but I honestly can't imagine that this was Mrs. Calhoun's dream. I'm sure this wasn't the life she'd expected. I doubt she ever thought she'd have to work this hard or struggle so much."

"I would agree with you there."

"I feel sorry for her. Maybe that's not the right word. But I feel for her. I can't imagine she thought she'd have a house full of essentially disabled men."

"Rye is not disabled."

"No, he's not. He's the pillar keeping the house up."

"His mom sounds like the foundation."

"Yes. The girls and Jasper contribute to the stability. Even though Jasper has his struggles, he has a lot of emotional strength and that helps everyone."

"What you're saying is they're all in it together. They make it work by being a family."

Ansley fell silent. She heard what her mom was saying, and her mother was right. They'd made it work, and perhaps it was because Rye had assumed leadership, becoming the head of the family, but it didn't sit right with Ansley. She wanted to marry a man who'd put her first, not last.

"It sounds like you have a lot to think about," her mom said. "Which is good, because Rye hasn't proposed. You two aren't in a serious relationship yet. If you have doubts, now is the time to extract yourself before anyone is hurt ... and before any of his family gets attached to you."

RYE STOOD OUTSIDE the trailer, rooted to the spot. He didn't mean to overhear Ansley's conversation, but the windows were open, and her voice carried. And once he was there, next to the doorstep, he froze, unable to do anything but listen.

He wished he'd never overheard any of it.

He couldn't remember when he last felt so much shame. It was like being caught outside in your underwear. He felt embarrassed and exposed.

He understood what she was saying, and he understood why she was uncomfortable, but it didn't make it any less painful for him. This had always been his fear, too. That his family wasn't good enough for others. That his world would be found lacking.

When he heard her say good night to her mom, Rye finally found the presence to move, but he couldn't return to the house. Instead, he walked across the backyard, through the side gate, to the driveway and his truck. He didn't know where he was going to go, he just had to go somewhere, away from here. Away from *her*.

It was better to know now how she felt, but it was the worst way possible to discover her thoughts. She'd been so blunt with her mom, her opinions almost brutal.

He hadn't expected it of her.

He'd thought she had more compassion. He'd thought

she'd adore his mother. Why didn't Ansley talk about his wonderful mother to her mother? Why didn't she mention how hard everyone worked today to make Ansley feel welcome?

Chest on fire, Rye drove, but he didn't know where he was going. All he knew then was that he'd been right to keep women away from his home. He'd been right to avoid romantic attachments.

But somehow, he'd convinced himself that Ansley was different, and because he wanted her to be the right one, he thought she'd be okay with everyone. That she wouldn't mind the main house or the trailer. He'd thought she'd realize they were all doing their best and she'd be proud of the way they pulled together.

Instead, she just saw the wounds and the flaws and all the Calhoun weaknesses.

Rye drove through downtown Eureka, and then onto Highway 22, driving to where, he didn't know. He passed the office for Calhoun Roofing, seeing it tonight through her eyes—a tiny little business, in a very humble building, with its practical exterior and unassuming interior.

Because that was who the Calhouns were. Practical unassuming people.

He should be relieved to know how she felt, and yet his disappointment was excruciating. He felt profoundly let down, her criticism so sharp, so personal.

He'd promised he wouldn't just cut her out again. He'd

promised he'd talk to her. He'd communicate. But how did one communicate about this?

There was no way he could return to the trailer tonight, not if she were there. He didn't want her at his house anymore. He needed her gone by the time he returned, or he would say something he might later regret.

Indignation warred with hurt, shock giving way to fury.

How dare she speak about his family that way? This was his family, and he loved them. From the moment Jasper was born, Rye realized his life would never be the same. He wasn't just a teenager, but an older brother with a responsibility to a baby whose brain had been damaged during birth.

He remembered his father saying, *it's not your mother's fault, and it's not the baby's fault. These things happen and so we have to do our best, we have to circle the wagons and look out for each other.*

Rye had taken that message to heart. He had spent every day of his life since then protecting his family, and just when he thought he'd found the right woman, he discovered his family, the family he loved, horrified her.

Rye swallowed the lump in his throat and rubbed a hand across his forehead, thinking he'd never forget the things he'd heard her say.

He loved his brother, his sisters, and his parents. They weren't perfect, but they were his family, and if Ansley couldn't see how important they were to him, then she needed to leave and leave now.

He pulled over onto the side of the road, shifted into park, and turned off the ignition. For long minutes, he sat on the highway's shoulder, gut churning, chest on fire. Every breath burned, every time he swallowed, he swallowed acid and pain. Finally, he grabbed his phone and sent Ansley a text. *I'm needed elsewhere and had to leave this evening. I tried to come tell you but you were on the phone. I hope the rest of your trip goes well.* And then he pushed send.

Aware that his family would also have questions, aware that his mom might try to intercede and convince Ansley to stay, he sent her a text. *I can't talk about it now, but Ansley and I are done. Let me know when she's gone. I won't return until then.*

His phone immediately rang. It was Ansley. He pressed ignore. His phone rang again. It was his mom. He declined this call, too. He wasn't hiding. There was just no way he could trust himself to speak to anyone right now.

Chapter Eleven

ANSLEY READ AND reread Rye's text, feeling a cold trickle of dread seep down her spine, into her limbs. He'd heard her.

She knew, without knowing anything else, that he'd heard some of her conversation with her mom. Possibly all of it.

Ansley sank onto the gold plaid couch, legs weak, heart racing. This couldn't be happening. This couldn't—

She called Rye again. He declined the call, not even bothering to let her go to voice mail.

He'd blocked her again.

Her eyes stung and she blinked back tears, her phone grasped tightly in her hand. She waited a half hour before trying to call him again, but his phone was off.

It was happening again. He was shutting her out, but this time it was her fault. This time, she'd said things that had to have hurt him terribly. Ansley couldn't move, couldn't walk, couldn't think. Instead, she sat glued to the couch, cold and clammy, feeling as if she'd throw up any second.

Mrs. Calhoun appeared at the trailer door, opening it slightly to peek in. Her gaze met Ansley's and her expression fell. "I'm sorry," she whispered.

"He's not coming back," Ansley said faintly.

Rye's mother shook her head.

Ansley swallowed hard. "I have to talk to him. I have to explain."

"What happened?"

"He heard me talking to my mom. I said some things..." Her eyes filled with tears, and she struggled to finish her sentence. "I shouldn't have said."

"About him?" she asked, coming to sit on the couch next to Ansley.

"About how different everything here was from ... my home."

Mrs. Calhoun's lips parted and then she pressed them closed. "Rye is pretty protective," she said, the exact words Josie had said the night of the art show.

"I wasn't trying to be unkind."

"No, but honesty can be painful."

Ansley had nothing to say to this. She couldn't remember ever feeling so awful before. This was her fault, 100 percent her doing.

"Want me help you pack?" Mrs. Calhoun said, breaking the silence.

Ansley wiped away the tears clinging to her lashes. "He wants me gone."

His mother nodded.

Ansley packed, and put her bag in her car, but before

leaving she went to the main house and said her goodbyes. It was the proper thing to do. The only thing to do. There were hugs—a very long hard hug from Rye's mom—and a fierce hug from Jasper who asked her to come back and visit soon and then she was in her car, fighting the tears while she reversed and then drove away from the house.

Ansley didn't know where she was going to go. But she knew this—she was not going to go home without speaking to Rye. And even though she felt terrible—beyond terrible—and even though she still wanted to throw up, she was determined that they have a proper conversation, face-to-face.

Instead of leaving Eureka, she checked into a motel, and spent a sleepless night going over everything she wanted to say, while trying to anticipate everything he might say, before dragging herself out of bed for a shower.

It wasn't going to be an easy day. She dreaded the next couple of hours, but she wasn't going to just run away. Running away solved nothing.

Ansley grabbed some coffee and a cinnamon roll at the coffee shop next to the motel before driving to Calhoun Roofing's office. As she expected, Rye's blue and white Chevy truck was already in the parking lot. She parked next to his truck and entered the office, through the unlocked front door.

The reception was empty but the bell tinkling on the front door drew Rye from the back. He stopped when he saw her.

For a long moment, he said nothing, his jaw granite hard. "I thought you left town," he said as the silence grew unbearable.

"I'm driving back this morning, but I had to see you before I left."

"Why? Seems that everything that needed to be said was said yesterday."

"You and I didn't talk."

"No, but I overheard you on the phone. It was more than enough. Your feelings were clear." He fell silent and looked away, jaw still clenched, expression harsh.

Ansley swallowed around the knot thickening her throat. "I'm sorry that I hurt you."

He shrugged. "I'm glad to find out how you felt. Saved us both a lot of time."

"I was overwhelmed, Rye."

"Yeah, I got that, but there's no need to make excuses. My family is not for you. It's as simple as that."

Pain flickered through her, hot, brutal. "This isn't about your family—"

"It's completely about my family. It's only about my family."

Ansley fought to hang on to her composure. Crying would be a disaster now. "I fell for you practically at first sight. I care about you so much."

"That's not the issue though, is it?"

He was hard, so hard, and he was shutting her out again and this time she feared he'd never let her back in. "What exactly do you think you heard me say to my mom?"

"I heard enough to know my family made you uncomfortable and that you couldn't imagine ever living here."

So, he'd heard pretty much everything. She drew a slow breath. "It was an emotional reaction, Rye, not necessarily a logical one. I was scared."

"Scared?"

"Your mother copes with a lot. In comparison, my mother has had it so easy. My family has had it easy. There has been no struggle, not financially, and certainly not with disabilities. I admire you and your mother. I admire your sisters. I admire Jasper—"

"What about my dad? Do you admire him, too? Do you admire our house? Do you admire my trailer? Do you admire the sacrifices made?" His gaze locked with hers, his expression ruthless. "Now I admit I walked into the conversation and might have missed something positive. Maybe you said some nice things about my mom, or perhaps you praised Josie, who has put you on a pedestal—"

"Rye, please."

"Please what? Please be nice? Please be gentle? Why? You were ruthless last night. You tore us apart."

Ansley couldn't reply. She had no words, nothing to fix this or to take his pain away.

He walked toward her, tension rippling through him.

"From the beginning, I warned you off. I knew my life, my world, was not for you. But you couldn't accept it. You had to see for yourself. And once you saw it, you rejected it, and not gradually over the course of a week or even a few days. No, you rejected it immediately, from the moment we pulled up in front of the house, your lip was curled and you were turned off. Don't think I didn't see it. You might be a talented artist but you're a lousy actress. And I don't blame you, but I do wish you'd saved us this scene."

"Rye, I'm sorry. I really am. And I don't dislike your family. I wasn't judging them. I was confused and trying to process my reactions by talking with my mom. I'm sure it sounded offensive, but it wasn't meant that way. I came here because I missed you. I wanted to see you. I wanted to be with you."

"Sadly, I come with so much baggage," he said quietly, mockingly, stopping in front of her. He tipped her chin up, his brown gaze burning through her. "I'm sure when you return to Marietta, you won't miss all of this."

She blinked back tears. "I will miss you, Rye. I don't know how not to miss you. You feel like you're supposed to be my person. From the moment I met you, it felt like we were supposed to be together. It doesn't make sense. There's no logical explanation. I've just always been drawn to you and feel good with you. I feel like me with you—"

"Until you enter my house and see the ramps and the old furniture and my dad just sitting there in front of the TV."

Her eyes burned. Her heart burned. "I didn't mean it like that. I just felt bad that you have to take care of everyone. I felt bad that you haven't had the freedom my brothers have—"

"I don't need pity, Ansley, not from you, not from anyone." He dropped a kiss on her mouth, a slow, deep kiss full of regret and longing, before lifting his head and drawing away. "Goodbye, Ansley. Drive safely. Get home in one piece."

FIFTEEN MINUTES AFTER the door closed behind Ansley, it opened again and his sisters entered the Calhoun office. Rye rose from his desk, certain there had been an emergency.

"What's happened?" he demanded. "What's going on?"

"Where's Ansley?" Josie asked.

"Gone."

"Why?"

"I'm sure you know why. Mom must have called you," he answered, sitting back down, already too tired of talking to deal with his sisters standing up.

"Did you break up?" Hannah asked, grabbing a chair and rolling it close to his desk.

Rye gave her a hard look. "What do you think?"

"She was talking to her mom." Hannah gave her brother an equally hard look. "Girls talk to their moms. They'll say things when they're still trying to figure something out. Moms are a safe place. I talk to Mom. I tell her things that I would never tell you or anyone else."

Josie sat down on the edge of his desk. "I don't just talk to Mom," she said. "I talk to Dad, as well. He's not always the most communicative, but you'd be surprised at the good advice he can give, if you give him a chance."

"Not sure what you think you're accomplishing, but you're failing," Rye said, leaning back in his chair. "So, leave, both of you, before I throw you out."

"You can't," Hannah said, nodding to his arm in a sling. "Not like that."

"The point is," Josie continued calmly, "you can't be upset with Ansley talking to her mom. Talking to a mom is different than talking to a girlfriend. Ansley called her mom because that's what family is for, and it's what we have always done." She gestured to Hannah. "At least that's what we do. We go to each other so we don't burden you—"

"You're never a burden," he said.

"We just know you already worry a lot, and we want to make things better for you, so we talk to each other, and it helps. Talking something through helps more than you know. It's something you could do more of. You always try to handle everything yourself."

Rye did not need to do this with both of his sisters at the same time right now. Together they were an intimidating tag team. "Of course, Ansley is allowed to talk to her mom. I would never suggest otherwise. I'm not a total jerk."

"You're not a jerk at all," Hannah said. "But you do think you know what's best for everyone, and that's probably a mistake."

Rye rolled his eyes.

Josie leaned forward and touched Rye's arm. "What did Ansley say that was so upsetting?" She held her brother's gaze. "You can tell us. We're part of the same family."

"It wasn't complimentary," he said shortly.

"We figured as much." Hannah glanced at Josie. "I mean, we're not always complimentary about our situation. We're poor."

"That's just it. Ansley didn't realize how … rough things were." He shook his head and rubbed a hand across his face, wishing he could forget what he'd heard, but he was afraid it would stay with him forever. "She also thinks she'll play second fiddle to the rest of the family, and didn't want to share me with everyone. Oh, and she most definitely did not want to live in my trailer."

A faint smile hovered at Hannah's mouth. "No one wants to live in your trailer."

"Our house isn't much better," Josie added. "I hate it. I've spent my life coming up with plans and ideas to make it better, but there's never enough money or energy. And a couple years ago, I realized I don't want to fix up that house. It'd be better to start fresh, design something new. Our house will never be beautiful, no matter how much money we pour into it."

"Yes, but it wasn't just the house. If you'd heard her ... she sounded so shallow." Rye spit the words out as if they hurt his mouth. "And spoiled. She has grown up with far more than us, and she thinks—expects—to have the same standard of living when she marries. And since we know I can't provide that for her, it's better that it's over—"

"Why can't she have the same standard of living with you? You wouldn't be the only breadwinner, Rye. She'd be bringing in money, too." Hannah waited for him to say something but when he didn't, she added, "She might even outearn you, and maybe that's what's bothering you."

"No. It never even crossed my mind." He drummed his fingers on the desk. "It's great if she can pay her bills and then some."

"Have you two ever discussed money?" Josie asked carefully. "Have you talked openly about what you earn and where the money goes?"

"*No.*"

"That could be part of the problem."

Rye rose and stepped over Hannah's legs that were blocking his path. "I would never question her about her income, or her expenses."

"Why not?" Hannah asked. "Because I certainly would never marry Ron without a candid conversation about money—what he earns, what I expect to earn, and how we'll budget."

"That's different," Rye said. "Ron has money."

"And so does Ansley." Josie slid off the desk. "Did you see what her paintings were going for? After commissions she made over nineteen thousand with that one show, and she's been booked for another show this winter."

"I'm not comfortable discussing her money," he said stiffly, going to the water cooler and filling up a glass.

"Because you think it's something you're supposed to be in charge of," Hannah said. "You think it's the man's job."

He turned around, gave his sister a hard look. "I've never said that."

Josie's brow furrowed. "Wouldn't it be nice to know you don't have to manage it all on your own? Wouldn't it help knowing your person, your partner, could help support your family?"

He shook his head, uncomfortable, and unable to continue this conversation. His sisters meant well, but it was too much, too soon. "Ansley isn't my person. The differences between our lifestyles are too extreme. I have a fixed amount every month to live on. I have a strict budget so we can make ends meet. Calhoun Roofing pays for the big stuff, and then my rodeo income is for the extras. Unlike Ansley, I don't have the freedom to just do what I want—"

Rye fell silent, his words ringing in his ears. *I don't have the freedom to do what I want.*

And then just as swiftly, *but she does.*

She's free. Free to reject me, free to criticize, free to find someone better, someone with fewer problems...

Rye turned his back on his sisters, beginning to understand his rage.

He wasn't just upset with Ansley for what she said to her mother about his family, he was upset with Ansley for having options he didn't have.

He was upset because she could choose her future, and choose what she wanted to do, and choose where she wanted to live, and he couldn't.

Deep down, he resented her freedom. Because he wanted to be free, too. He wanted what she had, and he was afraid he'd never have it.

Just like that, he heard her voice again, heard the one-sided conversation with her mom and he knew she wasn't shallow, or spoiled. She was trying to figure out where she fit in his world, which was why he'd invited her to Eureka. He needed her to know it wouldn't be easy and she hadn't found it easy. And now he was punishing her for being honest.

But would he have been happier if she'd pretended all was good? Would he have respected her if she hadn't taken a good hard look at his family and realized there were issues?

No.

Rye walked to the front door and looked out the glass to his truck in the parking lot.

He glanced at his watch. She'd been gone maybe thirty-five minutes. Could he catch up to her? He could if he left now. But he'd need a little help.

Rye turned around, looked at Josie. "Call Ansley and tell her you're going to meet her in Whitefish. Tell her you know things went badly with me and you're on your way. Pick a coffee place you like, and once she agrees, call me, and let me know where to go."

Josie and Hannah both stood.

"You're going after her?" Josie asked, eyes wide.

"I am. And we're going to communicate like two mature adults should."

Rye knew the roads like the back of his hand. He'd spent every weekend for the past eleven years driving and he knew where the speed traps were and the places he could go fast. Provided his truck didn't break down, he should reach Whitefish fifteen minutes after Ansley.

Driving, he glanced into the rearview mirror and saw that he looked rough. No shower last night, no shave this morning, no sleep, either, as he'd crashed at the office and couldn't get comfortable resting in a chair. But he wasn't going to sell his looks. He wasn't chasing her down to play Prince Charming. He was going after her to apologize because her concerns about his family were valid, and even though his pride had been hurt, he cared about Ansley too much to lose her without a fight.

ANSLEY HAD BEEN surprised by Josie's call. She'd thought

Josie was in Missoula with Hannah, but apparently, she'd heard about Ansley and Rye's situation and was racing home to try to fix things. Not that the situation could be fixed. Even if Ansley hadn't had doubts, Rye's reaction made it clear that there was no fixing this. There was no going back. It was over. Done. It had to be done. This was just too hard. Romances were roller coasters but this was one of those rides that dropped you from a horrifying height, letting you plummet all the way down. It wasn't fun. There was no pleasure in the drop. It didn't make her feel good, or more alive. It just made her sick. She was so tired of feeling heartsick.

Ansley parked on Second Street and walked the block to Folklore Coffee. She wasn't in the mood to meet with Josie, but Josie had been so worried about everything and was making a herculean effort to meet Ansley that Ansley couldn't refuse the stop in Whitefish.

The coffee shop had a bustling business which looked like mostly locals at this hour. She got in line to order something, and then texted Josie to see what she'd want to drink.

Whatever you're having, Josie answered. *I should be there soon.*

Ansley ordered two caramel macchiatos then found a table and waited for the order to be called. As she rose to get the drinks, the Folklore Coffee's door opened and instead of Josie arriving, Rye walked in.

Ansley froze. What was he doing here?

He walked to the table and hugged her, a long hard hug that made tears start in her eyes. "I'm sorry," he said.

She still couldn't process that it was Rye here, and she blinked, trying to chase the hot tears away.

"I was an ass," he added, still holding her close. "You didn't deserve that. You try so hard, and I see it." He stepped back but didn't let her go. "I'm the problem here, not you."

She didn't know what to say. She didn't know what to feel. She looked up into his eyes and they were pink. Lines bracketed his mouth. Dark circles formed shadows beneath his eyes. Rye looked stressed and exhausted, but he was here, and she didn't know what to make of it. But she felt a tiny ray of light. If he'd come after her, there was hope.

"Ansley," the barista called again. "Your order is ready."

"I'll get it," he said.

She nodded and sat down, grateful to take her seat because her legs were shaking, and she was trembling head to toe.

Rye returned to the table with a small carboard tray holding the two cups. He placed one cup in front of her and then the other in front of himself.

For a moment, they sat in silence. Ansley had cried the first half hour of her drive out of Eureka, thinking it was over, telling herself she was glad it was over. But with Rye across from her, she knew she didn't want the relationship to end, just those huge, horrible drops that made her feel as if she was falling. She was tired of falling. She needed something firm beneath her feet. She needed something solid and safe.

She held her cup between her hands, letting it warm her. "I owe you an apology as well," she said lowly, glancing up at Rye before looking back at her cup. "What I said to my mom had to have been hurtful, and I feel terrible you heard. The last thing I would ever want to do is hurt you, or embarrass you, and I did both."

"My situation in Eureka isn't easy. I recognize that."

"But you do an amazing job of taking care of everyone." She met his gaze. "You told me the night of the cocktail reception that you were proud of me. Well, I'm proud of you. You work really hard, and you never complain. I wish I was as giving and selfless as you. I wish I'd been more supportive of you. Instead, I was only thinking of myself, and I wasn't kind, and I'm ashamed of myself—"

"I'd rather know how you truly felt. I'd rather have us confront the problem together than pretend there's no issue."

Her eyes stung again, fresh tears filling them. "Do you really feel that way?"

He took her hand in his. "I love you, Ansley. I want you in my life. I want to figure out how to make this work and we can, and will, if that's what you want, too."

She blinked. "It's what I want."

"Good." He squeezed her fingers. "But there are obstacles."

She nodded. "I had a hard time with Eureka."

"It wasn't an easy visit, no."

"I didn't just struggle with your family. I think it was also the town. I think I arrived prejudiced as I love Marietta so much. Marietta is a special place for me. We met there during the rodeo, and I fell for you there. I've imagined opening a gallery of my own there, and I didn't realize how attached I've become to my Marietta dream until I was in your town, trying to imagine myself there, and it wasn't easy."

"I thought it was my family."

She needed a moment to figure out how to say what she needed to say without offending him all over again. "Your family has different dynamics than mine, and perhaps as the youngest in my family I've been sheltered more than my older brothers. I was rather overwhelmed, and to be honest, the part that was hardest for me was seeing your mom in your home."

Rye's eyes narrowed. "Why my mom?"

"Because she reminds me so much of Josie, and I could picture your mom being Josie when she was younger..." Ansley searched Rye's eyes, trying to make him understand. "Your mom is beautiful, and kind, and yet she's had a hard life, and there isn't a break coming for her. Even if she stops working, she still has your dad and brother to take care of."

"Did Mom say something to make you feel bad? I've never known her to complain—"

"*No.*" Ansley pulled her hand away from Rye's. "She's lovely, sweet, kind. She welcomed me with open arms, but I kept comparing her life to my mom's. I kept thinking what a difficult life she's had, and it made me feel sad. It doesn't seem fair that I've had so much, and she hasn't."

"Things weren't always this hard. When dad worked it was better. We weren't rich, but it wasn't such a struggle."

Ansley exhaled, unsettled. "Want to go outside, just walk a bit?"

He nodded and tossed his coffee cup, but she kept hers.

Outside the cool, fresh autumn air helped calm her. They walked a couple blocks before Ansley spoke again. "I have an idea," she said, glancing at Rye.

"I love ideas," he said, a hint of a smile playing at the corners of his mouth.

"Well, hopefully this is a good one."

"Good ideas are the best kind."

She smiled, relaxing a little. Even if this wasn't a good idea, at least he wasn't making her more nervous. "What if we were to come up with a plan? What if we didn't try to come up with a permanent solution today, but discussed what we could do today so that we could be together more, and then sometime in the future, after we see how it's going, we consider other options?"

He lifted a brow. "In theory, it sounds good. But how does that work?"

She took a last sip of her coffee and then tossed the cup

away as they neared a trash can. "Maybe we start out in Eureka—"

"When you say we, do you mean you'd move there?"

She nodded. "And when your sisters finish school and enter the job market, we could look at moving somewhere else. Perhaps toward Marietta, or maybe even here, to Whitefish. It's a really cute town. Reminds me a little of Marietta."

"Lots of tourists and lots of money," he agreed.

"I just think we don't have to decide what we want or need in five years. We just need to figure out what we need now. And what I need now is more time with you. Or full-time with you. You're what I want, Rye, and the rest ... it can wait."

"But you don't love Eureka, and my family home wasn't comfortable for you."

"I shouldn't say I dislike Eureka. The truth is, I don't know Eureka. It might really grow on me. I might realize that it's the perfect place for me. And if you were there, I would be happy there."

"And my family home?"

"It was a hard day to visit, Rye. The curtains were drawn. It was dark. Your dad wasn't in the best mood. It was a little claustrophobic. But, you don't live in the house, you have your place—"

"I can't put you in the trailer."

"We can spruce it up. Get some new furniture, hang

some paintings on the wall." She gave him a sly smile. "It would mean moving some of your ribbons and awards, but if you don't mind me beautifying, it could be really cute."

"Now you're overreaching. That trailer will never be cute."

She shrugged. "I follow Tiny Houses on Instagram. I have some ideas, and I bet Josie does, too."

He stopped walking and faced her. "You don't have to make all the sacrifices, Ansley."

"I'm not making all of the sacrifices. I'm saying ... let's try to figure this out together." She clasped her hands, her expression hopeful. "You know, we could be a proper team. I could be a good team member, too. Maybe I can't ride in rodeo events, but I can compromise, and I don't know why we couldn't find a happy medium because, Rye, I love you. It was love at first sight and I know it seems fast, but I don't want anyone but you."

He said nothing and her insides flip-flopped, somersaulting with hope and fear, love and anxiety and she needed him to say *something*. "Rye? Did you hear anything that I just said?"

"Every word," he said, pulling her into a dark doorway and pressing her against the brick wall. "But right now, I don't want to talk. I just want to kiss you."

His head dropped and his mouth covered hers, and the kiss was absolutely consuming. It was impossible to know how long the kiss lasted. All she knew was that she'd turned boneless, and she was melting into him. Thank goodness he was holding her up because her legs were useless at the moment.

RYE KISSED HIS beautiful Ansley until he was done for. He kissed her until the fight was gone, and there was no resisting her, and no resisting his heart. He loved her completely. He'd loved her from the moment he laid eyes on her, and he was one who didn't believe love could happen like that. He didn't believe that love could sweep one completely off one's feet. He'd never believed that love could change one from the inside out, but he'd been changed—transformed by her love and light, her warmth and bright, fierce, inspiring spirit.

It was as if God knew he needed someone exactly like Ansley, someone with backbone, someone with passion, someone just as deeply loyal, and foolishly stubborn, as he was. There was even a good chance that she was more stubborn, but then, she might need to be, considering how hardheaded he was.

At last, when Rye lifted his head, he clasped Ansley's lovely face in the palm of his hand. "You won," he said, smiling faintly. "You've won my heart, you've proved me wrong, you are everything I ever wanted and didn't dare to dream I'd ever have."

"I didn't win," she said huskily, leaning into him. "I just found you, and I wasn't going to let go. You are the one for me. I knew it immediately, felt it all the way through me. Having grown up in a family of strong men, I needed a strong man, a man with integrity, a man willing to put his family first, a man who'd always do the right thing. Rye Calhoun, you always do the right thing, even if it's not the right thing for you. You do it for others. You do it because you put those you love first. I love that about you, but you have to be a little bit selfish. You have to protect your dreams. They matter just as much as everyone else."

"I always believed I'd have my chance. I believed one day it would be my turn. And now it is."

"Now it is," she agreed, kissing him on the mouth and then smiling mischievously into his eyes. "I adore you, you know. I'd do anything for you. And I mean that. I think I'd be happy in Eureka. I think I'd be happy—"

"No. No not this again, Ansley."

She reached up, placed a finger against his lips. "Hear me out. It doesn't have to be forever. It could be for three years, five years, just keep your mind open and solutions will come. We'll figure this out together."

"What about your uncle?"

"My mom is lining up a full-time caregiver who will be live-in. There's also a possibility one of my brothers might be heading to Montana and decide what to do with the ranch, so he'd be on the property, too."

"You've just made friends in Marietta. You've been happy there."

"I have," she agreed, lightly tracing his cheekbone and

then down along his jaw, "but I can be happy here, too. I'll just need some time to adjust, and Josie is still living at home until January, and she'll be a big help. I've never had a sister—"

Rye stopped her flow of words with another fierce, hungry kiss. He loved this mad, beautiful woman, and she was saying all the right things but in his heart he knew it wouldn't be an easy move, or a painless adjustment.

He lifted his head to look into her intensely blue eyes. "I do want to marry you. We just have to figure out the logistics."

"They're not that complicated. We marry, I move, and I join the Calhouns."

"You're being awfully optimistic."

She pressed her finger to his lips. "There will be problems, but as Team Calhoun we can overcome them."

"Last night you weren't so certain."

"Last night, I wasn't looking at the big picture and today I am. I want a life with you, and a future with you, and I know if we talk to each other, and we take time to listen to each other, we can have a wonderful life together."

He looked deep into her eyes, seeing her fire and strength, and it reassured him. He didn't want anyone else on his team. "Will you marry me, Ansley Campbell?"

She laughed, a joyous bubble of sound. "Yes, Rye Calhoun."

Chapter Twelve

R YE AND ANSLEY wandered around Whitefish for an hour, talking, kissing, making plans, before Rye spotted a jewelry store and insisted they go in and look at rings.

Ansley didn't want Rye to buy anything, but he wanted a ring on her finger, and even if money was tight, he would make it work. He pointed out several large white solitaire diamonds, the stones so white they glittered in the light, but Ansley shook her head.

"I don't want a big rock," she said, moving down to another display cabinet. "I want something more personal … more us."

"What's wrong with a nice diamond?"

"Nothing, but I paint and use my hands a lot and I don't need a huge statement ring. A pretty band would be perfect, maybe even a band with a couple tiny diamonds set in it."

The sales assistant had been listening and directed them down one more case where he drew out a black velvet tray filled with bands, plain, engraved, and some embedded with diamonds.

Ansley's gaze swept the tray and almost right away she pointed to one. "That ring, with three diamonds."

The ring was platinum, and the diamonds were tiny, but they glittered against the contemporary band. She tried the ring on and smiled. "This one," she said, extending her fingers and watching the light catch the stone. "If it's in our price range."

It wasn't a flashy ring. It was a clean simple design, but it did look good on Ansley's hand. "You don't want to try any others?" Rye asked her.

She shook her head, her hand forming a fist, her gaze never leaving the ring. "No. This is perfect. I was hoping to find a band with three diamonds."

"Why three?" he asked.

"I fell in love with you over the three days of the eighty-fifth Copper Mountain Rodeo. I never want to forget that weekend, and how magical it was to spend time with you."

Rye paid for the ring and until Ansley could have it sized, she slipped it on the chain around her neck, wearing it inside her shirt against her chest. They had lunch together and then Ansley said she needed to continue home, that her mom would worry if she didn't return before it was dark.

Rye kissed her at her car, pinning her against her door with his lean hips to keep her from leaving. She didn't mind. She didn't want to go. They'd struggled to get to this point and now that they had, she just wanted to be with him, forever.

Her head was spinning by the time he lifted his head. Ansley blinked, dazed. "Wow," she whispered, pressing two fingers to her trembling lower lip. "I'm not going to be able to drive if you keep that up."

"I hate to see you go."

"I know, but we'll see each other soon."

He pushed back long strands of hair from her cheek. "When?"

"Whenever I can get away again—"

"No," he interrupted. "I'll come to you this weekend. My turn to drive."

"You're sure?"

"Absolutely."

She stared into his eyes, the dark irises bright with heat and desire. "I won't tell my family about our engagement yet. Then we can break the news to my mom together."

"What about my family? Should I keep it a secret from them?"

"No." She smiled. "They're quite invested in our romance. Your mom called your sisters and your sisters raced from Missoula to save us. I think they need to know how grateful we are."

"We are grateful, aren't we?" he murmured, nuzzling her neck, making her sigh.

"Very, very grateful," she agreed, gasping a bit as his teeth scraped a very sensitive spot, sending bolts of delicious sensation through her.

"When will we get married?" he asked.

She shivered against him, his mouth and hands lighting

her up. "As soon as we can."

"I like that answer."

BACK HOME RYE was met in the driveway by his sisters and then his mother appeared on the doorstep. They were all looking at him waiting for news.

"It's okay," he said, unable to hide his smile. "We're good."

"How good?" Josie asked anxiously.

"She said yes," he answered, suddenly feeling shy.

"Yes to what?" his mother asked.

Rye gestured to the house. "Can we all go inside?"

"Not until you answer Mom's question," Hannah said. "Yes to what?"

"I asked her to marry me, and she said yes. I bought her a ring. We're engaged."

Rye's sisters shouted and started jumping around. His mom was smiling, too, and the girls were asking a dozen questions, one right after the other.

Rye shook his head at the noisy celebration. "I promise to tell you everything, but I need a shower and some sleep and then later this afternoon I'll fill you in."

Two and a half hours later Rye stirred, slowly waking. His head felt fuzzy. He felt strange. Carefully he rolled onto his side, looked at the clock. It was almost four in the afternoon. Still staring at the clock, he tried to clear his head. What happened this morning? Was it real, or just a dream?

But then he reached for his wallet from the nightstand and pulled out the receipt for the Whitefish jewelry store and laid back down. It wasn't a dream. He'd proposed, she'd said yes, and he'd bought Ansley a ring. Smiling crookedly, he got up and walked into the kitchen for water. He drank a tall glass and then leaned against the counter.

He was going to get married. They would be planning a wedding. His smile grew. He couldn't believe it, and yet he'd never felt so good, so hopeful about anything.

A knock sounded on the trailer door, and he opened it. It was his mom on the doorstep.

"I wanted to talk to you before your sisters started screaming and jumping up and down again. They're still very excited," she said. "They've got Jasper worked up, too."

Rye studied his mom's expression. His sisters might be thrilled but his mother didn't seem as happy as she had earlier. "Come in, let's talk." He watched his mom walk around the tiny living area before sitting on the edge of the gold plaid sofa. "What's on your mind?"

"I was curious about your plans. I didn't know if you and Ansley had discussed the future—"

"We have."

"Where will you live?"

"Here." He hesitated. "We're going to fix up the trailer—Ansley has lots of ideas—and it will be a good starter home."

"No, it won't. Don't do this. Don't bring her here."

"Mom."

"I mean it. Your sisters don't even want to live here. Don't bring Ansley here, don't start your marriage like this."

His eyes narrowed. "We do struggle, Mom, we all do. But I didn't realize you were that unhappy here."

"I'm neither happy nor unhappy. I'm existing. Just as Dad is existing, and Jasper is existing—correction—no, he's happy. He's happy because he chooses to be happy every day. He knows he has limited years and he's determined to make the best of them, but the rest of us..." She shook her head. "We're not living up to Jasper's example. We just make do. We get by. Because that's what we tell ourselves we have to do." She regarded Rye steadily. "But we can make different choices. We aren't obligated to be stuck, and let's be honest, releasing you from obligations will make me happy, and that's a pretty big deal for me."

Rye felt as if his mom had knocked him over the head with a two by two. "What choice would you like me to make? Choose to leave you all? Choose to move somewhere else?"

"*Yes.* That's right. That's exactly what I want you to do. Put yourself first. Choose love. Choose happiness. Don't be a martyr. Find a new place." Her eyes locked with his. A spasm of pain tightened her features. "And if it's possible, if we're lucky, take us with you. Because this isn't paradise. This doesn't have to be our home. We all have options."

Stunned, Rye just stared at her. "What about the property? What about the Calhouns' legacy?"

"I wouldn't say this to your dad, but it's not much of a legacy. All the good land has been sold off. You have a couple acres for the horses, but there is nothing here that matters. The house has a newish roof but other than that, it's nothing special. It's a plain house built a hundred years ago, built for practicality, and it's served us well, but it shouldn't be a prison. We shouldn't be trapped here."

"You feel trapped?"

She hesitated, then nodded. "Sometimes, if I'm being honest. I look around the place and think, please, God, don't let me die here. Please, God, let there be more adventure, more life, more happiness in store for me." Her voice cracked and she glanced away, tears filling her eyes. "I shouldn't tell you this. I don't want to burden you—"

"It's not a burden. You're my mother. I'd do anything for you."

"I know you would, but that's not your job. I'm not one of your responsibilities." She brushed away the tears and mustered a smile. "The bottom line is, you have options, far more options than you think."

Rye's chest ached with bottled air. "Why didn't you ever say any of this before?"

"Because it didn't matter before. You seemed happy here, or at least, content to continue. I try not to think too much.

I try not to feel too much. I try not to focus on things that might not come true, but between us, I would love to do something else. I would love to try something else. I would love to think that my future won't be exactly like the past nineteen years. I love your brother and I love your dad, but there's not a lot of freedom. I wouldn't mind feeling as if there were a few possibilities. Perhaps that's selfish. Perhaps women ... mothers ... aren't supposed to feel that way, but I wasn't always a mother. I was once a girl and I had so many dreams. I was going to travel and explore the world. I was going to go to all those different wineries around the world and pitch in during the harvest season. I knew someone who was from Kelowna who did that in Germany and Australia. She went from harvest to harvest and ended up seeing the world. I wanted to do that, too. I've always had this thirst for adventure. But then I met your dad, and fell in love, and the rest is history."

"You regret marrying Dad?"

"No. But I do wish he hadn't got hurt. I wish we'd had better insurance. I regret decisions his father made. I regret that no one in the Calhoun family knew how to run a ranch and racked up decades of debt, leaving your dad to sort it out, and then you to deal with it. Now here we are, the product of generations of bad choices and I don't want you to get trapped here, like your dad did, and his father before him. You're tough, but that toughness also makes you inflexible, and life requires flexibility, and a willingness to adapt. Change. You have to change, Rye. You have to put you and Ansley first, and then you can help the rest of us, but if you're not happy, none of us will ever be happy. We're that dependent on you." She rose and brushed a tear off her cheek. "Now, if you truly want to stay here, I can be good with that. If you are happiest here, I can be happier here. But, Rye, if you think there's more for you somewhere else, then do what you need to do."

RYE DIDN'T SHARE any of this with Ansley. It wasn't something he wanted to discuss on the phone. Instead, he'd talk it out with her once he was in Marietta.

He drove down Friday afternoon, arriving at Bramble House late Friday night. He was meeting Ansley for breakfast in the morning at the Main Street Diner and then he'd share everything his mom had said. He couldn't wait to see Ansley. Morning couldn't come fast enough.

She was there at Main Street Diner when he arrived and he swept her into his good arm, lifting her off her feet. "That was the longest week," he said, kissing her.

"I agree. At one point I wasn't sure today would come."

"Let's get a table, I've lots to tell you."

The hostess seated them at a window table, but neither of them were interested in anything outside. Rye took her hand, and she held it tightly, even after the waitress filled their coffee and took their order and walked away.

"I don't know where to start," Rye said quietly, and it was true. He didn't know how to put everything his mother had said into words. The last time he and Ansley had been together, they'd talked about Eureka and converting his trailer into a cozy little house, and now it was all changing. "Remember how you said my mom seemed sad?" he asked.

Ansley nodded.

"You were right," he said. "I never knew that. I didn't realize what she was feeling. I didn't know how trapped she felt."

Ansley pressed his fingers. "She probably didn't want you to know."

"After I returned from Whitefish, it all came out. She doesn't want to stay in Eureka. She wants to move."

"But what about your family property? And Calhoun Roofing?"

Rye shook his head. "We'd sell it. Close it. We'd start over, start somewhere fresh." He glanced down, feeling her platinum band on her finger. "You've had this sized."

Ansley smiled, her fingers curling around his. "I wanted to wear it. I needed to wear it. I missed you."

"I missed you, too." He turned the band again, rubbing his thumb across the little diamonds. "I need you. I need your courage and fire. I need your smiles and laughter. You have a way of making all things seem possible."

"All things are possible," she said, holding his hand tightly. "We just have to stick together."

"We'll do it here, in Marietta," he said. "You're happy here and if we found a place close to town, my mom would be happy, too. I don't want her feeling isolated anymore."

"I agree." Suddenly tears filled Ansley's eyes. "And I promise to be a good daughter-in-law. I promise to be a good sister to Jasper and your sisters—"

"I have no doubt about it."

She hesitated. "I have something to share, too." Her head lifted and her blue gaze met his. "Some of my family has come out this week. It seems my brothers want to meet you, make sure your intentions are good."

"They know we're engaged."

"I didn't tell them. I only put the ring on after they'd all arrived and demanded information."

"Then how?"

"My mom." Ansley made a face. "She wasn't trying to get them all out here, but she mentioned to Van that things were looking serious between us, and within two days the brothers were flying in. My uncle's house is pretty full, so full in fact that three of my brothers are bunking down at the Wyatt's."

"When do I meet everyone?" he asked, sitting back to allow the waitress to set their hot plates in front of them.

"Today." Ansley reached for the salt and pepper. "If you're up for it."

He thought for a moment, shrugged. "Might as well get

the introductions over. It can't be any worse than your first impression of us in Eureka."

Ansley wrinkled her nose. "I wouldn't count on it. The Campbell brothers are a whole thing." She pushed the salt and pepper across the table, but he wanted the hot sauce.

"Long as they're friendly."

"No one should throw a punch, if that's what you mean."

Rye suddenly laughed. "Sounds interesting."

"So you don't mind if we head up after breakfast?" she asked.

"No."

She suddenly frowned. "Oh, they still think I'm moving to Eureka, and just to lay all the cards on the table, there was some pushback."

"Because Eureka is a long drive from Marietta?"

"There was concern that I was abandoning Uncle Clyde, and it seems from what he's told Mom, my uncle has grown attached to me." She laughed and shrugged. "Who knew?"

Rye had picked up his fork but for a moment he could only look at Ansley, all gold and glowing, so full of sunshine. He didn't know why she loved him, but he wasn't complaining. "Good thing we're staying close."

THEY LEFT ANSLEY'S car on Bramble in front of the bed-and-breakfast and drove together to Cold Canyon Ranch in Rye's truck.

"Tell me everyone's names," Rye said as they left Highway 89 and headed east for the mountains.

"My mom is Andrea," Ansley said, "and my dad's name is Callen, but he's not here, thankfully. It's going to be hard enough with the brothers." She exhaled as if suddenly nervous. "The oldest is Vander, he's a navy fighter pilot, and then it's Knox, he's a tech guy and lives in Austin, and then it's Lachlan, Duncan, and Fin, he's the youngest. Fin's my favorite. We were pretty close growing up. He's eighteen months older than me but we were just a year apart in school."

Arriving at the house, Rye parked next to the vehicles already there, two cars and two trucks. Ansley's mom came out of the house and met them in the driveway. She looked more Ansley's older sister than her mom, wearing stylish jeans and a pink and white striped T-shirt that showed off a trim figure. Her long highlighted blonde hair was pulled back into a ponytail. "So good to meet you," Andrea said, giving Rye a hug. "I can't tell you how glad I am that you're here."

"I understand your sons are here," Rye answered.

Andrea exchanged glances with Ansley. "Don't let them intimidate you," she said, patting his back. "Just like their dad, their bark is worse than their bite."

"That's reassuring," he said, smiling at her. "But to put

you at ease, I'm not worried."

"He's a professional cowboy, Mom," Ansley said, linking her arm through Rye's. "He deals with tough animals for a living."

"That's good because your brothers are wanting to talk to him for a few minutes without you there."

Ansley groaned. "Mom, that's not happening."

"I don't mind," Rye said. "In fact, it might be better that way. They'll have questions and we can talk freely without worrying about your feelings."

Ansley tugged on his good arm. "But what about *your* feelings?"

He smiled down at her. "Not easily hurt."

Ansley looked at her mother. "I don't think this is a good idea, Mom. I don't."

Her mother shrugged. "He's a man. He can handle himself."

Rye eased his arm from Ansley's hold and kissed her forehead and then her mouth. "Don't worry. I'm fine."

"He's right," Andrea said. "It's not as if your brothers will hit a one-armed man."

Rye laughed. "Where are they?"

"In the living room."

Still smiling, Rye climbed the farmhouse steps and opened the front door. It wasn't a long walk to the living room, and they were all there. Brother after brother after brother. Rye counted five. So, all five of Ansley's older brothers had made it to Cold Canyon Ranch. Interesting. They must have been seriously concerned.

The living room had been buzzing with conversation, but once they saw him all conversation ended, the deep voices falling silent. Rye almost smiled. He'd been through so much in his life that facing five Campbells didn't intimidate him. He would have preferred they were all seated, and that there was a chair for him but no matter.

"We've never met," Rye said, his gaze sweeping the room. "I'm Rye Calhoun. You're Ansley's brothers."

There was a murmur of agreement and one of the brothers introduced each of them, pointing at them as he did so. "I'm Van, and that's Knox, Lachlan, Duncan, and Finlay."

Rye inclined his head. They were big guys, tall and broad shouldered, and nearly all fair like Ansley. "What brings you to Montana?"

"You do," the man—could have been Lachlan—standing in front of the fireplace said. "Dad couldn't be here so we thought we should meet the man who has captured Ansley's heart."

"I'd do the same," Rye said. "I have two sisters."

"Either of them married?" Fin, the youngest, asked.

Rye shook his head. "Hannah, she's been seeing someone seriously, but I'm not okay with it. Not okay with him."

Van crossed his arms over his chest. "Why?"

Rye shrugged. "He's not good enough for her."

"And what if we don't think you're good enough for

Ansley?" the brother by the fireplace shot back.

"I'd say you're probably right," Rye answered easily, smiling. "But then, I don't know if any man is good enough for her. Your sister is pretty much perfect."

The guys laughed, some shaking their heads.

"Wait until you really get to know her," the one Van had introduced as Knox said. "She's tough. She knows what she wants and, apparently, she wants you."

"Which is why we're here," Vander added. "We thought you'd appreciate the support."

"Do I need support?" Rye returned.

"Everyone needs help," one of the brothers sitting on the couch answered. "Especially if you're organizing a big move."

Rye's eyes narrowed. "I'm not sure I follow."

"I think we're handling this badly," Vander said. "I think we should have asked for his help first. He might not even be interested."

"Interested in what?" Rye hated that he felt like he'd been dropped into the middle of a scene and he'd missed the key setup.

"We have a situation, and it crossed our mind that you could be the answer to our problems."

"If you were a religious man, I'd say an answer to our prayer, but I don't know where you stand up in terms of faith," the one who was probably Duncan spoke.

"I talk to God," Rye said flatly. "But not sure what He's got to do with any of this."

"Let's cut to the chase then." Van was comfortable taking charge. He was obviously the oldest. "We have a big piece of land here in Montana. Even though my dad and uncle are estranged, Dad is still part-owner. Our grandparents left Cold Canyon Ranch equally to both of their sons. Uncle Clyde has run the ranch all these years, but he has no children, which leaves the ranch to us."

"Our father wants nothing to do with it," the brother on the couch said. "He's happy in Texas and that's where he calls home."

"Most of us have made our homes in Texas," Van added. "No one is ready to move to Paradise Valley, which is why Ansley is here."

"I thought one of you was interested in this place," Rye said.

"Possibly, but if you thought this could be a good home for you and Ansley, then that is what we'd do."

Rye took a breath. "I'm not sure I'm following."

"You're a cowboy. You come from a family of cattlemen. You know what to do with Cold Canyon Ranch. You'd know how many head of cattle you can run on the property. You'd know which crops to plant. You'd know how to bring value back and stop the financial drain on my uncle," Van said.

Lachlan nodded. "Uncle Clyde hasn't made the necessary decisions to provide for his future. Short of selling the ranch, there's nothing set aside for him. He has nothing liquid. In light of this, he is dependent on our family for care and financial support."

This was a story Rye was all too familiar with. "I know, and I'm sorry your uncle is ailing. I'm sorry none of you can see yourself here in Montana. It can't be easy making decisions for his care from Dallas or wherever you live."

"We wouldn't have to, if you were here," Fin spoke up.

Rye suddenly saw where they were going with this. Ansley's brothers wanted him to take on the ranch and for Ansley to care for Clyde, but that wasn't what Rye wanted for either of them. "I don't see that happening."

"Why not?" Duncan asked. "This is a big piece of land and could be prosperous again. It would take hard work but eventually—"

"No." Rye gritted his teeth. There was no way. It didn't work. He wanted his mom close to town, near people, and he didn't want Ansley having to take care of her uncle. They could hire a nurse and Ansley could visit, but he wasn't going to turn her into a caregiver. She had dreams, and he would protect her dreams even if it meant that it inconvenienced her family.

"That was an awfully quick no," Lachlan said. "Ansley could still paint. There are a number of bedrooms here. It's not a long drive to town and your brother would get exceptional care at Marietta Medical."

Rye shook his head, temper rising. "You have it all figured out. I'm supposed to move my family here, take over the ranch, ask my family to squeeze into this farmhouse so you don't have to worry about *your* uncle or *your* nest egg."

For a moment there was only silence, then Fin smiled crookedly. "It doesn't sound very appealing like that, but it's an option. I don't know about you, but I like having options. Options aren't decisions. They're just another opportunity, something to think about when you can't sleep at night."

"We don't expect you to make a decision today," Van added. "If it were me, I couldn't make a decision without talking with my family."

Rye wasn't happy. This wasn't the conversation he'd anticipated them having. He thought he was coming to the house to meet Ansley's family, not have her brothers try to take charge of his life. No wonder Ansley wanted to get away from them.

The front door opened and suddenly Ansley was there looking at the room full of brothers. She glanced at them and then at Rye, a question in her eyes. It was obvious something was wrong from the tension humming in the room.

She looked at her brothers, and then back to Rye. "What's going on?"

"We're talking about some options with Rye."

"Oh?" Her voice rose to match the lift of her elegant brow. "What options?"

"It crossed our mind that Rye could be the answer to the problem of Cold Canyon Ranch, and we've been running our ideas past him."

Ansley's jaw tightened. She didn't appear reassured. "I'm in the dark here," she said. "Someone, please fill me in."

For being such big guys, they suddenly looked unsure, and no one rushed to speak. She looked at each of the five before focusing on Rye. "It looks like they're being cowardly. Want to tell me what's going on?"

Rye hesitated, not wanting to come between family, but he and Ansley had agreed no secrets. They had to talk. It was essential to communicate. "Your brothers think I should live here with you, and you could take care of your uncle while I run the ranch."

"That wasn't the suggestion," Vander interjected. "We wouldn't want Ansley to become Uncle Clyde's nurse. Mom's arranging for a professional caregiver to live in, but yes to running the ranch. He's experienced and we thought he might enjoy working close to the Wyatts since he knows them from the circuit."

Ansley's eyes narrowed, her furious gaze sweeping the living room. "How dare you go behind my back and make plans for my life? Just because you don't want to live here doesn't mean I should have to live here. Mom knows I recommended selling the place after Uncle Clyde passes, and then you guys could divvy it up however you want. I don't need it. I don't want it."

"But it's a family property," Knox said. "It's been in the family for nearly a hundred years."

"But if no one in the family is willing to come here and manage it, then let it go and stop trying to make decisions for me. Rye and I want our own path, and our own life, and it blows my mind that you thought it was okay to dangle this place in front of Rye as if he's going to be grateful for the opportunity. This is not his place, and the Campbells aren't his family—"

"Now hold on," Duncan said. "You led us to believe that you wanted to marry him. You talked about the future, and if you get married Rye becomes a Campbell. He becomes one of us."

"No!" Ansley practically shouted. "No, Duncan, that's not how it works. He's a Calhoun. If we marry, I become a Calhoun. Rye and I don't do what's best for the Campbells. We do what's best for the Calhouns."

Silence followed her speech. The brother by the fireplace shuffled his feet. The one on the couch stretched his legs out.

Temper still blazing, Ansley marched into the center of the room. "You disrespected me, and you disrespected Rye, and I'm ashamed of you. You should have come to me first. You should have asked me what I thought, and if I thought there was potential, I could have run it past Rye in private. Truthfully, I wouldn't have run this idea past Rye as it's insulting to even think he'd want to be here on this ranch, in this house. This isn't his home. And it isn't mine."

"It's a special piece of land," Rye said, trying to soften her words. "I'm a big believer in family legacies. I've done my best to take care of my grandfather's property in Eureka. I've taken over my dad's roofing business. I'm very loyal to family, and I'm not insulted, but it doesn't sound like this is the right move for Ansley. Ansley is not a country girl. She has dreams that are bigger than being a rancher's wife—"

"That's not it at all," she interrupted, turning to face Rye. "I don't care if I'm a rancher's wife, a cowboy's wife, a roofer's wife. It's not about your occupation. It's about us— you and me—being respected. I can paint anywhere. I can paint here. I can paint in Eureka. I can paint in Bozeman if that's what you wanted to do. I just want us to find the place that is our place, one that feels right for me and you." She glanced at each of her brothers. "Now butt out and mind your own business. I won't stand for your interference."

LATE THAT AFTERNOON, following a very late and awkward lunch, Rye slipped out of the back of the house to go for a walk. He took the gravel road that wound to the high pastures up until it turned to dirt and kept walking. It was a significant climb, but he welcomed the exercise and the quiet. He could hear the birds as the sun began to set, sparrows, crows, and a circling hawk, which made the crows even more vocal. In the distance, he heard a cow low, and wondered if it was on the Wyatts' property or if it was one of the cows the Wyatts were running on the Campbell ranch.

There was so much to like about Cold Canyon Ranch. There were intriguing possibilities in being in Park County. If he didn't have to consider his family's needs, he would jump at the opportunity to start a life here. This was a beautiful part of Montana, some of the best grazing land, as well. He could give up the roofing and focus on being a rancher, which was his first love. He could give up competing, too, which would give him more time to devote to Ansley and his family, and the family he and Ansley would have one day.

But he couldn't just consider himself. He had to think of his family, and Jasper would do better here, and he would get better care in Marietta. There were outstanding doctors and specialists just thirty miles from the ranch. If there was an emergency, help would be close by.

If he and Ansley didn't want to be on the ranch, they could find a place that suited them better, and just because he wasn't working the Campbell ranch, it didn't mean he couldn't find a ranch hand position elsewhere. He'd have to prove himself, but he wasn't worried about that. Rye was good with challenges, and like his mom, he was ready for something new.

He heard a motor and turned to look at the road. Ansley was riding a four-wheel all-terrain vehicle, charging up the road toward him. Rye stood in the middle of the road waiting for her to reach him. "Where did you get that from?" he asked.

"It's Tommy Wyatt's. He's home for the weekend, and he came over to meet my brothers and, since they were all busy, I asked if I could borrow it to come find you."

"You are very resourceful."

She turned the ATV off but remained seated. "Mind some company?"

"Not if it's yours."

"Yeah, wasn't about to bring any of the brothers. I'm still so mad at them."

"Don't be mad, Ansley. They thought they were doing something good."

She huffed an indignant breath. "They should have talked to me."

"I agree."

"And if they had, I would have told them no way you'd be interested in moving here—"

"Actually, I wouldn't mind living here, working here," he said, crossing to where she sat and lifting off her goggles so he could see her eyes. "I like this area and you have the best neighbors next door."

"That's true."

"But I also wouldn't want you having to drive from here into town to open your gallery every day. The weather is harsh in winter, and I'd worry about you—"

"I don't have a gallery." Ansley cut him short, laughing. "But one day, yes, I'm hoping."

She swung her leg over the ATV seat and stood up, stepping into his arms. "Let's spend some time house hunting. There's no reason to rush. I'd rather find the right place for all of us instead of trying to squeeze us into a place that won't work."

"Like the Campbell farmhouse?"

"Way too small. I don't know where we'd put everyone."

He kissed her head and then her mouth. It was a light warm kiss, filled with sweetness. "There's a lot of good communities between Marietta and Bozeman, and Livingston, too."

"It'll be fun to look for a place, *our* place," she said with some satisfaction.

He kissed her again, a deeper kiss, a kiss of absolute love and affection. "So, when are we going to get married, Ansley? We never set a date."

"Whenever you want to. I'm not interested in a big wedding. I'm not interested in all the fuss. I just want you. And I want us to be together. These past few months have been tough with us living in two different places, and trying to meet when we could. I'm just ready to be with you twenty-four-seven."

"Maybe a Christmas wedding? That would give us a month to plan. Is that enough time?"

"Do you know what the weather is like around here? If we have a lot more snow—"

"Oh, we will definitely have a lot more snow, and I'm not thinking of a garden wedding. Maybe something at a hotel, and let them do all the work?"

"Wouldn't that be a lot of money?"

He thought for a minute. "What about at Bramble House? It's a good place and it'd probably work for a small wedding, although if all your brothers come, it's not going to be such a small wedding."

Ansley laughed. "They'll come, but they're all single so that saves money."

"We'd have my family, plus Ron." Rye's tone hardened. "Or I could tell him it's family only."

Ansley tugged on his vest. "We could also just elope and deal with the consequences."

Rye pictured her five older brothers and shook his head. "If your dad is anything like your brothers, eloping might not be a good idea. I have a feeling everyone wants to see you married. You're the only girl, and the baby."

"Then let's talk to the Bramble House tonight when we go back to town and see if they have a day open."

"I love it when we communicate. Look how much we get done."

She laughed and wrapped her arms around his waist. "You will have your cast off before the wedding, won't you?"

"Yes. Thank goodness."

She reached up to stroke his jaw, her nails lightly grazing the bristles of his beard. "Can't wait to marry you. Can't wait until I'm yours forever."

"The time will pass quickly. We have a lot to do."

"I'm excited," she said. "Excited about our future."

He kissed her. "I love you, Ansley."

She smiled against his mouth. "I love you, Rye Calhoun, and I can't wait until we have a little Calhoun of our own."

Epilogue

I N THE END, it was the Wyatts who helped Rye and Ansley find their dream house.

With Lachlan deciding to move to the Campbell ranch, Rye and Ansley spent the next few weeks diligently looking for their future home despite November's wind and chill. The snow from the storm a week ago still covered the ground in white and for a girl from Texas, Ansley was learning about driving in snow and on black ice.

Every weekend, Rye drove to Marietta so he and Ansley could see different communities and different properties. There were a few possibilities, but none were quite right and then one day just before Thanksgiving, Sam Wyatt called Ansley, and said a place was coming on the market and it was special. He and Ivy knew the owners and they thought Ansley and Rye should see it right away, as they didn't expect the house to stay on the market long.

Rye drove down that evening, and early the next morning, Ivy and Sam met Rye and Ansley at the Howe property, along with the Realtor. Unlike some of the other real estate they'd looked at, this wasn't a ranch or a farm, but it did have seven acres and it lay halfway between Bozeman and

Marietta, making it convenient for everyone.

Ivy knew the Howe family well as she'd worked with their daughter Ashley for years, helping her ride again after a terrible riding accident left the young teenager paralyzed. The family had adapted the home, the barn, and even the walkways to make everything accessible for Ashley, but with Ashley now at college in Southern California, the parents wanted to move west with her, and had made an offer on a small ranch in San Juan Capistrano, a thirty-five-minute drive from Chapman University.

Because they'd made an offer, the Howe's wanted to sell their Montana property as quickly as possible and were pricing the place aggressively to make a quick sale. When the Realtor didn't seem very confident in giving the tour, Ivy took over, showing off the large four-bedroom house with the vaulted beamed ceilings and enormous windows with views of the nearby mountains. The house, just fifteen years old, was full of light and all modern conveniences. It had also been modified four years ago to accommodate the daughter's wheelchair, and the new accessible features would be ideal for Jasper.

Ansley and Rye glanced at each other again and again. It was without a doubt the nicest house they'd seen—not just spacious—but downright luxurious with gorgeous finishes, a huge professional stove, a roll-under sink, pull out lower drawers for the dishes, marble kitchen counters, heated limestone floors in the bathroom, and a large fully accessible bedroom suite with a proper accessible bathroom for Jasper, including a roll-in shower.

Ansley was sure the house—even without the attached land—would be way out of their budget, but Sam and Ivy seemed so excited to show them the house that Ansley kept her fear to herself.

Leaving the house, they went down a wide paved path to a lovely little mother-in-law house which had been used as a rental property, first by college students, and then later by a traveling doctor. But now, the house and the mother-in-law quarters were empty, and Ansley followed Rye through the adorable tiny house with its own kitchen, living room, master bedroom and a tiny guest room. Like the main house, the tiny house had matching windows and a vaulted ceiling and tons of charming touches.

Rye took Ansley's hand and gave it a squeeze. She knew what he was thinking. She was thinking the same thing. This would be perfect. *If only…*

They still had to see the large clean barn, and then finally, the small stand-alone building which had been the gym, which had played such an important part in Ashley's rehab. Like the rest of the house, the gym was empty and while it wasn't very large, it had a high ceiling, big windows, and a small half bath—accessible, of course.

Just as it had been Ashley's gym, Ansley thought it would be an ideal space for Jasper. He could stretch in here and do his necessary therapy. The walkway between the gym and the house was paved, allowing Jasper to move about the property with the freedom he'd never had in Eureka.

"This would be yours," Rye said, hooking his thumbs over his belt. "It'd be your own studio. Your private space."

Ansley shook her head. "No, this would be better for Jasper. He needs it more."

"He doesn't. He's getting a huge bedroom. You're not. Take the studio. I would, if I were you."

Through the open door she could see the house and barn, the tiny house, and the paddock. It was a truly amazing place, but it wasn't something she could, or should, want, not when finances were so tight. She drew Rye out the door so they could have some privacy.

"I love how much you love me, Rye, but I don't need all this. It's breathtaking, and there's the barn for you and the studio for me, but truly, all I need is for your family to be comfortable and happy."

"They'd be so comfortable here, believe me."

"But how would we afford it?" She took his hands, pressed them to her chest. "Neither of us wants to carry lots of debt."

"We won't. Selling the house and business in Eureka gives us enough for a decent down payment, and that's without touching any of your money. I think if we pool our resources, you contribute some of your income and me with mine, we can swing this.

Ansley searched his eyes. "I don't want you to do this for

me."

"It's not for you, it's for us. But if this isn't the right place, we can keep looking. We're not getting married for another month, and once we're married, we still don't have to rush."

"Have you *really* looked at the numbers?" she asked.

"Sam and I had a long conversation before I drove down. I didn't want to get your hopes up if it wasn't in our budget."

"It's such a nice place," she breathed. "It's really beautiful."

"It is."

"But you don't have a new job yet so doesn't that make things ... difficult?"

"Last week, Lachlan offered me a job, working the Campbell ranch with him. I haven't said yes yet, but it's an intriguing idea. Not sure what you think of it."

"I think you should do what makes you happy."

"I am. I'm marrying you very, very soon. And you know I like being outside. I'm not cut out to be a desk guy." He hugged her close. "So, what do you think? What's your gut saying?"

She pressed her cheek to his chest. "My gut is saying this is perfect. It's perfect for your family. It's perfect for us. It's close to Marietta, close to Bozeman, close to Uncle Clyde and the ranch."

"And you could keep painting," Rye said, kissing the top

of her head.

"And we'd all be together," Ansley answered, snuggling closer. "One big happy Calhoun family."

Rye laughed softly. "One big happy Calhoun and Campbell family because we're not leaving our families, we're just bringing them together."

"Oh, I like the sound of that," she cried, lifting her face for a kiss.

He was happy to oblige her. He loved her mouth. He loved everything about her. "Me, too."

The End

Dear Readers,

It's always so much fun to start a new series, and that's what TAKE ME PLEASE, COWBOY does—we kick off the 85th Copper Mountain Rodeo, Tule's 10th Anniversary (how can that be?!?), and I'm launching a brand new Montana set series, The Calhouns & Campbells of Cold Canyon Ranch.

The Calhouns & Campbells of Cold Canyon Ranch brings together two different families, from two very different backgrounds, both coming together in Marietta, Montana as they fall in love and begin new lives. I'll be so interested in hearing what you think and hope you'll take a moment to post a review after reading Take Me Please, Cowboy, whether on Amazon, BookBub, or your favorite reviews site.

I love being in touch with my readers as well, and am active online in my private Facebook Group, as well as on Instagram, and through my **newsletter**. I use my Facebook Group and newsletter to share my plans for upcoming reader events, including the 3-4 private reader lunches and teas that I do every year in different parts of the country. Tell me where you live and maybe I'll soon be coming to see you!

Jane

The 85th Copper Mountain Rodeo Series

Book 1: *Take Me Please, Cowboy* by Jane Porter

Book 2: *Tempt Me Please, Cowboy* by Megan Crane

Book 3: *Marry Me Please, Cowboy* by Sinclair Jayne

Book 4: *Promise Me Please, Cowboy* by C.J. Carmichael

See Carol Bingley's story in....
The Untold Story of Carol Bingley by Jane Hartley

Exclusive Excerpt:
Tempt Me Please, Cowboy

The next book in the 85th Copper Mountain Rodeo series

H E WAS EXACTLY the kind of trouble she needed.
Six feet and then some of lean muscle packed into jeans, boots, and a white T-shirt that every woman in a ten-mile radius of Grey's Saloon here in Marietta, Montana, was going to dream about tonight.

Herself included.

And that wasn't even getting to the dirty-blond hair, a little too long and the kind of messy that led straight to more dreaming, plus a set of amused green eyes that were a health hazard all their own.

Sydney Campbell stopped pretending to do her brand-new job as the worst bartender in the history of the old saloon that had been in her family since a branch of Greys escaped the east. They'd found Paradise Valley and decided that looking for copper in the nearby hills was thirsty work. Better still, that they should address that problem. They'd been doing exactly that ever since.

She paid no attention to her uncle Jason's irritated muttering about firing her even though he'd only just grudgingly hired her in the first place. Because unlike the many people packed into this place tonight who were very careful with the current proprietor and his legendary bad mood of about twenty years and counting, *she* knew he was all bark.

Well. Mostly.

And anyway, she wasn't the only person staring.

Because she wasn't the only person in the saloon with eyes.

"I'm supposed to be doing normal things like normal people," she reminded her uncle when he scowled at her, and then smiled angelically at him when that scowl deepened.

"I didn't realize 'normal' was on the table," he growled.

But he left her to it.

This was the main benefit of letting her entire, over-involved extended family think that she was having a nervous breakdown. That her arrival in town heralded an epic collapse of uncertain nature. That she was *in the throes* of a cataclysmic personal event.

Sydney hadn't meant to let them all think that. Not really. But she hadn't corrected them, either.

What else could explain her sudden decision to relocate to tiny little Marietta for an indeterminate amount of time this fall? Sydney usually only came to Montana for Christmas, family weddings, peremptory summons from her perpetually unamused grandmother, and the like. She flew in, smiled like a well-adjusted and potentially well-rounded person for no more than a long weekend, and then flew back to reality on the red-eye.

Because the reality for most of her adult life was that she was busy, and not in the way everyone liked to claim they were *so busy so busy so busy* these days. Sydney spent night and day in her office at Langley, where she rarely knew or cared if it was night or day because she was lost in all the data that was always scrolling across her many screens and through her head. She was the kind of busy that when her phone buzzed, she always had to answer it, and she was expected to appear in a nearby office within minutes or at the Pentagon within the hour.

She was so busy that when she actually got to go home, she sometimes had to take a minute or five to remember that yes, in fact, she had a small, soulless apartment in nearby McLean, VA, chosen years back so that she was never *too* far from work. But she was usually *at* work, so every time she actually went back "home" she felt as if she was staying in a hotel. She'd never bothered to put up pictures or decorate. It had come finished and she left it that way because it was easier. No muss, no fuss.

She had no pets. She saw no people outside of work because she had no time to see anyone. Her friends and family had to content themselves with erratic phone calls and texts at odd hours.

Only other people with all-consuming jobs understood what it was like, and that it wasn't sad. That she was not depressed or riddled with ulcers or whatever they liked to think, simply because her job was the significant and consuming relationship in her life and had been since she'd been recruited out of Georgetown. Everyone else used words like "workaholic" and "stress case" and so on, never understanding that those were compliments in Sydney's world.

Some of her friends and family claimed she was a spy. Others preferred to call her a flake.

Sydney was neither, but she neither confirmed nor denied it when people said these things to her face. She could only imagine what they said when she wasn't around, because she knew her family enjoyed nothing more than diving deep into the psychoanalysis. Preferably over drinks served right here in this saloon.

It wasn't a stretch for them to imagine it had all become too much for her, because they thought it *should have* been too much for her years ago.

That wasn't the truth of things, not precisely, but Sydney had decided to go with it and it had already borne some pretty excellent fruit. Her cousins, usually notable for their benign mockery and sarcastic references to everything under the sun and especially to each other, were forced instead to attempt pleasantries. They'd gotten the news through the lightning-fast Grey family grapevine last night and had called her in a wave earlier today.

Most of them were bad at pleasantries, being genetically predetermined toward intensity.

Or maybe they were just unused to Sydney actually answering her phone.

What she'd realized was that she should have pretended to be fragile years ago. It was hilarious.

But tonight, she wasn't feeling the least bit fragile.

She tracked his progress through the saloon. Slow and lazy and intent all at once, just like him.

When she'd met him the first time, long ago, she had not been pretending to be fragile. She barely knew that word. That night she'd been after oblivion and she'd managed to get a fairly good grip on it. It was the night before Christmas that year, and she'd squeaked into town last minute on a flight that had skated into Bozeman—and bounced a few times while it was at it—right before they'd started cancelling all flights coming in and out ahead of an expected snowstorm in the mountains.

Sydney had decided that instead of attempting the drive out to Big Sky, where her grandparents lived and hosted Christmas almost every year, she would stay in Marietta and head over very early in the morning with her uncle after he handled the booming Christmas Eve business at Grey's Saloon. When they could see how bad the storm was going to be, since there was a big gap between *newscaster bad* and *real Montanan bad.*

Besides, she had discovered over time that everyone benefited when she put some space between her job and her family, since her family liked to talk about her career like it was her toxic boyfriend.

Some people called it "blowing off steam" and that night, Sydney had gotten into the tequila to see just how steamy she could get. And she'd been having a grand old time. She'd been hanging out with a girl she'd used to play with in summers long past, when her airy, careless mother would park her kids in Montana for most of June, July, and August and take off to follow her bliss—meaning her latest lover—wherever it took her.

Sydney and Emmy Mathis had been summer friends. Close when they saw each other and fine when they didn't, and Sydney had been delighted to discover that held true once they were grown, too. Emmy now lived in town because she'd married the one and only Griffin Hyatt, another summer-in-Marietta guy who was now a tattoo artist at such a high level that people traveled from all over the world to little Marietta, Montana, for a little ink directly from his hand. He and Emmy had come out with a circle of friends as well as their sharp-eyed grandmothers—who drank more than everyone else—and they'd all been in a festive mood that Christmas Eve.

The Grans, as the grandmothers were known all over Crawford County, had been drinking all of Griffin's tattooed and bearded friends under the table. Emmy had long since shifted to Cokes. Sydney couldn't really say how many shots she'd had, which to her mind was the point and purpose of shots. That was the sort of data she didn't need to hold on to, so she didn't. It was all part and parcel of the Christmas spirit.

Though she did remember, with perfect clarity, when she'd decided she needed to step outside to see if a burst of frigid air might sober her up a little before her uncle Jason cut her off. Something she had no doubt he would then want to discuss before dawn as they inched through new-fallen snow all the way to Big Sky, no thank you.

That was what she told herself, but it wasn't really the reason. He would cut her off when he felt like it no matter what state she was in, and his lectures did not require an inciting incident. The real reason was that Sydney wasn't a sentimental person. She wasn't forever surfing about on the tides of various emotions like Melody, her impossibly dramatic mother, who Sydney loved dearly and also was very happy to see but rarely.

She wasn't like her mother. She could never be so careless and emotional. *She* didn't like to think about the fact that the air was just... different in Marietta. That even in the crystal clear cold of that December night with a storm sitting heavy in the hills, there was something about standing outside and taking such a deep breath that it was like inhaling the stars.

Sydney didn't wax poetic. She dealt in facts. She put data and details together, synthesized seemingly unrelated tidbits of information, and drew connections no one else saw.

That was some damn fine poetry right there.

But she didn't let herself think things like that and she

certainly didn't say things like that, so she'd told the alarmingly clear-eyed Grans that she was getting some air.

Of course you are, dear, Gran Martha Hyatt had said serenely. *That will freeze the alcohol right out of your bloodstream, I'm sure.*

Perhaps it's not the alcohol that needs the breathing room, Gran Harriet Mathis had added in a similar tone.

Both with smiles that Sydney had chosen to ignore, because the old women were knowing and strange but they didn't *actually know* anything about her. No one did, and not because she was secretive, as her older sister Devyn liked to claim. But because there was nothing to know about her except what was classified, and anyone who needed to know that already did.

She had hurtled for the door to the outside, maybe a little too desperate to get away from those knowing old lady smiles, thrown it open to charge straight out, and had instead slammed into the person coming in.

Directly into him.

So hard that he'd had to take a step back and grip her by the arms to keep them both from toppling over and doing a header on the icy sidewalk, straight into the snow.

But he had risen to the occasion, instantly.

She thought about that now as he did his usual thing, wandering through the saloon, greeting people he knew, and pretending he didn't know exactly where Sydney was. Or notice that she was looking right at him.

Sometimes she was the one who pretended not to see him, and that was fun too.

But either way, she knew this game. And every time they played it, everything in her turned bright and achingly hot with that same longing that had rushed into her on a cold sidewalk in December, filling her up in place of all those Christmas stars, an intoxicant all its own.

That first night, they had stayed out in the dark together, holding on to each other a whole lot longer than necessary to simply remain upright. Sydney had been laughing, telling herself it was all that tequila, and he'd looked a little bit like he'd been punched straight in the face.

Like he was dazed, somehow, and not from their collision.

He wasn't fragile either.

And it was true that she'd spent a lot of time in the years since, five years to be exact, thinking about that particular poleaxed expression he'd wore in those first frigid moments. She remembered them as a blinding rush of heat. She didn't have a lot of nights in that bed of hers in her barely used apartment. She mostly slept, when and if she slept, on the couch in her office or on the floor. And yet every single one of the nights she actually went home involved her lying in that strange bed, pretending to sleep, running through moments like that one.

Almost like she was analyzing them. Looking for connections. Drawing conclusions.

You're going to catch a chill and freeze to death, he'd said, *and it will be my fault for letting you stand out here without a coat.*

She'd learned so many things about him in that moment. It was his voice. She heard the Texas in it. The drawl. She already knew that he was strong because she could feel it all around her. He could have lifted her straight up from the ground if he'd wanted and she had the happy little notion that he did want that. She knew that he was taller than her. She knew he was chiseled to perfection, there in jeans and boots that told truths about his form and the heavy coat he'd already unzipped, happily, so she could see there were no lies on the rest of him.

He was all muscle. All man.

There was no getting past the fact that he was wildly, astonishingly hot. She'd told herself then and later that it was the tequila and maybe that had helped, but it had been five years now. There was no getting around the fact that it was him, too.

And that little hint of Texas was like hot sauce on top, making everything smoke.

I'm from generations of good Montana stock, she had replied, smiling wildly for no good reason. *I'm not saying I'm going to take a nap in a snowbank, but I'm also not going to freeze to death in three seconds.*

I'm from Texas, darlin', he'd said, in case she hadn't worked that out. *And I might.*

He hadn't let go and she hadn't pushed the issue, because she really didn't want him to let go. She liked that he'd called her *darlin'* like that, like she was the kind of woman men used endearments on when she knew she wasn't. She never had been. Sydney was spiky, combative, blunt. Everyone told her so at work, and those were compliments.

But he'd drawled out *darlin'* like he meant it. And she'd watched, outside in the hushed dark of Marietta on a Christmas Eve with a storm coming in, the way the corner of his mouth had curled.

Just a little bit.

As if it was hers alone.

Looking back, she liked to think it was the tequila talking when she'd grinned up at him, opened up her mouth, and said, *But if you're worried, we could always warm each other up.*

Like she was the kind of *darlin'* who flirted with men that way.

Or at all.

But that night, she had been. And her reward was that she'd watched his dark green gaze go smoky like his voice.

Glad I was here to keep you out of that snowbank, he'd drawled. *I'm Jackson Flint.*

Find out what happens next...

Get now!

More by Jane Porter

Oh, Christmas Night

Love at Langley Park series

Book 1: *Once Upon a Christmas*

Book 2: *The Christmas Cottage*
Coming in December 2023!

The Wyatt Brothers of Montana series

Book 1: *Montana Cowboy Romance*

Book 2: *Montana Cowboy Christmas*

Book 3: *Montana Cowboy Daddy*

Book 4: *Montana Cowboy Miracle*

Book 5: *Montana Cowboy Promise*

Book 6: *Montana Cowboy Bride*

Love on Chance Avenue series

Book 1: *Take Me, Cowboy*
Winner of the RITA® Award for Best Romance Novella

Book 2: *Miracle on Chance Avenue*

Book 3: *Take a Chance on Me*

Book 4: *Not Christmas Without You*

The Taming of the Sheenans series

The Sheenans are six powerful wealthy brothers from Marietta, Montana. They are big, tough, rugged men, and as different as the Montana landscape.

Christmas at Copper Mountain
Book 1: Brock Sheenan's story

The Tycoon's Kiss
Book 2: Troy Sheenan's story

The Kidnapped Christmas Bride
Book 3: Trey Sheenan's story

The Taming of the Bachelor
Book 4: Dillion Sheenan's story

A Christmas Miracle for Daisy
Book 5: Cormac Sheenan's story

The Lost Sheenan's Bride
Book 6: Shane Sheenan's story

About the Author

New York Times and USA Today bestselling author of 70 romances and fiction titles, **Jane Porter** has been a finalist for the prestigious RITA award six times and won in 2014 for Best Novella with her story, *Take Me, Cowboy*, from Tule Publishing. Today, Jane has over 13 million copies in print, including her wildly successful, *Flirting With Forty*, which was made into a Lifetime movie starring Heather Locklear, as well as *The Tycoon's Kiss* and *A Christmas Miracle for Daisy*, two Tule books which have been turned into holiday films for the GAC Family network. A mother of three sons, Jane holds an MA in Writing from the University of San Francisco and makes her home in sunny San Clemente, CA with her surfer husband and three dogs.

Thank you for reading

Take Me Please, Cowboy

If you enjoyed this book, you can find more from all our great authors at TulePublishing.com, or from your favorite online retailer.

TULE
PUBLISHING

Made in the USA
Las Vegas, NV
06 September 2023